THE MYSTERY OF A BUTCHER'S SHOP

THE MYSTERY OF A BUTCHER'S SHOP

GLADYS MITCHELL

ISIS
LARGE PRINT
Oxford

First published in Great Britain 2010
by
Vintage
a member of The Random House Group Limited

Published in Large Print 2011 by ISIS Publishing Ltd.,
7 Centremead, Osney Mead, Oxford OX2 0ES
by arrangement with
The Random House Group Limited

British Library Cataloguing in Publication Data
Mitchell, Gladys, 1901–1983.
  The mystery of a butcher's shop.
  1. Bradley, Beatrice Lestrange (Fictitious character)
  - - Fiction.
  2. Detective and mystery stories.
  3. Large type books.
  I. Title
  823.9'12–dc22

ISBN 978–0–7531–8922–1 (hb)
ISBN 978–0–7531–8923–8 (pb)

CONTENTS

CHAPTER
ONE

Inconsiderate Behaviour of a Passenger to America

It was Monday. Little requires to be said about such a day.

Charles James Sinclair Redsey, who, like Mr Milne's Master Morrison, was commonly known as Jim, sat on the arm of one of the stout, handsome, leather-covered armchairs in the library of the Manor House at Wandles Parva, and kicked the edge of the sheepskin rug.

Mr Theodore Grayling, solicitor, sat stewing in an uncomfortably hot first-class smoking-compartment on one of England's less pleasing railway systems and wondered irritably why his client, Rupert Sethleigh, had seen fit to drag him down to an out-of-the-way spot like Wandles Parva when he could with equal ease have summoned him to his offices in London.

Mrs Bryce Harringay, matron, lay prone upon her couch alternately sniffing languidly at a bottle of smelling-salts and calling peevishly upon her gods for a cool breeze and her maid for more eau-de-Cologne.

Only the very young were energetic. Only the rather older were content. The very young, consisting of Felicity Broome, spinster, dark-haired, grey-eyed, red-lipped, aged twenty and a half, and Aubrey Harringay, bachelor, grey-eyed, brown-faced, wiry, thin, aged fifteen and three-quarters, played tennis on the Manor House lawn. The rather older, consisting of Mrs Beatrice Lestrange Bradley, twice widowed, black-eyed, claw-fingered, age no longer interesting except to the more grasping and avaricious of her relatives, smiled the saurian smile of the sand lizard and basked in the full glare of the sun in the charming old-world garden of the Stone House, Wandles.

The train drew up at Culminster station, and Theodore Grayling alighted. There would be a luxurious limousine to meet him outside the station, he reflected happily. There would be tea under the trees or in the summer-house at the Manor. There might possibly be an invitation to stay to dinner. He had eaten Rupert Sethleigh's dinners before. They were good dinners, and the wine was invariably above criticism. So were the cigars.

The road outside the station was deserted except for a decrepit hansom cab of an early and unpromising vintage. Theodore Grayling clicked his tongue, and shook his head with uncompromising fierceness as the driver caught his eye. He waited, screwing up his eyes against the glare of the sun, and tapping his stick impatiently against the toe of his boot. He waited a quarter of an hour.

"They've forgot you, like," volunteered the driver, bearing him no ill-will. He flicked a fly off the horse's back with the whip, and spat sympathetically.

Theodore Grayling laid his neat case on the ground and lit a cigarette. It looked a frivolous appendage to his dignified figure. He glanced up and caught the cabby's eye again. Common humanity compelled him to proffer his gold case, the gift of a grateful client. The cabby lit up, and they smoked in silence for two or three minutes.

"Wouldn't hurt, like, to take a seat inside while you're waiting," suggested the man hospitably. "It's full 'ot to stand about."

Theodore Grayling shrugged his shoulders.

"Doesn't look as though anyone is coming to meet me," he said. "I want the Manor House, Wandles Parva. Know it? All right. Carry on."

The driver carried on.

The young man who received the lawyer in the fine hall of the Manor House looked apologetic when Grayling asked for Rupert Sethleigh.

"Come into the library," said the young man. "It seems a bit awkward to explain. In fact, I can't exactly explain it — that is to say" — he paused, as though anxious to be certain that he was using the words he wished and intended to use — "it is very difficult to explain it. I mean, the fact is, he's gone to America."

Feeling more than surprised, Theodore Grayling followed the young man into the library.

"I'm Redsey," the young man said. He was a big, untidy, likeable fellow, although his usually frank

3

expression was marred at the moment by a look of strain and anxiety, and his nervous manner seemed at variance with his whole appearance. He stooped down and straightened the corner of the rug which he had been kicking, and invited the lawyer to be seated.

"So your cousin has gone to America?" said Theodore Grayling, pressing his finger-tips together and gazing benignly down at them. "When?"

"To-day." The young man seemed definite enough on that point. "Early this morning."

"To-day? What boat is he on?"

"Boat?" Jim Redsey laughed unconvincingly. "It sounds a bit daft to say so, but I don't know. Cunard Line, I believe — yes, I'm sure it was — but the actual name of the boat —!" He knitted his brows. "I *did* know it," he said, "but it's gone now."

"To America," said Theodore Grayling pensively. "Strange! Very strange! Perhaps you can tell me why he requested me to come down here this afternoon in order to discuss and effect certain alterations in the testamentary disposal of his property!"

"Eh?" said Redsey, startled. "Do you mean he — he *asked* you to come down here to-day? I say" — he chuckled feebly — "he must be off his chump, don't you think? Look here, my aunt will be down to tea. We had better discuss the thing together."

The lawyer raised his eyebrows, but then nodded and turned to study the backs of the books in one of the glass-fronted shelves. Redsey, with an inaudible but heartfelt sigh of relief at what was evidently the termination of a disquieting conversation, lounged on the arm of a stout leathered-covered armchair and picked up a sporting periodical from the table.

On the lawn outside the library, two young people, the boy of fifteen and the girl of twenty, were still playing tennis. Their fresh voices and the clean, strong cello note of rackets striking new balls came clearly into the room through the open French windows. These windows, together with part of the tennis-net, a stretch of level green turf and, occasionally, the figures of the white-clad players, were reflected darkly and strongly in the glass doors of the bookcase towards which Theodore Grayling was turned. The lawyer, however, was concerned at the moment neither with the books in the bookcase nor with the pleasant images which were reflected in the glass. He was puzzling over the news which had just been given him by the young man lounging on the arm of the massive armchair. At the end of five minutes' fruitless pondering he shook his head, and, swinging round from the bookcase so suddenly that the startled young man beside him dropped his well-illustrated periodical on to the floor, he demanded with unusual abruptness:

"And do you know that your cousin has invited the Vicar of Crowless-cum-Boone to spend a few weeks here to catalogue all this" — he waved his hand round to indicate the solemnly splendid library — "and to give him some advice about his Alpine plants?"

Jim Redsey's mouth opened. He tried to answer, but no words came. He turned exceedingly pale, became stammering and confused, and, in order to gain time, stooped and picked up his sporting paper from the floor. Having placed it with meticulous care in the very centre of the table, he moistened his lips, furtively wiped clammy hands on the seat of his plus fours, and tried again.

"No — I — er — no. No, I didn't know they were coming — that is — he was," he stammered confusedly. "As you know — I should say — as you probably don't know — I am only staying here until I hear about a job — a post I've been promised. It's in Mexico, this job. I don't quite know what sort of a job it is. I believe I sweat round on a horse or something, and generally try and get the other *wallahs* to put a bit of a jerk in it, and so forth. Anyway, I'm rather keen to get out there, and so on, and I've given up my digs in Town, so I'm sort of filling in time down here until I hear definitely. Of course, it was rather decent of Sethleigh to have me here at all, especially as we don't really know each other frightfully well. Our respective maters didn't exactly hit it off, you see. They were twins, and my mater always thought Aunt Poppy, that was his mater, put one over her, and a dirty one, too, by beating her into the world by a short head — two hours or something, I believe it was. By doing so, she collected the bulk of the boodle when the old lad died — the house and property, you know — while my mater got fobbed off with the loser's end, a beggarly thousand quid. Not," concluded the young man thoughtfully, but with a certain amount of animation, "that a thousand quid wouldn't come in handy to pretty nearly all of us; but, still, one can see my mater's point of view. After all, when you expect something and get handed something else, only less so,

I suppose you do feel a bit peevish about it. She always felt as though she'd taken a dirty one below the belt. As I suppose you know, the referee dismissed the appeal, too. Oh, yes. She ran it through the courts, and never forgave Aunt Poppy the judge's summing-up. Idiotic name for an aunt, Poppy, I always think. Makes you wonder whether she's on the variety stage or something. It's a sort of a fruity name, if you know what I mean. And my Aunt Poppy", he concluded sorrowfully, "was anything but fruity. Anything but."

"Quite, quite," murmured the lawyer absently. "But, you know, I am quite at a loss to understand your cousin's going off to America like this," he went on, reverting to the matter in hand with some abruptness. "And without a word of warning, too! It is not at all the kind of thing Rupert Sethleigh would do. I've known him for many years now, and the idea of his going off to America without a word of warning — no, no."

Jim Redsey mentally substantiated this theory. A vision of Rupert Sethleigh rose before him. A conventional, smirking, fattish fellow, he remembered. One who always appeared a little too well dressed, a little too well fed, a little too self-satisfied; that was Rupert Sethleigh. He was smug. He was contemptible. He considered every word before he uttered it and every action before he performed it. It *was* difficult to imagine him rushing off to America without warning. It was more than difficult, thought Jim Redsey, who liked to be fair-minded; it was impossible. Rupert Sethleigh was five feet seven and a quarter in his socks, the wrong height for such impetuous behaviour.

"And what motive had your cousin for going off like this?" the lawyer demanded brusquely, cutting across the current of Redsey's thoughts.

Jim smiled uncertainly. The lawyer glanced down at his restless, fidgeting fingers.

"Motive?" The sinister word struck oddly and uncomfortably on the ear. "What do you mean — motive?"

Before the lawyer could answer, noises off, in the parlance of the stage, announced the entrance of Jim's only living female relative. It was significant that this was the first time in his whole life that Jim felt glad to see her. She appeared in the hall doorway of the library and petulantly demanded her tea.

Mrs Bryce Harringay was what used to be known as a magnificent woman. She was tall, large, and spirited. By virtue of her relationship to the absent Rupert Sethleigh she was accustomed to claim his hospitality, invade his house, order his servants to wait on her, his cars to transport her, and his meals to suit her convenience. This occurred summer after summer with almost unfailing regularity. Rupert loathed her whole-heartedly. So did Jim. It was the one bond between two exceedingly diverse natures. The one opinion the cousins held in common was that any social gathering, however enjoyable otherwise, was irretrievably ruined by their aunt's presence. Conversely, they held that any function, however tedious or harassing, was at least tolerable provided that their aunt could not be there. Her conduct on public occasions, they agreed, was only one degree less trying than that of a female

8

lunatic suffering under the delusion that she was a cross between Lorelei Lee and the Queen of Sheba. Jim, given the choice between being afflicted by the plague or with the burden of conversing with his Aunt Constance, would undoubtedly have chosen the plague with all its attendant horrors.

Mrs Bryce Harringay usually was accompanied on her visits to the Manor House by her son Aubrey, a likeable, intelligent boy, and by her pomeranians, Marie and Antoinette, who might have been likeable, intelligent animals but for the inordinate amount of pampering they received from their mistress, and the storms of abuse they incurred from other people. Yappy, snappy little brutes were Marie and Antoinette, with a propensity for sly thieving. Jim Redsey was never quite certain whether his loathing for his Aunt Constance exceeded his loathing for her pets, or whether he detested the little animals rather more than he detested their mistress. In moments when time hung heavily upon his large, powerful hands, he was wont to ponder the problem. He was a slow thinker.

On this particular occasion it happened that his aunt was unaccompanied by her favourites. Having demanded her tea, she lowered her thirteen stone of stately flesh into a comfortable chair, disposed her draperies, which were diaphanous but full, in a graceful and modest manner, folded her hands in her lap, sat bolt upright, fixed Jim Redsey with an accusing glare, and observed with venom:

"James! What is this I hear?"

"I — er — may I present Mr Grayling — Mr Theodore Grayling," babbled Jim, avoiding her basilisk eye.

"Long ago I had the pleasure of making the acquaintance of Mr Grayling," replied his aunt coldly. She flashed upon the family lawyer a gleaming smile. Her dentist was an artist in his way. "You might have imagined that fact for yourself," she continued, shutting off the smile promptly as she turned to her nephew.

"Yes, Aunt Constance," agreed Jim jumpily.

"That is," his aunt went on, "if you possessed the brain of a bat. Which, of course," she concluded roundly, "you do not, and never will, possess! Now listen to me. I have made the most appalling discovery!"

Jim gave forth something between a moan and an incipient bellow of fear. The lawyer and Mrs Bryce Harringay stared at him with misgiving, and then glanced at one another.

"Oh, well, you know — oh, well —" began Jim thickly. "All for the best, I mean. What I mean to say — all these things sent to try us, and all that. I suppose —"

"I agree," said Mrs Bryce Harringay frigidly, "that it will certainly try me most sorely, James, most! And your Manifest Sympathy is most touching, especially as the lady in question is entirely unknown to you."

"Eh?" said Jim feebly, taking out his coloured silk handkerchief and wiping his face. "Er — oppressive this afternoon, isn't it? What? *Lady* in question?"

10

He sank down, perspiring with relief.

"Certainly. Mrs Lestrange Bradley has taken the Stone House."

CHAPTER
TWO

Farcical Proceedings during an Afternoon in June

"The mater," observed Aubrey Harringay, picking up the fourth ball and dropping it into the string bag, "is a sort of walking *Who's Who*. She gets to know all about everybody."

"Is that the lot?" asked Felicity Broome, poking about with her racket among the laurels.

"Four. X for Xenophon, P for Pandora, K for Sybil Thorndike, and this last little chap with the black smudge on his shirt, he's Q for Quince."

"K for what?" asked Felicity, abandoning her tactics among the shrubbery and commencing to lower the tennis-net.

"Sybil Thorndike. Didn't you see her at Hammersmith as Katharina the Shrew?"

"Of course I didn't. And you're not to tell me about it. I'm too envious." Felicity smiled sweetly. "You don't mind, do you?"

"Doesn't your pater care about the theatre? Moral scruples and what not?"

"Father hasn't any morals. He's a clergyman," said Felicity, with perfect gravity. "We can't afford the theatre, that's all. What were you saying about your mother?"

"The mater? Oh, yes. I was about to remark that she is now putting that reverend bird over there through her version of the Catechism. You know: What is your name? — de Vere or Snooks? Who gave you this name, your ancestors who came over with William One —"

"Who?"

"Billy the Lad. Also ran, Harold Godwinson. Don't you know any English history?"

"Idiot! Go on."

"Yes. Well, if you say your people didn't come over with Bill, she wants to know whether you collected your meaty handle with the assistance of letters patent for making bully beef in the Great War, daddy, or what? Especially what. I say, I wonder whether there are cucumber sandwiches for tea? Of course, if you answer to the name of Snooks, you're damned."

Felicity sat down in the middle of the court and shaded her eyes with a slim sun-kissed arm.

"But he isn't a reverend gentleman," she said, narrowly observing Theodore Grayling, who was being personally conducted from garden bed to other garden beds by the majestic Mrs Bryce Harringay. Her loud, juicy voice came clearly across the grass, although the words she said were indistinguishable.

"How twiggee he isn't a padre?" asked Aubrey, sitting beside Felicity and clasping his white-flannelled knees.

"Hasn't a dog-collar. Use your eyes, little boy. I'm going in now to get washed before tea. Coming?"

"Let's go in through the library. The windows are open. I expect old Jim is in there. I say, he's got the hump to-day or something. Have you noticed?"

"I don't think he is very well," returned Felicity, as the boy hauled her to her feet. "He looks so dreadfully white and tired. And he is rather a jolly man usually, isn't he?"

"Don't know him frightfully well, you know. His mater and old Rupert's mater never hit it off or something, and my pater, who was the brother, got himself cut off with the proverbial bob for hectic proceedings with the lasses during his youth — the mater jolly well reformed him, though, after they married — and he couldn't stick either of his sisters, so I've hardly ever met Jim until this holiday.'

"You like him, though, don't you?" asked Felicity, as they strolled towards the house.

"Oh, he's all right." Aubrey tucked her racket under his arm with his own, and she passed before him up the steps and in at the open French windows.

Jim Redsey, still weak from the shock of his aunt's remark, sat up as the two entered.

"Hullo, Jimsey," said Felicity. "I say, are you all right? You look dreadfully white."

"Touch of the sun, I expect," returned Jim, with a sickly grin. "Both want your tea, I expect. Ring for it,

14

Stick, will you? Your mater jolly well handed me a kick in the ribs just now, so you owe me something for that. I thought something serious was up, but it seems she has only heard about a woman named Lestrange Something-or-other who has taken the Stone House on the far side of the village. Your mater seems to loathe the dame pretty freely."

The brown-faced boy grinned.

"Well, I don't know what she said to give you a nasty knock," he said, "but you do look as though something's got you in the gizzard, old lad."

"You don't feel sick, Jimsey, do you?" asked Felicity, pursuing the subject with motherly interest. "You are a horrible greenish-white colour, you know. You look simply beastly, poor old thing."

"As though you're going bad, you know," contributed Aubrey sympathetically but not very happily. "Sure you're fit?"

"Quite sure, thanks," replied Jim shortly. "What about tea?"

"On the lawn?" suggested Felicity. "It's lovely out there. Come along and wash, Aubrey darling."

"You can't say that as Yvonne Arnaud said it in *Tons of Money*," said Aubrey, grinning, and pressing the bell as he passed by it in following Felicity out of the room.

Having ordered that tea should be served on the lawn, Jim Redsey hoisted his feet over the arm of his chair and closed his eyes. As, however, his thoughts behind closed lids seemed even more wearying, worrying and confused than when his eyes were open, he stared absently at the glass doors of the bookcase opposite. The figures of his aunt and the lawyer were reflected in these glass doors. They were deep in conversation, or, rather, in a dissertation on roses, emphatically delivered by Mrs Bryce Harringay in a peculiarly penetrating voice, as they crossed the lawn in front of the library windows.

Jim's eyes narrowed. Was this the chance he had been waiting for all that long day? With the two youngsters up aloft, and the two older birds preoccupied with each other and even making off in the right direction, could he sneak out without being seen?

He crept to the French windows, concealed his large form behind the curtains and peered out. His aunt and the lawyer were walking away from the house towards a rockery covered with Swiss mountain plants with which Rupert Sethleigh's late gardener had been making some experiments. Mrs Bryce Harringay was still talking, this time on the subject of the rockery.

"Yes, very interesting, of course. No, I have never been in Switzerland. The Riviera, of course, but not Switzerland, no. Yes, Rupert has been looking after these himself since Willows was dismissed.

"No, he doesn't really care about gardening, but the Vicar of Crowless-cum-Boone is coming on Thursday — I think Rupert said Thursday — to look at these plants, and so Rupert felt bound to attend to them himself now Willows is gone. Oh, a nasty sullen fellow. Had no idea of his place. Of course, it was a pity Rupert struck him. I never think it wise to give these people a real grievance, do you? Oh, yes, the Vicar of Crowless is quite an authority upon Alpine plants —

quite. He lectures, you know. And spends his *life*, they say, in Kew Gardens. Oh, his wife runs the parish. A most *capable* woman, most."

"Well," said Theodore Grayling, seizing upon this opening before Mrs Bryce Harringay could change the subject, and wisely deciding that if he was to obtain a hearing at all he had better be as dramatic as possible, "I do hope the Vicar of Crowless will not be disappointed when he arrives and finds that your nephew has gone to America. Not that there is any reason against going to America," he added, noting with satisfaction that Mrs Bryce Harringay was turning purple with amazement and emotion. "I have always longed to visit our great sister-country; I have an admiration for America which —"

In defiance of all the canons of good taste and correct behaviour, Mrs Bryce Harringay seized the lawyer's arm and shook it violently.

"What *are* you saying?" she asked. "Rupert is not going to America! My younger nephew, James Redsey, a rather unsatisfactory boy, is trying to get a post out in Mexico, but *Rupert* would never dream of leaving England. He says he will never even cross to France again, because sea-travelling upsets him so much!"

"But I have just received definite information from Mr Redsey that his cousin sailed for America this morning!" cried the lawyer. "It is not a case of his dreaming of going! He is gone!"

Perceiving that his aunt and the lawyer had their backs to him and were absorbed in conversation, Jim Redsey stepped quickly out on to the gravel path and walked swiftly round the side of the house to a small gardening-shed which stood about fifty feet from the garage and stables. He unlocked the little shed, disappeared inside it, and shortly afterwards emerged carrying a heavy spade. Drawing from his pocket a large, dark, richly coloured silk handkerchief, he wound this about the shining edge of the tool, secured it with a natty piece of green twine, and carried the spade along to the stables. Here, after a hasty glance round him to make certain that he was not being watched, he kicked open one of the wooden doors and thrust the spade under a heap of straw in the far corner. Then, automatically dusting the palms of his hands one against the other, he stepped out into the sunlight again and walked briskly back to the house.

Felicity and Aubrey had not gone immediately upstairs after leaving Redsey in the library, but had loitered a moment in the fine hall. An idea struck Aubrey.

"Tea won't be ready for a little while," he said, "and you wanted to see the view from the top of the old Observation Tower. It's great. You can see the sea and everything. Come on."

The Observation Tower was the only portion of the original building left standing. It rose high above the roof of the house, and at the top of it was an outside platform surrounded by a stout iron railing. Up the tower Aubrey and Felicity climbed, and were standing on the platform admiring the fine view, when Aubrey drew Felicity's attention to the stealthy movements of his cousin Redsey. They watched him with interest and amusement. Suddenly his movements became more interesting still.

"I shall go immediately to the Vicarage," Mrs Bryce Harringay was announcing as Jim Redsey reached the little gardening-shed, "and find out what the vicar knows about this mad freak. The whole thing is most astonishing, annoying, and ridiculous! And what is more, I don't believe a word of it! Rupert gone to America indeed! Either my nephew James was wilfully deceiving you — a not inconceivable idea, I may say! — or else he has been misled. James was always an idiot! But the vicar will know, I should think, one way or the other, because he witnessed Rupert's last will, and so, I suppose, is in his confidence, which is more than can be said", she concluded bitterly, "of his nearest relations."

The lawyer coughed sympathetically, and Mrs Bryce Harringay led him at a rapid pace, which was unsuited to the heat of the afternoon, across the lawn, into the park, and over to a path which meandered into the beautiful, thickly wooded outskirts of the demesne. On the farther side of these woods was a small wicket gate which opened on to the main Bossbury-London road. All this formed a short cut from the Manor House to the Vicarage.

To Jim Redsey's surprise, therefore, there was no one on the lawn when he returned from his visit to the gardening-shed and the stables, except for a man-servant who was setting the tea on a small table outside the summer-house. Jim turned to him for information.

"Mrs Bryce Harringay, sir? I think I caught sight of her and the gentleman walking towards the woods, sir. They've disappeared now."

"Towards the woods!" cried Redsey. "Good God!"

He bounded across the springy turf of the lawn, took a fourteen-foot flower-bed in his stride and leapt a clump of low-growing bushes like a steeplechaser. Into the longer coarse grass of the park he plunged like a swimmer dashing into the waves, and so galloped into the woods.

He yelled as he ran — the loud, terrifying and terrified yell of the panic-stricken man.

"I say! Aunt Constance! I say! Grayling! Grayling! I say! Stop! Stop a minute! Half a minute! Dash it! I say! I say! Hi!"

A turn of the narrow woodland path, and he sighted them. Attracted by his wild cries, the magnificent orange-clad figure of his aunt and the neat black form of the lawyer halted and looked back. A tall, loose-limbed, untidy, overheated young man in a suit of plus fours and a pair of golfing shoes, his tie flying loose and a dank lock of fair hair straying into his eye, came flying up to them. He halted, panting heavily, and leaned against a tree.

"Really, James!" his aunt protested frigidly. "You are a most offensive-looking object, most! You are *perspiring*, boy!"

"Sorry! Yes, I know," gasped Jim. "Beastly hot weather. Damned well out of training! Had to run the hell of a way after you! Came to tell you — came to tell you —" he rolled his eyes wildly and racked his brains.

20

What had he come to tell them? Must think of something. Something feasible. Must think of something quickly. "Came to tell you —" A wave of relief flooded over him. "Tea-time!" he shouted triumphantly. "Came to tell you it's tea-time! Tea-time, you know. Hate you to miss your tea. So beastly, you know — so — er — so beastly disappointing, you know, to miss your tea. I mean to say — tea. What is life without a nice cup of hot tea? Cold tea, you see, such beastly stuff. I mean to say, cold tea — well, you feel as though you've put your shirt on the hundred to eight winner and the bookie's caught the fast boat to Ostend. No? Yes?"

He pushed the lock of hair out of his eye and smiled feebly.

"You are puerile, James," observed his aunt, commencing to swell ominously. "I suppose fresh tea can be made for us! Pray return to your other guests! Mr Grayling and I are going to the Vicarage to discover the Truth about Rupert."

"The truth about Rupert?" Jim Redsey stared helplessly at her. "You don't know what you're talking about! The vicar doesn't know the truth about Rupert! The truth about Rupert — ha! ha! ha!" And he went off into shouts of hysterical laughter, until the woods resounded with the terrible, crazy sound.

His aunt regarded him with horrified and the lawyer with pitying amazement.

"You are ridiculous, James!" announced Mrs Bryce Harringay. "Pray control yourself. A most foolish exhibition, most!"

Theodore Grayling grasped the young man by the arm.

"Come, Mr Redsey," he said sharply. "Come, now, come!"

"Not to the Vicarage," said Jim decidedly. "You come, now, come! Come along to tea."

"The Vicarage," began his aunt, eyeing him with contempt, "is not more than —"

Jim set his jaw. The spasm of hysteria had passed. "Look here, Aunt Constance," he said stubbornly, "you can't go to the Vicarage now. Besides, you would only be wasting your time if you did go. I assure you — you must take my word for it — the vicar knows nothing about Rupert, nothing at all."

He turned to Theodore Grayling with gregarious Man's instinctive confidence in a member of his own sex.

"I say, Mr Grayling —" His eyes were eloquent.

"Quite, quite! With pleasure!" said Theodore Grayling, rising to the occasion nobly. "Tea. Very nice. Very welcome. Come, Mrs Harringay." Gallantly he offered his arm.

"But the vicar will be out after tea," objected Mrs Bryce Harringay, obstinately determined not to abandon the project on which she had set her heart. "He always takes a Boys' Class at Bossbury Mission on third Mondays. He is never at the Vicarage after five o'clock."

"Then," remarked Theodore Grayling, glad to find a simple way out of the difficulty. "I fear we should scarcely catch him."

He drew out his massive gold watch, a gift from a grateful client, and held it out towards Mrs Bryce Harringay, who gazed at it, snorted angrily, and, with as good a grace as she could muster, allowed herself to be escorted back to the summer-house by the lawyer. Jim walked behind them, his large frame blocking the narrow path as though fearful that they might take it into their heads to make for the Vicarage after all. As he walked he sweated. It had been a near thing.

On top of the old Observation Tower, Felicity Broome and Aubrey Harringay were looking at each other in amused surprise.

"But why the spade —?" began Felicity.

"All dressed up and nowhere to go, too! Going to dig for buried treasure to-night, perhaps!" contributed Aubrey.

"You don't think he's got a touch of the sun, do you?" asked Felicity, in some anxiety. "And then to go dashing all over the park like that — it's positively dangerous this weather. What do you think is the matter with him?"

"Heaven knows, sweet child." Aubrey balanced himself precariously on the iron railing which ran round the platform on which they stood. "Perhaps he's going to bury one of the family heirlooms in the shrubbery. How's that for an idea? And he wants the mater to hold his coat while he does it!"

"You're making yourself so filthy, climbing about on that railing, that I think we'd better go and wash if we want any tea at all," retorted Felicity, giggling at the picture of the stately Mrs Bryce Harringay holding anybody's coat for any conceivable reason whatsoever. "How's that for an idea? I wonder if Rupert will be in to tea? Where is he to-day, by the way? Not still in bed, surely?"

"So long as he isn't among us, I don't see that it matters where he is," said Aubrey, abandoning his perilous gymnastics and beginning to descend the stairs. He leapt down the last eight in a highly spectacular manner and then turned to finish his remarks. "Personally, I don't care a dime where Rupert is, as long as he isn't with me. I can't stick the chap at any price. Most frightful outsider that ever lived, I should think. Awful bounder — and his friends are worse. And it makes me jolly sick, I can tell you, young child, to be lugged down here by the mater, who's got the hide of a hippopotamus when it comes to saving money by sponging on other people."

"Really, Aubrey," protested Felicity, rather horrified by the scalding candour of the young.

"Yes, I know it sounds a bit thick about one's own people. But it's the truth. I'm fond of the mater, of course, but I can spot her weak points. She won't tip taxi-drivers, you know, and grouses because I do. And down here it makes me jolly well squirm to be forced to eat the chap's beastly grub and sleep in his rotten, over-furnished bedrooms, and be taken out in his putrid car and accept his greasy favours, and pretend I'm grateful!"

"But I haven't seen him all day," said Felicity, reverting to the original topic. "*Is* he out?"

"Dunno. Cheer up, angel," replied Aubrey, brightening visibly at the sight of the chap's beastly grub, which was tastefully and lavishly laid out on a table shaded from the sun by a brightly striped awning. "There *are* cucumber sandwiches!"

CHAPTER
THREE

Midsummer Madness

I

The night was hot. Felicity Broome, tossing on her small single bed at the Vicarage, found sleep an impossibility. She counted imaginary sheep, she thought over the events of the day, she played an imaginary set of tennis, she visualized the top of her dressing-table and recalled to mind which aunt had presented her with each of the pretty but inexpensive adjuncts which reposed on it, and upon what festival, anniversary, or occasion she received the gift — but all was to no purpose. Hot and wide-awake she remained. She flung off first the coverlet and then the sheet. She sat up. She seized the pillows and banged and punched them. She lay down again. The pillows still felt as though they were filled with lumps of wood instead of soft down feathers. Felicity groaned and flung her slim body restlessly about.

A car went by along the main road. Somewhere in the house a man was talking interminably. Her father, she knew. The vicar seldom retired to bed before twelve.

A bat flew into the room, fluttered uncertainly round in a jerky, frightened fashion, and flew out again. Somewhere an owl was calling. Two men went by, their heavy boots ringing sharply on the road.

There was no moon, but through the wide-open un-curtained window she could see the stars clustered gem like, remote and shining, in the clear night sky. Felicity slid out of bed and walked to the window. She leaned out into the glimmering faëry darkness.

Away to the left lay the thickly wooded park of the Manor House. The trees were like a drifting cloud, felt rather than seen. Mysteriously attractive they loomed, shadowy, awesome, and inviting.

Felicity ran a comb through her short dark hair; soft and shining was her hair, like silk. She gave it a toss to settle it into place, then she pulled on a pair of rubber-soled gymnasium-shoes, tightened the string of her pyjama trousers, thrust her arms into the sleeves of her old school blazer, and climbed cat-like down the porch on to the Vicarage flower-bed.

Her father's study was at the side of the house. Felicity was thankful for this. She felt instinctively that, broadminded as the vicar undoubtedly was, he could scarcely be expected to approve of his motherless daughter's present walking costume. Felicity slipped noiselessly across the lawn, vaulted the low stone wall which separated the Vicarage garden from the churchyard, and flitted like some slim, entrancing ghost in and out among the gleaming tombstones. She reached the ancient lych-gate, climbed profanely over it, and dropped down into the road. This was a mere sandy lane which acted as tributary to the main Bossbury-London thoroughfare, which ran clean through the centre of Wandles Parva village.

Around her and above her head, beneath her feet, before her and behind, were all the scents and sounds and silence of night. Felicity breathed them in — breathed long and deeply. The firm, long, winding road, the quiet hedgerows, filled her with nameless joy. She longed to travel in their company to the world's end and into the fields of asphodel that grace the heaven of youth.

The main road was deserted. Not even a car passed by. The lights of the village were out. The village itself lay behind her. Beyond was ecstasy. The solitude itself was adventure.

Less than five minutes' easy walking brought her to the little wicket gate which opened into the Manor House park. Felicity pushed at the gate. It was not locked, but appeared to be stuck fast. She pushed again. Standing at this portal which bordered the enchanted land she imagined so attractive, her courage failed her. The gloomy woods were black with heavy shadows. The place looked lonely, not with the loneliness and charm of quiet solitude, not even with the loneliness of death, but awesome with the loneliness of living things whose thoughts were not as hers. The true witch-magic of a wood on a midsummer night when the trees are heavy with leaves, and every leaf, however still the forest, has a voice and a secret all its own, affrighted and unnerved her. She was in half a mind to retreat; to leave the pagan temple for a safe and

Christian pillow. The factor of the fast-shut gate decided her. To make it an excuse of cowardice was to condemn herself. Retreating a dozen steps, she darted forward, placed one hand upon the topmost rail, and vaulted neatly over it.

It was eerily dark among the trees. They whispered to Felicity their strange and awesome secrets. They were old. They had some mystery in their keeping, and they leaned towards her with their gloomy branches and brushed her cheek with their summer-heavy leaves, trying to attract and snare her — trying to tell her something which she could never understand. Felicity trembled, and her courage failed her. She remembered that in the centre of this great deciduous wood some bygone owner of the Manor House had planted a circle of pines. Tall, straight, and stark they waited, towering into heaven; and in the centre of their circle stood the Stone of Sacrifice. Felicity had heard queer tales about the Stone. It was a solid block of granite, roughly triangular in shape, and once, so ran the legends, it had been the altar of some prehistoric temple to the sun. Priests of a lost religion had sacrificed upon it to their god the flesh of rams or cattle or the blood of human kind. What dread ecstatic dances, what strange and awful sights, what deeds of violence and cruelty the Stone had witnessed, the girl could only guess. She turned, and began to retrace her steps.

Suddenly she stumbled upon the narrow pathway which led towards the Manor House, or, conversely, to the road. Irresolute, she halted and glanced round. All the blood in her body came racing to her head. In the near distance, and among the shadowy trees, she saw a steady gleam of light.

II

"Aubrey dear," said Mrs Bryce Harringay for the fifth time. She had commenced by saying it lovingly. She had continued by saying it coaxingly. Then she had proceeded to put it petulantly, and at length she resorted to command. This also having failed to produce the desired reaction on the part of her son, she had fallen back on a fond and foolish mother's last hope — entreaty.

"All *right*, mater," her heir returned, also for the fifth time. He sighed, thrust a picture postcard of Hobbs into a copy of *The Hairy Ape*, laid Mr O'Neill on top of the piano and followed his mother up the stairs.

"Good night, Jim, old man," he remarked as he passed out of the room. Jim Redsey looked up from his own book and nodded. He looked harassed and ill.

At the top of the stairs, Mrs Bryce Harringay paused.

"Good night, Aubrey dear. Now do try to be down in time for breakfast to-morrow morning. Remember — 'Punctuality is the politeness of princes.' So charming of them, I always think. So you will make a special effort, won't you?"

"Righto. Good night, mater, Sleep well. Oh, do you want me to come and goggle under the bed for you?"

"Well —" said Mrs Bryce Harringay hesitatingly. It was a strong woman's one weakness, this fear of burglars under the bed.

"Righto," said Aubrey good-naturedly. He preceded her into the room and switched on the electric light, for the wealthy Rupert possessed his own electric plant and paid his own electrician to look after it. Having looked solemnly under his mother's bed, Aubrey stepped across to the window and, pulling back the edge of the blind which Mrs Bryce Harringay's maid had already drawn down, he peered out. Although the hour was late, it was not dark outside. He could perceive the outline of the summer-house, and some formless shadows which were the roses and the flowering garden-beds by day. Suddenly a shaft of light shone broadly out on to the gravel path, and, from the library below, a man stepped out and walked towards the stables. Aubrey watched him go, and in a few seconds observed that he returned and apparently switched off the electric light.

"For goodness' sake, Aubrey, come away from that window and let me go to bed," said Mrs Bryce Harringay petulantly. "Here is Louise. Good night, dear."

"Good night, mater. So long." And he slipped out. The maid bestowed upon his back the special smile she kept for every member of his sex, and turned to attend her mistress.

Aubrey shot into his own room like lightning, kicked off his pumps, pulled on a pair of rubber-soled gymnasium-shoes, flung off his dress clothes and climbed into shorts and a sweater, then tiptoed to the door, regardless of the wild disorder he was leaving in his bedroom. As quickly as he could manage to do without making a noise, he shot downstairs and into the library. It was in darkness, but a strong scent of roses with which the hot night filled the room informed him that the French windows were wide open. Fearful of being too late to see the fun, he stepped out on the gravel path, slipped quickly aside on to the short, friendly turf of the lawn which would deaden the sound of his footsteps, and ran towards the garage and the stables.

"Elementary, Watson, you goop!" crowed Aubrey, as, coming within sight of the stables, the circle of light cast by a hurricane lamp met his gaze. "So there you are, Jimsey my buck! Now we shall find out what the spade is for. Perhaps he's robbed old Rupert's safe and is going to bury the spoils! I wonder what the little game *really* is, though?"

Seeking the shelter of a thick clump of laurels, he lay with his face as close to the ground as was possible, and waited patiently. He crushed a spider, which was tunnelling a panic-stricken way between his shirt and his body, by the simple expedient of rolling on it, scratched his left ear, which was beginning to itch maddeningly, and held his breath so as not to betray his presence. He had not long to wait. A muffled oath, in a voice unmistakably belonging to his cousin James Redsey, who had dropped the spade with a clatter upon the brick flooring of the stable, was followed by the appearance of a large black shadow looming against the starlit-scented dimness of the night, and Redsey passed by at a swift pace, carrying the hurricane lamp in his left hand and the spade across his right shoulder. He seemed in great haste, and was obviously bent upon some secret and important errand.

"Got gymmers on, like me," thought Aubrey, noting Redsey's noiseless footsteps, "Silly ass to tread on the very edge of the turf like that, though! Any idiot could trace him to-morrow."

He allowed Jim about thirty paces' start, then, moving like the shadow of a cat, sinuous, gliding, and without a sound, he began to follow him.

When they were well away from the windows of the house, Jim abandoned the cover afforded by bushes and flowering plants, and struck out boldly across the park. On this open ground, Aubrey had need to exercise much care in order to keep his presence secret. At irregular intervals, Jim Redsey halted and looked round as though some sixth mysterious sense were warning him that he was being followed. Rejoicing at the absence of the moon, Aubrey, who was bending nearly double in his determination to avoid being discovered, sank down and lay full length in the dew-drenched grass of this open country and was soaked to the skin by the time they reached the outskirts of the Manor Woods. Here Jim made his last halt before plunging in among the trees.

He was immediately lost to sight, and a less venturesome person than Aubrey Harringay would have paused at this juncture and contemplated abandoning the chase. Such a thought, however, did not enter

Aubrey's head, so, although the chances were decidedly in favour of his running full tilt into his cousin in the confusion engendered by the countless tree-trunks and the darkness, he plunged in after Jim and was immediately swallowed up among the trees.

III

Human curiosity is a strange and awe-inspiring thing. Felicity Broome's first impulse on beholding the gleam of light among the trees had been to turn and run. She was on the path; she could find the road. Inside ten minutes she could be safely between the sheets of her bed. The upbringing of the modern girl, however, can scarcely be said to encourage the instinctive adoption of first impulses. More powerful than this deterrent was the force of curiosity. *Who* was walking in the Manor Woods at night? Why was he armed with a lantern? Could it be poachers? But what was there to poach? The recollection of Jim Redsey's stealthy, strange manoeuvres with the spade flashed into her mind. Felicity, her fears forgotten, her curiosity lusting to be sated, crept cautiously along the path to get a nearer view.

The first thing she saw was the Stone. There it crouched, a loathsome, toad-like thing, larger than ever in the semi-darkness. She herself was sheltering behind a pine. Away from her — in that most strange of symbols, a complete and perfect circle — stretched its tall upstanding brothers, a ring of witch's sentries

34

guarding unhallowed ground. Ten yards, or thereabouts, from the Stone, lantern in hand, like some gigantic, lumbering, hag-ridden will-o'-the-wisp, was Rupert Sethleigh's cousin Redsey. Just as Felicity recognized him, he set down the lantern and began to dig.

IV

In less than a minute, Aubrey Harringay realized that he was hopelessly lost in the woods. The tree-trunks, crowding together, barred his progress. He tore his socks and shorts on briars and brambles, his woollen sweater caught on to low-growing branches, his face was soon scratched and bleeding, and, although he had explored the woods from end to end in daylight, he began to realize that they seemed a different place by night. He halted and listened. Suddenly, a few yards in front of him and a little to his right, the gleam of the hurricane lamp intensified the surrounding gloom.

"Doggo!" thought Aubrey, hastily stepping aside and concealing himself behind a tree. He had gained the middle of the wood. He crept forward, from tree to tree, until he was in sight of his cousin. The hurricane lamp, now standing on the ground, shone on the glinting surface of the quartz-encrusted triangular block of granite which went by the name of the Stone of Sacrifice, or the Druids' Altar. The tree behind which Aubrey's wiry body was concealed chanced to be a massive, smooth-trunked beech, but immediately in front of him, surrounding the rude stone altar which occupied the centre of the clearing, was a circle of sighing pines whose tall, straight trunks rose dread and awesome, towering into the night sky like guardian spirits of the brooding Stone.

Jim Redsey walked into the circle of light caused by the hurricane lamp and began to dig. The light loam was easy to move. Jim's arms and body moved with rhythmic grace. The pile of earth beside him grew and grew.

"Great jumping cats!" said Aubrey to himself. "The chap is trying to get through to Australia! What *is* the little game? Is he walking in his sleep?"

Having effected a cavity some six feet long and of a fair depth — Aubrey judged it to be about three feet down — Jim laid down the spade. Then he stepped down into the hole very carefully and disappeared from view.

"Chap must be off his chump!" thought Aubrey, more amused than uneasy at these curious manoeuvres. "Must be sleep-walking! Thinks he's in bed now, I expect. Wonder whether I ought to wake him up? Old Tompkins says it's dangerous to wake up sleep-walkers. They go loony or something. Wonder what I'd better do? Anyway, I'll pinch the spade before he can do any damage with it."

He was about to act upon this idea when Jim Redsey's head and shoulders appeared above the hole in the ground, and he stood up, stepped carefully out on to the sparse grass of the clearing, and walked away from Aubrey towards a clump of hazel bushes. Scarcely had he disappeared within their depths when Aubrey, worming his way snakewise over the short grass, approached the spade, seized it by the handle, and wriggled back into cover, dragging the spade after him. Felicity, more surprised than ever, witnessed this performance, but made no sign.

Jim reappeared as suddenly as he had gone. He seemed hesitating and uncertain, and stood gazing at the bushes in either surprise or dismay — in the darkness it was impossible to tell which it was. He disappeared again into the same clump, and after a few moments, during which Felicity and Aubrey, from opposite sides of the clearing, could both hear him charging about and swearing softly but bitterly as he did so, he again appeared and began searching other clumps of bushes near at hand.

Nearer and nearer to Aubrey he approached. Aubrey considered the wisdom of retiring from the scene, but realized that to do so without attracting Redsey's attention would tax all his woodcraft, even without the additional burden of the spade. Hampered by the latter, which was large and heavy, he knew that he must be heard. Of course, he might have left the spade behind and so glided away, but, having once acquired, as it were, the flag of the opposing forces, he felt that death in its company would be preferable to the dishonour of abandoning it. He remained hidden where he was. Redsey, groping blasphemously among the bushes in quest of some object or objects unknown, the non-appearance of which seemed to be causing him the gravest uneasiness, suddenly seized his ear. Aubrey let out a yell which caused Mrs Bryce Harringay, far away in the Manor House, to stir in her sleep. Leaping up, and clinging fast to the spade as representing the spoils and the trophies of war, he sped through the woods towards the Manor House, and his mother. Luckily for himself, he stumbled upon the path and flew down it, turning as it turned, doubled on itself, and ever straining every nerve to detect the sounds of pursuit.

Behind him, but less fortunate, in that he had missed the narrow path, and was thus in imminent peril of rushing into a tree or tripping over briars and brambles and small low-growing bushes, Jim Redsey crashed and stumbled.

Suddenly Aubrey burst from the woods on to the vastness of the open park. A good half-miler in the school sports, he galloped on. Jim Redsey, extricating himself from the mass of brambles into which he had fallen, and swearing softly and continuously as he denuded his hair and person of clinging blackberry stems, realized that his quarry had escaped him and that further pursuit was hopeless.

Perplexed and worried, he reached the house just as Aubrey Harringay, having deposited the spade on one of the flower-beds where he assumed the gardener would find it early in the morning, was pulling the sheet up past his chin and wiping the perspiration off his face with it.

Felicity had recognized Aubrey, although she realized that Jim Redsey, in full cry after the lad, had failed to do so. When all sounds of pursuit had died away, and Felicity's fluttering heart had resumed its normal beating, she began to realize that she was alone in a large and terrifying wood, and that the hour was very late. Visions of a peaceful bedroom came to her.

"But, before I go —" she thought to herself.

The lineal descendant of Eve in Eden crept cautiously forward until she stood beside the hole which James Redsey had seen fit to dig. She peered into its depths and shuddered. To the daughter of the spiritual adviser to the parish, the six-foot hole presented the appearance of a freshly dug grave!

CHAPTER
FOUR

Spreading the News

I

Mrs George Willows was getting breakfast for the children. The day was Tuesday, the time ten minutes to eight and the temperature a pleasant sixty-five degrees in the shade. Mrs Willows was a small, anxious-looking woman who hovered round the half-dozen or so lusty young Willows as a foster-mother bird might hover round a nest full of young cuckoos.

The cottage would have filled the heart of an American motion-picture producer with unadulterated joy. It was thatched, it was floored with slabs of stone, and it had a small outside porch covered with pink rambler roses. A long narrow path led up to the door; on one side of the path a stretch of garden was devoted wholly to vegetables; on the other side blazed a bed of summer flowers. The cottage boasted four rooms and an out-house, for George Willows was no farm labourer; he was a gardener. Until the afternoon of June 15th he had been Rupert Sethleigh's gardener. Since that day he had been Major Farquar's gardener every afternoon, and general odd-job gardener to those who could afford him in the mornings and on Saturdays. At the moment when Mrs Willows was pushing Tommy Willows out of the front gate and latching it sternly behind him, and at the same time was admonishing George Willows, junior, who was showing signs of desiring to climb a tree in his best school shorts, her husband was putting a load of gravel down on the paths of the Cottage on the Hill, half-way between the village of Wandles Parva and the neighbouring town of Bossbury.

Mrs Willows waved to Emily Willows, who, with little Cissie Willows in tow, was about to turn the corner in the lane on the way to school, and then, with a sigh of gratitude to the powers that provide schools and teachers to come to the rescue of harassed parents, she retired to the kitchen to prepare breakfast for her husband. George was supposed to have done this job yesterday, but had not been able to procure the gravel and get it delivered at the Cottage until the late afternoon, when he was engaged at the major's and could not spare time to deal with it. Therefore he had gone off at six o'clock that morning and hoped to be home to breakfast by nine.

Mrs Willows glanced at the clock, cut the rind off four rashers of bacon, laid two eggs beside them on the blue-ringed plate and placed the frying-pan ready to hand. This done, she changed the table-cloth for a freshly ironed one, walked out to the gate again, and, shading her eyes with her hand, looked down the sandy lane in order to catch the first glimpse of George, which

41

should afford her the signal to dart into the kitchen and start cooking his food.

Far away, and very faint in the clear delicate air of the morning, she could detect the note of the school bell indicating to the tardy that the time was five minutes to nine. Soon the bell ceased. The bees began to hum. The hazy blue of the sky deepened and the sun's warmth became more intense. Mrs Willows sighed. George had had nothing but a piece of bread and butter and a cup of tea before going out that morning. A man ought not to shovel and roll gravel with so little as that inside him, she felt sure. She sighed again, and longed for a cup of tea. She bent, and pulled a noxious silver-weed out from among the pansies. Then she went in again and glanced at the kitchen clock. It was twenty past nine.

At a quarter to eleven Willows came home.

"I was getting that worried and upset, I nearly came to look for 'ee," volunteered his wife.

Willows, an affectionate but taciturn husband, seated himself in a chair, hitched it up to the table, and, having waited in silence while his wife placed two rashers and an egg on his plate and the same on her own, grunted, and attacked his food with appetite. Mrs Willows, who had carried on a losing fight for some years on the grounds of being compelled to eat two rashers and an egg for breakfast whether she wanted them or not, sighed for the third time and picked up her knife and fork.

After ten minutes of steady mastication, Mr Willows pushed aside his empty plate and reached for the

42

cheese. Then he looked across at his wife, who was hesitating before the second rasher.

"Well," he said, with the assumed ferocity of the self-conscious, affectionately disposed working man, "can't 'ee say something, like?"

"I don't know as I got much to say, Geordie," replied Mrs Willows timidly. "Could 'ee eat up another bit o' bacon if I put it on your plate?"

"Now that'll do from you, my gal!" responded Mr Willows, eyeing her sternly. "You eat un up, and no nonsense! Here I feeds 'ee, day in, day out, as very few men feeds their wimmin-folk, I'll lay, and that's your gratitude! Where'd 'ee be now, I wonder, if I 'adn't see 'ee et well, eh?"

"In — in 'eaven, Geordie, I shouldn't wonder," replied Mrs Willows, desperately anxious to give the answer which would placate him by coinciding with his own opinions.

Mr Willows snorted.

"Then you et un up," he replied pithily.

"Nice goings-on in the village last Sunday night, I 'ear," observed Mrs Willows tentatively, when, breakfast over, her husband prepared to settle down in the doorway with a pipe.

"You're right, my lass. There was. Who's bin talking wi' you about it?"

"Oh, young Percy Noon was passing on his way to work and stopped to say thankee for them there young shallots. Said I'd tell when 'ee came 'ome. Percy says as how Squire Sethleigh's gone off to the States sudden like, and young Mr Wright, up where 'ee bin working this morning, is going off's 'ead. Give I a turn, it did, to think of 'ee working there along. Percy did say as how he went clumping young Farmer Galloway over the head wi' a hog-pudding in the bar of the 'Queen's Head', and as how Galloway he took and give un the biggest thrashing out, and Bill Bondy, not liking to interfere, held the watch and see fair play. And Squire's cousin, that young Mr Redsey, Percy do say, was lying dead drunk in the middle of it all."

"Well, that's the news that was round the village yesterday," said Mr Willows. "There's more to tell this morning. Made me late for my breakfast, going off along to know the truth of it."

"Well, there now! If I didn't watch and wait at the gate, wondering what had come over 'ee at all to be so late for breakfast," said Mrs Willows.

"Ah! Very likely 'ee did wonder. 'Ee'll wonder more when I do be telling 'ee all. There's bin a murder done at the butcher's in the market down in Bossbury."

"A murder? Lawk a-massy I! 'Ee'll sleep home tonight, Geordie, won't 'ee?"

"Happen I will. Nothing much doing at the major's this afternoon. The roses can do wi' a spray, for the green fly is mortal busy up along of 'em, and I set the lad to weed the gravel yesterday, so he can go on wi' that again. The chrysants is coming on nice, and the strawberries looks a treat. But what ails you? You don't want for company wi' all the little 'uns in the 'ouse wi' you!"

"I be mortal feared o' that there murder, Geordie!"

Mr Willows took the pipe out of his mouth and spat with accuracy and finality.

"There won't be any call for 'ee to be worriting, my lass," he observed. "Nobody don't want to murder 'ee. Happen 'ee 'en't important enough to be murdered. What's that clock say?"

II

"And what I say is," pronounced Mrs Eulalie Blenkins to the assembled meeting of mothers in the Chapel Parlour, "I say it's a judgment on Henry Binks. A man was never meant to make his living out of killing the dumb animals and offering their carcasses for sale. I'm a vegetarian myself, though I can't persuade Robert into it, I'm sorry to say. I was converted to it when I lived in Blackwater. A good mistress she was, and not hard to please. 'But there's one thing, Sarah,' she says — not liking to call me Eulalie as it's such a mouthful, and disliking Polly as being a sort of a skittish name, so she always called me Sarah, which is not unsuited to me, Robert's second name being Abraham — 'there's one thing,' she says, 'that I can't abide. And that's butcher's meat,' she says. 'We're all vegetarians here, and Christian Science too,' she says, 'and if you'll promise to be likewise, well, I like your looks,' she says, 'and I'd like to give you the place.' So vegetarian I been ever since, though I stuck out about the Christian Science on account of being a Wesleyan, and you can't get your money from the State

45

Insurance, you see, without a certificate from the doctor."

An older woman leaned forward.

"But what's all this got to do with Henry Binks?" she asked. "A very respectable man. Sober, too."

"He hasn't done nothing that I know of. At least," amended Mrs Blenkins piously, "I hope it isn't him that's done it. It's what he found." She lowered her voice to a blood-curdling whisper. "Human joints, my dear, all hanging up on the hooks where he generally hangs his beef and lamb on a Tuesday morning!"

There was a hushed and horrified silence, and a long pause. Then one bold spirit, running her needle in and out of the seam of a nightshirt destined to cover the nakedness of darkest Africa, enquired breathlessly:

"Human joints? Why, whatever do you mean, Polly Blenkins?"

Mrs Eulalie Blenkins glanced around her. The minister's wife and the rather dull book from which she was accustomed to read aloud to the assembled sisterhood of matrons had not yet put in an appearance, so Polly hitched her chair a little more closely to the questioner's and replied softly, while the rest of the circle also hitched up their chairs and strained their ears and paused in their work to listen:

"Yes. This morning first thing he found them. Of course, Henry Binks lives over his shop in the Purlcy Road, and he has also got the lease of a lock-up butcher's shop in the market, although the lock-up still goes under the name of Smith, which was old Tom Smith as used to live over Border's the grocer's in

Queen Street. He's gone now, poor old man, and Henry Binks that took over the lease of the lock-up in the market has never troubled himself to have the name painted out and his own put there instead. Well, Monday not being a good day in his line of business, Henry Binks never troubles to go down and open the lock-up till Tuesday, but every Monday he just contents himself with selling a few odds and ends at the shop in the Purley Road. Well, first thing this morning, then, being Tuesday, he goes down to the market shop, leaving his wife and son to manage the Purley Road shop as usual, and what does he find?"

She paused, with true dramatic instinct.

"I tell you what Henry Binks found," she said. "He found a body, a human body, all cut up into joints as neat as he could have done it himself, and all hung up on his hooks, as he could see when he took down the shutters. His very tools had been used to do the job and everything, so folks do say. The police is keeping them for fingerprints, my young nephew told me. An 'orrible sight it must have been! They say when Henry Binks see what it all was he fainted dead away, butcher though he is!"

III

"Fingerprints? We took hundreds of 'em. Identify the corpse? We can't, not yet awhile. Hold Henry Binks? On what charge? Oh, he's under observation, all right. You needn't worry. But there's nothing to arrest him for. *Scotland Yard?* 'Ere, you clear out of this, quick, else I'll run you in for obstruction!"

The only reporter the *Bossbury Sun* could afford grinned cheerfully at the harassed constable who had been left in charge of Henry Binks's little lock-up shop in the Bossbury covered market, and walked away briskly. The usual crowd of morbid persons who immediately rush to any locality where murder has been committed were lined up in front of the shop, anxious to be at the scene of one of the more unsavoury and horrifying crimes of the decade. The constable, having got rid of the young reporter, fixed his eye on a market sign which hung about three feet above the heads of the sightseers and resumed his stand-at-ease position. He wondered what credit — if any — would accrue to him for having been first on the scene after Henry Binks the butcher had made his appalling discovery that morning.

"Pity the murderer had the sense to take the head away with him," mused Constable Pearce. "Then we'd have known who the dead man is, and could have gone on according."

His superiors, Superintendent Bidwell, the deputy chief constable of the county, and Inspector Grindy, who had been placed in charge of the case, were discussing the same point.

"Damned nuisance about the head," said Superintendent Bidwell. "He's left us everything else, including the innards. He might as well have left the head, and saved us a lot of trouble."

The inspector guffawed heartily at what he took to be a feeble but well-intentioned jest on the part of his superior officer.

"No, I mean it," said the superintendent. "You see, it is going to be a brute of a case. To begin with, the murdered man is obviously a gentleman. Bath every day sort of look those limbs have got, if you noticed. And the hands and feet are well kept. Then look at the cleverness of dismembering the corpse in a butcher's shop! Nobody wonders what the chopping noise is for. It's the butcher getting ready for the next day's sales. Nobody is surprised to see a natty little car or what-not drive up to the market entrance and deliver stuff at any of those lock-up shops. As a matter of fact, I don't suppose there was anybody there to wonder or not to wonder. Once inside the shop, the chap had only to shove on Henry Binks's apron and overalls which he leaves hanging up in the shop when he goes home on Saturday night, because his wife won't wash 'em on account of the bloodstains, which turn her up, she says, so the laundry calls for the things on Wednesdays — and there you are!"

"Looks like a local fellow," said the inspector. "Special knowledge and all that. See what I mean?"

"If it isn't," said the superintendent decidedly, "— or, at least, if the dead man isn't a local chap, I'm not going to have anything to do with the case. I'll hand it over to the county where he belongs, or to Scotland Yard. I don't care which it is. A murder case is always dirty work, and in a case of this kind, where you've got to establish identity before you can get down to anything else at all, it's the very devil, and a confounded waste of time."

"Yes, the identification is going to be a tough proposition," said the inspector. "It isn't only the head. There isn't even a mark or a scratch on the body that you could use to prove it was anybody in particular. It's fattish and youngish — the doctor puts it as forty years old — and it's been well cared for. That's as much as you can say. Well, I'd better start by finding out who is missing. Then I shall have to check them all up, and perhaps we shall get on to something."

"As to that," said the superintendent, drawing out a paper, "you needn't bother about any of these. We know about 'em. All except this chap. Seems to be some sort of mystery here. He's the big bug at Wandles Parva, you know. Sethleigh. Suddenly taken it into his head to go to America, but nobody seems to know anything about it. His aunt, a Mrs Bryce Harringay, reported on the matter by letter this morning. You'd better go and look her up. Here's her description of him. It *might* fit the corpse."

CHAPTER
FIVE

Another Gardener

I

Again it was night. Tuesday night. Aubrey Harringay, who, to use his own expression, had "snooped under the mater's bally bed and scared away the beetles, bogies, bugs and burglars for her", retired at eleven-ten to his own room and lovingly turned back the bedclothes. Reposing secretly and a little grimly between the sheets was the spade he had brought back as the spoils of war and the relic of his adventures on the previous night. Aubrey drew it out, laid it gently on the rug, and remade the bed. Then he squatted down beside it, and pondered.

Aubrey was an intelligent boy. As he pondered he would have whistled but for fear of disturbing his mother. He was not actuated altogether by feelings of filial affection in not wishing to disturb his mother. Some men and women, he knew, were at their best in a crisis. Others were not. He sensed that Mrs Bryce Harringay must inevitably remain in the second of these categories. A crisis, he also sensed, had been reached. The police had been nosing about the house all the afternoon. They had asked questions. They had turned out all Rupert Sethleigh's letters and papers. They had driven the cook to hysterics and the butler to blasphemy. Aubrey himself would have enjoyed their visit but for two distressing and extraordinarily harassing thoughts. One was the thought of the spade he had hidden in his bed. It had been propped up against his wardrobe door and covered decently with his evening clothes until three o'clock that afternoon. He had planned to carry it down to dinner and rag Jim about it. But at three o'clock the police had arrived. They began asking for news of Rupert. There was bruited abroad the theory that Rupert had disappeared. It was rumoured that Jim Redsey had lied; that Rupert had never intended nor spoken of going to America. It was even darkly hinted that Jim Redsey could say a great deal about Rupert's whereabouts if he chose, but — with a significant pause — that he did not choose.

And there was an almost unrecognizable corpse down in Bossbury — fattish — aged about forty —

And Jim had dug a hole — rather like a grave — in the Manor Woods on the previous night. That was the second harassing thought.

And there was no doubt that Jim had got wind up — shocking wind up — especially when he saw the police coming up the drive!

Aubrey stood up. When in doubt, the old and experienced call canny. Youth is impetuous. Youth is inclined to be rash. Aubrey's rule, when he was seriously afraid of anything, was to make a wild dash at it. He had learnt to dive that way. He seized the spade and crept downstairs with it. He entered the drawing-room, whence came a narrow shaft of light beneath the door, and "stood easy" with the edge of the spade on the carpet.

"Oh, Jim, old bird," he said in an airy tone.

Jim Redsey, who was standing on the drawing-room hearthrug gazing earnestly at his reflection in an oval mirror which hung over the mantelpiece, turned with a start. His eye fell immediately upon the spade which Aubrey was holding.

"What the devil is that?" he cried. His eyes were almost starting out of his head with terror, and, as he pointed to the cumbersome implement, his hand shook so badly that he lowered it in haste.

"I hate to ask you, old lad," said Aubrey pleasantly, "but, as man to man, and without prejudice on either side — where *is* that blighter Rupert?"

II

"Those flannel bags," said Cleaver Wright, laughing as well as he could with a badly swollen lip, "are my flannel bags. Go and find your own moth-eaten and corruptible garments, and leave a gentleman's clothes alone."

George William Savile smiled. His perfect teeth were his great pride. He smoothed down his already sleek and shining hair and held the garments in question up to the light.

"Lulu," he said, "I appeal to you. Are not those my trousers?"

"Gawd only knows," responded the lady, indolently raising herself from the bed on one perfect arm and eyeing the whole tableau, men and trousers alike, with great distaste. "And 'E won't tell," she added, with the proverbial fatalism of the true Cockney. She slid down again and closed eyes that would have conquered Galahad. "And now get out, you — , — swine," she said. "Both of you!"

III

Felicity Broome was in a quandary.

"I suppose I ought to tell father," she thought, "but really he's such a priceless old ass, he'd only go and tell the wrong people and get somebody into trouble."

She looked at the clock. It was eleven p.m. "And it's at least ten minutes slow," she reflected. "I wonder whether Aubrey is in bed? He's young, but he's awfully sensible. I'll talk it over with him, and see what he can suggest."

She reconnoitred. All was well. She climbed out of her bedroom window, slid down the porch, and was soon at the gate.

After her experiences of the previous night, she felt nervous at the idea of traversing the Manor Woods. However, the way round by the lodge was so very much longer, and the thought of finding the gate closed when she eventually arrived there so disheartened her that she decided to summon all the resolution she possessed and dare the woodland path. She entered the little wicket gate, found the main path through the woods, and ran.

The drawing-room, like the library, looked out on to the lawn. Felicity saw a light shining through the curtains as she emerged from the darkness of the trees, and made directly for it. As she approached, she heard a heavy crash. Her heart leapt. Her pulses raced. Her head swam, and her knees knocked together. At the same instant the light went out, and Aubrey's boyish accents, raised in something between fear and horror, cried:

"Cheese it, you stiff! You'll do me in, you fool!"

The mother, that sleeping lioness which inhabits all of us, however weak and timorous we be, awoke to frenzied life in Felicity's breast. She dashed towards the French windows and banged frantically on the glass. Jim Redsey's voice exclaimed:

"Hullo! Who's that?"

Felicity banged again, and somebody inside the room switched on the light. A voice behind the curtains said:

"Who is it?"

"It's me!" said Felicity, with an ungrammatical terseness born of nervousness. "Let me come in! Quick, quick!"

A fumbling at the catch, and Aubrey opened the French windows. Except for himself, the room was deserted.

"Where's Jimsey?" asked Felicity, surprised. Aubrey carefully closed the French windows before giving her any answer.

"Gone to bed," he replied laconically.

"Who were you shouting at just now?"

"Me?"

"Don't be silly! Who was being unkind to you?"

"No one, dear child. I am the rose of Sharon and the lily of the valley. Nobody is ever unkind to me."

Felicity stamped impatiently.

"Naughty," said Aubrey, unperturbed. He bent and picked up the spade, which was lying across the splintered top of a small occasional table.

"I suppose you've heard the glad tidings that are round the village?" he asked.

"You mean the murder? Aubrey, that's what I've come to see you about. You know our dust-heap?"

"Survivals of mediaeval England," said Aubrey, grinning. "In other words, past pluperfect of the verb stinkay — to give forth an obtrusive odour with malice aforethought. I know it, yes."

"I agree it's time something was done about it," said Felicity with a grimace of disgust. "Well, this time it's excelled itself."

"Oh?"

"Yes. I always have to go and inspect it, because Mary Kate Maloney will throw food away if I relax my vigilance, and, between friends, we can't afford to be wasteful. Besides, it's wicked. Well, on the dust-heap I found a suitcase. It has Rupert Sethleigh's initials on it. In fact, I'm practically certain that it's the same

56

suitcase he lent Father when we went away for a holiday last month."

"And that's Mary Kate's neighbourly way of returning it," grinned Aubrey.

"I don't know about that. I thought Father had returned it — properly. What terrifies me is —" she paused, and a slight frown settled between her eyes — "the inside of the case is horribly stained with blood."

With no thought of waking his mother, with no thought for anything except Felicity's news, Aubrey whistled.

"My — hat!" he said, aghast. Added to his own surmises, theories, and fears, these seemed dreadful tidings.

"Yes, isn't it?" agreed Felicity, subscribing to the thought and not to the inadequate expression which clothed it. "You see — it's so awkward, with poor old Jimsey digging that ghastly grave and everything!"

"Eh?" said Aubrey, startled.

"I was in the woods last night — out for a walk," Felicity explained. "I saw him chasing you."

"Oh, I see. We're in this together then? Good! You know the Roberts have been here all the afternoon, don't you?"

Felicity's eyes widened.

"I can't believe it of Jimsey," she said. "Not the — not the horrid part, anyway. Aubrey" — she laid a hand on the boy's arm — "what *was* happening in here when I came along?"

Aubrey grinned. "Oh, I made the poor old thing a bit hairy, you know. I can see now the way I asked him about Rupert practically amounted to an accusation of murder. A bit thick, that. I mean, a man may think a man has dotted a man one over the nut in a fit of peevishness, or absent-mindedly, but a man has no earthly right to indicate to a man, even in the most measured and tactful terms, that a man suspects such to be the case."

"Yes, I see what you mean," said Felicity, without ironic intention. "And he was angry with you?"

"He had a shot at slamming that spade down on top of my head," said Aubrey, grinning. He pointed to the splintered table-top. "I was always a nut at the obstacle race when I was a small kid at Cliveton House," he observed carelessly.

Felicity shuddered. Maternally she stroked his black head to make sure it was still safe.

IV

At twelve-twelve before dawn on Wednesday, June 25th, Mrs Bryce Harringay awoke. She raised herself slightly in bed and listened. Yes, there was certainly a noise. Yes, they were still at it. What a mercy she had locked her bedroom door! Thanking Heaven — for the woman was pious in her way — that the house was not her house, and therefore the burglars were no concern of hers unless they actually forced their way into her bedroom and demanded her jewel-case, she turned over on to the other side and lay down again. It occurred to her that about an hour earlier there had been that awful crash. Probably the burglars murdering James Redsey! A nuisance, that! Still, her subconscious mind was busily adding, James could be spared. It occurred to her that the bedroom window was wide open! An easy method of access to her room if the burglars could climb forty feet of blank wall! The feat, she told herself, was not an impossible one. These cat burglars could climb anywhere. A fly had nothing on them when it came to scaling precipitous heights, she had heard. And there had been that ghastly murder in the neighbouring town of Bossbury! . . .

Mrs Bryce Harringay poked a plump and graceful foot out of bed. In less than five seconds she was closing the window. It is not easy to close a window without making any sound at all, but, fear lending her dexterity, Mrs Bryce Harringay managed it.

Then, with a curiosity which not even fear could allay, she peered out. There was no moon, but the luminous softness of a midsummer night, heavy with scents and secrets, and never becoming wholly dark between sunset and the dawn, allowed her to discern two, or perhaps more, shadowy figures as they walked across the lawn. One of them seemed to be carrying an electric torch. She could see the moving disc of light it cast on the grass.

"Making their escape with ill-gotten booty," thought Mrs Bryce Harringay, who carried a romantic heart beneath the layers of superfluous tissue which covered it, and who had been in her youth a keen student of the then infantile Silent Drama. With great, though entirely subconscious satisfaction to know that the booty was not her property, she watched the burglars until they disappeared into the shadows beyond the farther flowerbeds.

She was about to return to bed when a thought struck her. What of Aubrey? Was he safe? She decided hastily that of course he was perfectly safe. Burglars had no interest in boys. She went to bed and slept soundly.

V

The burglars, halting at the edge of the woods, held a short conclave.

"You will stay by the wicket gate and keep watch, then," said Felicity, "while I go and get it." She spoke in a whisper, less from fear of being overheard than because the spell of summer midnight was upon her. It was faëry time.

"Right you are," said Aubrey, in the same voiceless tone. "Bung it over the gate when you've collected it, and I'll bury it."

Felicity squeezed his hand, and they were soon among the whispering trees. Tripping over briar stems and trailing blackberry plants, almost crashing into treetrunks which suddenly loomed before them, losing the path and miraculously finding it again, at last they reached the wicket gate and the London-Bossbury road. Once on its level surface Felicity began to run. She ran like the wild deer, or the goddess Artemis who hunts them with her bow. Into the sandy lane she sped and over the lych-gate she scrambled. Across the silent churchyard, with its ghostly tombs, she ran, and vaulted over the wall.

Behind the Vicarage woodshed was a pump, and behind the pump a pig-sty, empty now, for the vicar was no swineherd. His was not the nature which can find pleasure in scratching a pig on the back with a ferrule of a walking-stick and pondering on the wonders of evolution. The pig-sty, then, was untenanted.

Felicity hoisted herself over the rotting wooden fence which surrounded it, and groped her way to the inner sty. She stooped low and entered the small roofed enclosure. Once inside, she produced the electric torch Aubrey had insisted upon lending her, and switched it on.

A suitcase was standing in the far corner. With a shiver of disgust, Felicity gripped its handle and carried it to the entrance. Here she switched off the torch, felt her way to the outer fence, dropped the suitcase over, climbed after it, and carried it back to the wicket gate where Aubrey was awaiting her coming.

"Got it? Good egg!" he whispered. "I'll see to it now. Good night. Don't make a row getting back."

"I think I'd better help you," said Felicity quietly.

"No." Aubrey sounded determined. "Cut off, there's a good kid. One of us is far less likely to be nabbed than two if anyone *should* come nosing about. I've only got to bung it over and cover it up, you see, and there's only the one spade, so we couldn't both do the job even if you did come."

Felicity took his black head between her hands and kissed him suddenly and surprisingly on the mouth.

"Have your own way," she said, half laughing. "And good luck. But it's such a horrid place to be alone in, Aubrey. Are you sure you won't be afraid?"

"Oh, I shall be all right. I've got the torch, you see."

So saying, he picked up the spade which was resting against the trunk of a tree, and, with the torch in his pocket and the suitcase in his other hand, he stepped away from her. The woodland closed around him, and Felicity was left alone. In the branches of the nearest tree a star hung like some wondrous gleaming fruit. It winked as she watched it. Straining her ears for any sound from Aubrey, she waited several minutes. The night drew near and touched her. She could sense its quiet breathing. But no uproar broke the stillness, neither sounds of pursuing footsteps, cries for succour, shrieks of fear, nor any other sounds. Trusting that all was well, Felicity went home.

VI

It was a horrid place. There could be no other opinion. Sinister, ghostly, grey, the Druids' Stone bulked menacingly large, and the ring of whispering pines, like courtiers round a cruel, evil king, stood tall and straight and still. Aubrey breathed deeply to restore his ebbing courage, dumped down the suitcase in the hole Jim Redsey had made the night before, and resolutely picked up the spade.

Suddenly an idea occurred to him. Of what use, after all, to bury the case where the police must certainly discover it? Hauling the case up to the surface, he dumped it on one side and began to fill the hole with great spadefuls of the loose light soil. Suddenly another idea occurred to him. His brown face twisted into a wicked grin that made him brother to a faun.

"Might as well give the inspector something to think about if he does come nosing round here," he said to himself. He thrust spade and case into the bushes, groped his way out of the murky woods, and returned to the house.

There was a case of stuffed trout in the hall. Aubrey, creeping in by way of the drawing-room, whose French windows had been left unfastened when he and Felicity had ventured forth in quest of the case, switched on the light, took off his jacket, folded it into a thick pad, and placed it against the glass. Then he raised his fist and dealt the folded coat a smashing blow.

Above stairs his cousin Redsey slept heavily, the prey of terrible dreams. Aubrey's mother, that stately, uncourageous matron, also slept. Her Roman profile, dignified even in slumber, and both her shell-like ears, were buried beneath the clothes. The tinkle of broken glass as it fell to the floor of the hall passed entirely unnoticed.

Aubrey seized the largest trout with both hands. To his excited imagination it appeared to present an expression of shocked surprise at being thus rudely disturbed. Switching off the light, he thrust the fish under his arm and ran back to the woods. Here he pushed the trout into what remained of the hole, drew

63

out the spade, and quickly shovelled back the rest of the earth and stamped it flat.

Then, with the circumspect aid of the torch, he felt for the case, intending to find some other hiding-place for it. To his consternation and dismay, it was not to be found.

Aubrey searched frantically. Throwing caution to the winds, he used the torch recklessly, careless of who might see the gleaming light. All was of no avail. The incriminating bloodstained suitcase had vanished.

VII

"I knew I heard burglars," said Mrs Bryce Harringay triumphantly to a nervously ill-tempered Jim Redsey and a heavy-eyed worried-looking Aubrey next morning.

"Burglars?" said Jim, with a short laugh. "What rot!"

"I object, James, both to your speech and the abrupt, I may say discourteous, tone in which you see fit to deliver it," pronounced his aunt coldly. "I repeat, there were *burglars* in this house last night. They have stolen a valuable trout from the case in the hall."

"Valuable?" snarled Redsey. "What tosh! A beastly lot of mid-Victorian atrocities, those trout! As a matter of fact, one of them isn't a trout at all. It's a roach."

"I do not affect to be a judge of fish," said his aunt, "neither am I an authority upon their names and habits. I merely remark that there *were* burglars in this house last night. I heard them. As proof I submit that

64

the trout is gone. I realize that I am but a poor subnormal specimen of humanity, belonging to the weaker sex at that; one who may be contradicted, insulted and corrected at random by any young man who happens to be a poor twelve at golf and an average — a *very* average — performer upon the piano. Nevertheless, I have ears and eyes equal to any in this country, and I insist that this house was visited by burglars last night! I myself perceived them stealing across the lawn in the early hours of the morning! And I repeat that they removed a valuable fish from the case in the hall."

"Why you keep harping on the value of the putrid fish I can't conceive," said Jim irritably, perceiving that his aunt was going to get the best of it as usual.

"If it were not valuable," said Mrs Bryce Harringay, in a tone which indicated clearly that the argument was at an end, "the burglars would not have taken it. If you are going to choke, Aubrey, will you please go outside!"

CHAPTER
SIX

Thursday

"Please yourself, my dear old thing," said Felicity despairingly. "I don't mind a bit."

The Vicar of Wandles smiled upon his daughter vaguely.

"But you know perfectly well that I'm never happy when I please myself," he said. "You please yourself instead. Did you notice whether I put Tacitus on the mantelpiece in the other room? I don't seem to have him with me."

Apologetically he drew a small clock from the large pocket of his black alpaca coat and placed it on the table.

Felicity went into the dining-room and retrieved the volume in question.

"Here you are," she said. "I don't want to upset you, sweetest, but we shan't have a single clock in the house that will keep correct time if you go pushing them into the pockets of your coat like that. And I mend those pockets so often," she added with a little sigh. "Now, about the tennis. Whom shall we have? Aubrey, his awful mother, and Jimsey. That's three from the Manor to start with. Then I owe Mr Wright an invitation, so that means asking Mr Savile and the unspeakable Lulu as well. That makes six. You and me, eight. Then I ought to ask Margery — she doesn't get much fun, poor kid — and Dr Barnes. No good inviting Mrs Barnes with them, because she's away. That's ten. We ought to have two more, I suppose, and make it up to a dozen. What about the major? We might just as well ask everybody at once, and get it over. Besides, it's cheaper than having two or three little stunts."

"What about Mr Sethleigh?" suggested the vicar. "You didn't include him with the Manor crowd."

A shadow crossed Felicity's brow.

"Darling, I keep telling you he has gone to America," she said. The vicar gazed at her in mild surprise.

"Really? That's very curious," he said.

"Why?" asked his daughter sharply.

Felicity's nerves were raw. She had not slept for thinking of Aubrey and his task of burying the blood-stained suitcase. A thousand times in fevered imagination she had sped down the Bossbury road with the horrid thing in her hand. In fancy she found herself groping her way into the dark pig-sty, terrified of what she might discover there.

"Why?" echoed the vicar. He thought deeply for a moment. "Why?" he repeated. "Well, he wants me to witness his will. I promised to go over there on Monday afternoon, when his solicitor was due to arrive, but I completely forgot it."

"But you did witness his will, darling. Ever so long ago. I was about sixteen at the time. Don't you remember?"

"Oh, yes, I remember that will. I thought it a very fair will, you know. But he was going to alter it. You see, according to the terms of the first will, the chief beneficiary was the young cousin of his, James Redsey. But Redsey has done something to annoy Sethleigh, I should imagine, because this new will, from what I can understand, cuts Redsey right out and leaves the bulk of the property to the boy Aubrey Harringay."

"But — but are you certain?" cried Felicity, going very white.

"Absolutely. I told the police all about it yesterday afternoon. They came here to find out all I knew about Sethleigh, but I didn't realize he had gone to America. What have the police to do with it?"

Felicity sat down. She felt that, without support of some kind, her trembling knees would give way and she would fall.

"Oh, dearest!" she cried. "You didn't tell them about the altered will?"

"Of course I did. Why shouldn't I? Especially as it hasn't been altered yet. At least, I suppose not, or Sethleigh would have been over here for my signature before this. Oh, you say he has gone to America, though. Did he see Grayling — it is Grayling, isn't it? — before he went?"

"No," said Felicity, moistening her upper lip with the tip of her tongue. "No, he — no, he didn't."

"Oh, well, then Redsey is still the heir. Perhaps Sethleigh will have recovered from his annoyance by the time he returns to England. I like the look of young Redsey. By the way," he broke off, "I think I must go into Culminster this afternoon. I want to see Crowdesley about the Repairing Fund. We must have something done to the west door soon. It's the finest bit of Norman work in the county, and it's simply going to ruin."

"Good idea," said Felicity, as cheerfully as she could. "Perhaps he'll give you lunch if you trot off at once. I expect he'll have something nice. Bishops generally do, don't they? And there's nothing but the cold lamb here, and precious little of that."

"I doubt if it would be a popular move to rush him for lunch," said the vicar, grinning boyishly. "I think it will have to be the lamb, and I'll go over there first thing this afternoon."

The one maid the Vicarage boasted knocked aggressively at the door.

"There's a lady across the half-door does be wanting his reverence," she announced grandly and with a truly Hibernian toss of the forelock. "Will I be after asking her within?"

"You will," replied the vicar, to whom Mary Kate Maloney was an unending source of joy. "And kindly refrain from instructing her to wipe her shoes on the mat, as you did the last visitor who came to call on me."

"Sure," retorted Mary Kate, with the readiness of her race to enter into any argument, however unprofitable, "and wouldn't that be foolishness itself, with no rain falling these twenty days and the road without as dry as Tim Nixey's throat, and the whole of the sky like brazen brass entirely?"

The vicar chuckled as she flounced out, and Felicity rose to receive the visitor.

"Mrs Lestrange Bradley," announced Mary Kate magnificently. One of her most striking virtues consisted of an enviable ability to grasp names the first time she heard them, coupled with the courage to repeat them aloud with confident heartiness.

A small, shrivelled, bird-like woman, who might have been thirty-five and who might have been ninety, clad in a blue and sulphur jumper like the plumage of a macaw, came forward with that air of easy condescension which is usually achieved by royalty only, and fixed the vicar with an eagle eye.

"Am I addressing the spiritual adviser of this parish?" she enquired.

Her voice was startling in that it belied her whole appearance. Here was no bird-like twitter nor harsh parrot cry, but a mellifluous utterance, rich and full, and curiously, definitely, superlatively attractive.

The Reverend Stephen Broome blushed nervously, and ran a bony finger round the inside of his clerical collar.

"Er — I suppose so. That is — yes," he replied.

"Then I am compelled to state that in my opinion the west door is a disgrace," said Mrs Bradley firmly.

"We were just talking about it when you knocked," said Felicity, quick to defend her father. "But the Restoration Fund, all told, only amounts to twenty-nine shillings and sevenpence, and what's the use of that, I should like to know? It's all very well for people to complain —"

Mrs Bradley looked at her for the first time. Felicity felt herself blushing beneath the long, cool, slightly ironic gaze.

"A lovely child," said Mrs Bradley at last. "And so angry with me."

She turned again to the vicar.

"Have it repaired," she said. "Send me the estimates. I will pay the bill."

"Oh, but I'm going to see the bishop about it this very afternoon," said the Reverend Stephen helplessly. "I mean, it is tremendously kind of you, but —"

"Oh, I'm solvent," said Mrs Bradley, with a hideous cackle. "As for going to see Reginald Crowdesley, you might as well save your time, young man. Look here, suppose I give you a cheque for the Restoration Fund, and then you can muddle along in your own way with it. I suppose he *is* a muddler?" she added, turning to Felicity again. "He looks like one."

The vicar chuckled appreciatively at this palpable home truth, but Felicity was too angry to reply. She was more angry still when the vicar invited Mrs Bradley to the tennis party on the following afternoon.

"Then that will make the twelve people you wanted, dear," he announced to Felicity in tones of such decided self-congratulation at having solved one of the domestic problems at last that she could do no less than smile and second the invitation.

"Although how I did it," she confided to Aubrey Harringay next day, "I don't know. She's a most infuriating woman!"

"Yes. The mater loathes her too," said Aubrey, grinning. "She's a psycho-analyst."

"A what?"

"Psycho-analyst. I don't know what they do, quite. I believe it's something mad but brainy. The thing was all the rage two or three years ago, and the mater was potty to be in the thick of it, as usual. She collects these new movements. Well, she tried to collect Mrs Bradley, who appears to be rather a brass hat at the business, but the old dame wasn't having any. Said that what the mater required was not a psycho-analyst but a copperplated tummy, because all her moods and tempers were simply due to indigestion and not to all these repressions and complexes at all. Of course, the mater was rather fed, and tried to get old Blessington — that's our solicitor — to start an action for slander or something. But old Blessington only told her not to be an ass, but to think herself lucky she'd had such good advice absolutely free of charge, and advised her to follow it up. So the mater tried the diet stunt, as recommended by Mrs Bradley, and has positively never looked back. Oh, and by the way! Rather a confounded nuisance! I ought to have told you yesterday, but we all went out in the car, and, anyway, I couldn't see that there was anything to be done. That case of Rupert's. It's gone."

"Gone?" said Felicity, puzzled. "But you buried it."

"No, as a matter of fact I did not bury it," confessed Aubrey. "And I wish I knew whether the silly blighter who boned it while I was gone for the fish was playing a practical joke, or whether — Oh, I don't know. What do you think about it?"

"As I haven't the least idea what you are talking about," said Felicity, "I'm afraid I'm not thinking very clearly about anything. What did happen, then?"

"I'm telling you. I poked the case and the spade into the bushes while I went up to the house to get something to shove into the hole old Jim made on Monday night, and, when I got back with one of the stuffed fish from the case in the hall, I found the spade all right but the beastly case had gone. I looked again yesterday, and I looked this morning, but there's no sign of it anywhere."

"But I can't think why you didn't bury it as we arranged," cried Felicity. "Now we don't know what has happened to it!"

"Well, I thought — the police, you see."

"What do you mean?"

"They'll nose about. Sure to. They may just as easily nose about outside the house as inside it. If they go into the clearing they'll spot the freshly dug earth. Then they'll excavate. Well, it wouldn't do for *them* to find the blood-stained baggage, would it, with old Rupert's initials as large as life on the lid? You see, my theory is this: Old Rupert murdered that man, whoever it was, and took the body into Bossbury to cover the tracks. Then Rupert thought it best to disappear. Then I think Jim and Rupert had a scrap in the woods, and Jim won, and Rupert got hairy and told Jim he'd tell the police Jim did it, and Jim got wind up because he couldn't prove an alibi, and perhaps even helped Rupert a bit and so forth, and there you are."

"Yes," said Felicity slowly, "there I am. And there are you, and you're a wretched little liar, Aubrey Harringay."

Aubrey, who topped her by an inch and a half — for he was a tall boy — grinned cheerfully.

"Of course," continued Felicity, knitting her brows and thinking it out, "the murdered man can't be Rupert. I mean, theoretically he is, but actually things like that don't happen to people one knows. Oh, bother! Here comes somebody looking for a tennis partner. Will you play again, or are you too tired?"

"I'm too tired to play with Savile," said Aubrey decidedly. "He's such a dud at tennis." So saying, he walked off.

The sleek-haired Savile, however, was looking neither for a partner nor an opponent. He had come in search of Felicity for another purpose. He approached her with his ingratiating smile.

"When I was over here last time, Miss Broome," he remarked, "your father offered to show me his Rabelais."

"Oh, it's nothing special," replied Felicity indifferently, "except for the French illustrations. I believe they are supposed to be rather fine, but I've never seen them. If you want to look at it you can go into the study now. I think Father is there."

"Thank you so much," said Savile, his sallow face flushing warmly. "I will go along, then, if I may."

74

"There are sandwiches and things in the dining-room," Felicity went on. "Please help yourself. It's rather a thirsty afternoon, isn't it?"

"Greasy bounder," remarked Aubrey, returning to her side as soon as Savile was out of sight. "I suppose it's all right to let him go pawing your pater's stuff about? Chap always looks dirty to me."

"Don't be silly," said Felicity, laughing. "And, look here! Why aren't you helping to amuse my guests instead of hanging about and being rude about people?"

"Your guests are all right," said Aubrey, with youthful optimism. "The major is still clinging tight to lovely Lulu — no, honestly, though, talk about 'the face that launched a thousand ships' — she *is* a glorious kid, isn't she? Young, too, you know. Not more than eighteen. Can't be. She is bucked at having the old lad on her hands all the afternoon! And the mater is busy having a row with old Jim, and Mrs Bradley is hobnobbing with the doctor, and Margery has gone home to feed her rabbits, but she's coming back immediately, and I — here am I!" He put his black head on one side and smiled at her.

"Yes," said Felicity absently. "Aubrey, I wish you had buried that suitcase after all. It seems to me that even if the police had found it, they couldn't have done much with it. But the thought that somebody was watching us all the time in those woods makes me crawl all over. I say, here comes Mrs Bradley. Do talk to her."

"Not I," said Aubrey, making a bee-line for the gooseberry bushes which bordered the kitchen garden and divided it from the lawn. "You do your own dirty work, young child! I'm going to have a squint at your historic dust-heap."

"I've been talking for hours," announced Mrs Bradley to Felicity. "How ill-natured one is always tempted to be when one gossips! The dear doctor was thus tempted. He fell."

"Did he?" said Felicity. She laughed. "Poor old thing! He loves to be malicious. Who was the victim this time?"

"Mrs Savile." She lowered her small, thin body carefully into a deck-chair and arranged her sulphur and green voile frock.

"You mean Lulu Hirst," said Felicity, sitting on the grass and gazing up into Mrs Bradley's shrewd yellow face.

"Do I? That's what the doctor seemed anxious to impress upon me."

"What is?"

"That I meant Lulu Hirst. But I've worked it out logically. Would you care to hear the conclusions?"

"Yes, please," said Felicity politely.

"What is your own opinion of the young person?" Mrs Bradley enquired.

"I can't stand any of them up at the Cottage," said Felicity. "They are such a queer crowd. Of course, one can understand Cleaver Wright. He is an artist."

"But I thought personal peculiarities as part of an artist's stock-in-trade had gone sadly out of fashion," demurred Mrs Bradley. "Where does he come from?"

"Somewhere in London."

"And now he lives in the Cottage on the Hill. Did he give it that name? No? I thought not. That was the always-correct Mr Savile's choice, wasn't it? Yes? I thought so. And Lulu —"

"Surnamed the Unspeakable," muttered Felicity darkly.

Mrs Bradley gave a sinister chuckle.

"How extraordinarily interesting!" she observed.

"I don't think it is interesting," said Felicity through her teeth. "I think she's a little cat!"

"That's where you are entirely wrong, child," said Mrs Bradley very seriously. "However, we will go into that later. I was about to remark that Lulu, in actual fact, is Mr Savile's wife."

"Then why doesn't she say so, and have done with it?" was Felicity's spirited demand.

"For the simple reason, child, that Savile, a man of average prosperity and under no obligation financially to labour for his bread, likes to consider himself a painter. The craze for defying convention, I seem to remember, was still rife in the quarter of London from which he came, and therefore I imagine he considered it highly improper to be shackled by the matrimonial tie. To such an apostle of free thought, free love, and, I darkly suspect, free food and drink at the expense of other and more indigent people, the idea of marriage convention would be singularly distasteful. But there is another side to his nature. He is in the most startling sense a rigid pedant. Therefore, as he knows the average person still looks upon the state of matrimony as a reasonable preliminary to cohabitation with a member of the opposite sex, he went through the form of marriage with Lulu Hirst according to the requirements of English law, and such law would unhesitatingly recognize them as man and wife. But once this enterprising fellow had compromised with the law of the land, his next intention was to effect a compromise with that of his immediate circle. Therefore he and his wife mutually agreed that Lulu should retain her maiden name of Hirst, and the awful secret that they had been branded with the matrimonial iron was to remain locked in their bosoms. Savile desired that Chelsea or Bloomsbury or Chiswick or wherever it is should not look down upon him. He must save his soul — and, of course, his face; a thing of far greater importance to most of us!"

She cackled with pleasure at the picture she had conjured up. Felicity smiled politely.

"Thus," Mrs Bradley continued, "*all* the conventions had been complied with, and there remained but to settle down to a life of humdrum ease in the country."

She shook her head sadly.

"There are none as despotically governed as the lawless," she observed tritely. "There are none as absurdly shackled by taboo and convention as those who desire to be free of these things. We change our masters; but it is as slaves we live and die."

With grace, strength, and precision, Aubrey Harringay cleared the gooseberry bushes like a steeplechaser and came up beside Felicity.

"Well, child," said Mrs Bradley. Aubrey smiled engagingly at her, but addressed himself to the girl.

78

"I say," he said, "I hope you don't mind, but I've been having a squizz at your dust-heap, as I said I would."

"But it *smells!*" said Felicity, wrinkling her nose in disgust. "And I do hope you turned up the bottoms of your lovely white trousers! It is such a dreadful place."

"Horrid. Yes," Aubrey agreed absently, glancing down at his flannels. "I say," he added unexpectedly, "what does your pater do with his false teeth?"

"But he hasn't false teeth!" cried Felicity, bewildered.

"No, I thought he hadn't," remarked Aubrey. He smiled amiably at them both and walked serenely away, leaving Mrs Bradley with a curious expression on her sharp-featured, sardonic face, and Felicity staring after him in perplexity.

Suddenly Mrs Bradley laughed. Her own teeth were even, strong, and white — the teeth of a relentless beast of prey; a creature tigerish, carnivorous, untamed.

"But why the country?" she said to herself. "Curious!"

CHAPTER
SEVEN

The Tale of a Head

I

The Bishop of Culminster sighed heavily and inspected his left leg. The leg, shapely, well gaitered, neat, and infinitely episcopal, satisfied his anxious scrutiny. He inspected his right leg.

"I do wish, Reginald," said Mrs Bryce Harringay, with pardonable asperity, "that you would Hurry Up. The car has been at the door now for twenty minutes."

The bishop smiled benignly upon her, but groaned in spirit. A long drive in the car with his autocratic sister-in-law was, in his opinion, a poor way of spending a lovely June day.

"I am more than ready, my dear Constance," he observed, following her down the steps and out to the waiting vehicle.

Mrs Bryce Harringay snorted and, climbing in, settled herself comfortably against the upholstery of Rupert Sethleigh's Bentley car.

"And where is Rupert?" enquired the bishop, as the car, handled by Rupert Sethleigh's chauffeur, started off with some of the bishop's gravel path rattling under the mudguards. "Could he not find time to accompany you?"

"It is about Rupert that I wish to speak to you." Mrs Bryce Harringay paused. It was a thousand pities to miss a chance of being really dramatic. "Rupert," she announced after due consideration, "Rupert has disappeared."

"Disappeared? Rupert? But — I mean — that doesn't sound like Rupert. It isn't at all the sort of thing Rupert would do," observed the bishop mildly. "I can't imagine it. People like Rupert don't disappear. Absconding clerks and company promoters, perhaps, but not Rupert. Oh, dear, no."

Mrs Bryce Harringay turned wrathfully upon him.

"I am tired, Reginald, of being told absurd things about Rupert. Anyone is liable to disappear. It isn't anything disgraceful! As a matter of fact, we thought at first that he might have gone to America."

"I should hardly have thought that going to America came under the heading of Disappearance, you know," remarked the bishop thoughtfully.

Mrs Bryce Harringay turned upon him the gaze she kept for those suspected of trying to be humorous at her expense, but the bishop's expansive urbanity disarmed her.

"We have had the police! We have endured the Press! The house has been ransacked! The garden-beds have been both photographed and trampled upon! This morning the lodge gates were besieged — literally *besieged* — by sightseers from the neighbouring

81

towns! Rupert's private papers have been com-
mandeered! So has the library, which I have been
compelled to place at the disposal of the authorities so
that the servants and ourselves may be put through a
humiliating questionnaire concerning our movements
during the past few days! And it is all James's fault!
Every bit of it!"

The bishop lifted whimsical eyebrows.

"Indeed, Reginald, it is so! I know that James is a
favourite with you. I think it is a pity. It seems that
James has told Various Lies" — the bishop's smile
broke bounds at the sound of the capital letters in her
voice — "and that Rupert never had any intention of
going to America, as James had falsely led us to believe
he had had, and, in fact, that he did not go, and that
James was fully aware that he did not go, and that, with
intent to mislead us all — deliberate intent, quite
deliberate — he concocted a whole series of Untruthful
Explanations in order to conceal the true whereabouts
of his unfortunate cousin."

"And where abouts *is* his unfortunate cousin?" asked
the bishop, when he had digested this elaborate thesis
on the subject of Rupert's disappearance and James's
perfidy.

"We do not know. It seems that James, in a fit of
animal passion which a civilized person cannot but
deplore, laid violent hands upon his cousin, and smote
him on the head."

"I doubt whether that would have had a great deal of
effect upon Rupert, you know," murmured the bishop
thoughtfully. "A thick-headed —"

"The blow," Mrs Bryce Harringay continued, ignoring the interruption, "caught Rupert under the chin and —"

"Laid him out," interpolated the bishop appreciatively. "Go on, Constance."

"Really, Reginald!" his sister-in-law remonstrated warmly. "One might almost imagine that you condoned, if not actually countenanced, this act of Sheer Barbarity."

"No, no. Oh, no," the bishop hastened to observe. "It is your pithy narrative style which evokes my admiration, not the unworthy subject of your discourse. You should have — you have a decided gift for exposition, you know. Pray proceed."

"Well," continued Mrs Bryce Harringay, somewhat mollified, "now comes the Really Mysterious part of the affair. The heartless and unprincipled James, for whom I find myself unable to feel anything but the most utter contempt, left his unfortunate cousin lying prone upon the damp ground at eight o'clock at night in that horrible place —"

"I shouldn't have thought the ground could be damp anywhere after this long spell of fine weather," remarked the bishop. "But what horrible place do you mean?"

"I told you. In the midst of the woods near the Druids' Stone. There is blood on the stone where the poor boy struck his head in falling. From that moment, Rupert has never more been seen."

"I think it is rather soon to speak with such finality," said the bishop. "I expect the truth is that Rupert is suffering from concussion and is wandering about, helpless from temporary loss of memory."

"Well," pronounced Mrs Bryce Harringay in funereal tones, "that is what we all *hope*. But such Terrible Things have been happening down in Bossbury, that really one wonders why people come to the country for peace and quietness!"

II

"I shall bathe," said the bishop three hours later. They had drawn up on a piece of flat grassy land at the head of chalk cliffs. Below them the sea foamed shorewards over low black rocks, for the tide was just on the turn. Across the water the sun shone in a great breadth of glory; above the waves and up and down the face of the cliff the strong-winged seagulls wheeled and swooped and screamed.

There was a precipitous way leading down to the beach. Mrs Bryce Harringay had already refused to attempt it. The bishop, however, had been sitting on the short grass at the top of the cliffs, inhaling the splendid air and longing for a swim. The chauffeur had been sent over to the adjacent town to get himself some food, and Mrs Bryce Harringay some literature and a box of sweets.

"I really must have a swim," the bishop observed, finding that his previous statement had had no effect.

Mrs Bryce Harringay looked pained.

84

"So soon after lunch?" she enquired coldly. "I think you are unwise."

"Rubbish!" said the bishop, with an incisiveness which Mrs Bryce Harringay's late husband would have envied. "I'll make my way down to the beach and see whether there is a suitable place for undressing. Some rocks or something. If there is no suitable spot, I shall come up again and undress in the car. You don't mind being left alone for a quarter of an hour or so, do you, while I bathe?"

"Since I observe Cooper in the distance, I do not object in the very slightest," Mrs Bryce Harringay replied. "Particularly if he has brought the magazines I asked for and not some others of his own or the shopkeeper's choice."

The bishop descended the steep little path and arrived safely at the bottom. He was fortunate enough to discover a small recess, scarcely large enough to be called a cave, which formed an admirable shelter. In about three minutes he was trotting joyously into the sea.

Mrs Bryce Harringay sat contentedly reading. Cooper, on the step of the car, smoked a cigarette. In the clear shallow water the bishop splashed and grunted. Far up the beach towards the town stood a solitary red-striped tent.

The bishop enjoyed his swim. After about fifteen minutes he came trotting back up the beach, happily puffing and blowing, seized his towel, and began to rub himself vigorously.

Suddenly a voice from above cried out:

"I say, come and look at this!" And a young man of about twenty-five hung his face over the top of the cave and looked in.

"Buck up and get dressed," he said. "I must show somebody what we've found, and there's only you, so you've got to see it. Excuse me. My feet are slipping."

And the face was withdrawn.

The bishop was in high good humour after his swim. He did buck up and get dressed. Inside ten minutes he was ready, gaiters and all.

"Smart work," said an approving voice above his head. "I suppose they've invented a patent method of doing 'em up by now, like the girls' Russian boots. I say, just come up here a minute. Right foot here — give us your hand — up-se-daisy!"

The bishop found himself on a small promontory which was occupied by a large young man in shorts and a shirt. He wore nothing else except a pair of extremely dilapidated brown suède shoes, brogue pattern, of a style which had enjoyed a short measure of popularity among men some years previously, but had since gone completely out of fashion. His face was bronzed, keen and very good-humoured. He grinned companionably at the bishop.

"That's my dug-out down there," he said, pointing to the striped tent. "A bit gay, isn't it? My sister chose it. I say, look what we've found! Isn't it a beauty?"

And he drew out from a hole in the face of the cliff a human skull, complete except for a deep cleft from the top of the crown to half-way down the forehead.

Twenty minutes later the bishop, rosy and smiling, climbed the precipitous little path again and rejoined his sister-in-law. Mrs Bryce Harringay glanced at her watch.

"You've been a very long time, Reginald," she observed. "I do hope you will take no harm from so prolonged an immersion in the water."

"Oh, I was not in the sea for more than a quarter of an hour," replied the bishop, taking his place beside her in the car. "Something else delayed me."

"Let me spread out that damp towel," said Mrs Bryce Harringay. "It will quickly dry in this breeze."

"On no account!" cried the bishop hastily. "I have a real treasure wrapped up in it which I intend to present to the Culminster Museum. I think I will leave it there with Brown as we pass. He can then examine it at his leisure, and I will call tomorrow and talk with him about it. I am proud of the Culminster Museum, and it is a very long time since I sent them anything. And, as I was instrumental in founding it, I feel it is my duty —"

"What are you talking about, my dear Reginald?" asked Mrs Bryce Harringay, frowning as Cooper took a very sharp corner at a greater pace than she considered safe.

"I am talking about a brachycephalic skull," replied the bishop happily. "A young man on the beach gave it to me. This type of skull, as perhaps you are aware, was common among —"

"A skull!" cried Mrs Bryce Harringay, seizing upon what was, to her mind, the essential point of the discourse. She shuddered delicately. "But, Reginald! How Extraordinarily Unpleasant!"

She withdrew herself hastily from the bundle wrapped round with the bishop's gaily striped towel.

"Pray keep it as far from my person as the strictly limited confines of this Inadequate Vehicle will allow," she commanded him.

The inadequate vehicle passed over a large stone at the side of the road, and she was flung forward a little in her seat. Her hand came in contact with the loathsome protuberance she had anathematized. Mrs Bryce Harringay gave a little shriek of distaste and withdrew her hand hastily. The bishop, more careful for his treasure than for his sister-in-law's feelings, removed the towel containing the antiquity to a safer place in the car.

"I think Broome ought to see this before I hand it over to Brown," he said. "We could drive round that way, couldn't we? He knows quite a lot about the Celtic era. Far more than I do, as a matter of fact."

They reached the Vicarage at Wandles Parva just as Mary Kate Maloney was carrying in the tea.

"Are there any more scones?" whispered Felicity, when the visitors had been announced.

"There will be a few more in the kitchen," replied Mary Kate in a sibilant tone, "but you'd sooner stop up the great cave of Kentucky with little apples than you would be filling the bishop's stomach when there's scones to his tea!"

With this dark prophecy she retired to the kitchen. The scones, however, to Felicity's almost visible relief, proved more than equal even to the demands made upon them by the bishop.

When the meal was over, and Mary Kate, to use her own expression, had "made them more room to their elbows" by clearing away the tea-things, the bishop triumphantly produced his treasure and it was reverently handed round.

"But look here, sir," said the Reverend Stephen Broome, who had been in the bishop's form when the latter was a junior master, "this looks too good to be true."

"To be sure," interpolated Mary Kate, who, with a dish of jam poised perilously above the bishop's bald head, was leaning against the back of her employer's chair and breathing heavily down the inside of his collar, "if a nice set of false teeth wouldn't improve the appearance of the creature entirely! I mind when me Auntie Molly Ann Maloney that's own sister to me father and him an orphan down in County Cork —"

The vicar looked up at her, and she subsided. Then he felt the skull all over gingerly with his fine strong hands, and gave it back to the bishop, after taking a final glance at the deep cleft.

"Where did you say you got it?" he asked.

"A young fellow camping near Rams Cove found it and gave it me. Very fine, don't you think?"

The vicar stroked his chin.

"I should say that skull is less than a hundred years old," he said.

"Rubbish, man!" retorted the bishop spiritedly. "Use your eyes!"

"I am doing so," returned the vicar mildly. "Probably the skull of somebody who tumbled down the cliffs there in our grandfathers' time, I should say. It's a nasty place just there, you know. And landslips are fairly frequent. I dare say if you searched about you'd find something more of the skeleton."

The bishop looked annoyed. Mrs Bryce Harringay was slightly but, to her brother-in-law's way of thinking, exasperatingly amused.

The pause which followed was broken by the irrepressible Mary Kate, who had no intention of allowing the Reverend Stephen to interfere with her enjoyment of "the company".

"I declare to God entirely," she remarked conversationally, "if the look of that same there is not calling into me mind the bones of the pig's face me mother would be boiling the meat off for a dish of collared head. Just so do them lads of butchers chop the head down, the way the meat will boil nice and tender off the bones of it!"

The vicar turned his head and glared at her. Mary Kate started precipitately, and saved the jam only by a dexterous flick of her free hand underneath the dish as the glutinous sticky compound came surging over the edge. Surreptitiously licking a somewhat grimy palm, she departed hastily in the direction of the kitchen.

"Well, there is nothing to be gained by argument in this case," said the bishop. "But I shall certainly present it to Brown as a museum specimen of a brachycephalic skull of the late Celtic period."

"I hope he will accept it in the same spirit," said the Reverend Stephen with delicate irony. "I say, though," he broke off, "I know what would be rather a joke! Let's send for young Wright and see if he can reconstruct the thing. He's very clever at modelling. May I send over and get him to do it?"

"With pleasure, so far as I am concerned," said the bishop stiffly.

"Felicity," said her father, "send Mary Kate over to the Cottage and ask her to get Mr Wright to come over here for a few minutes."

"I'll go myself. I promised to take Mrs Bradley's dog for a run this evening, so I can call there and go on to the Cottage."

Her father chuckled.

"I was under the impression that you didn't like Mrs Bradley," he said.

Felicity flushed and tossed her head.

"Oh, well, when you've been there to lunch and been there to dinner, as we have, you can't go on feeling unkindly disposed," she said.

Mrs Bradley was in.

"But Boller doesn't like strangers," she said. "You don't think he'll bite them, do you, child?"

Felicity giggled.

"I hope not. But I'm not going up there if you won't allow me to take the dog," she said. "I don't like those people. There's something funny about them. They are Londoners. What did they want to come and bury themselves alive down here for?"

"Take the dog if you like," remarked Mrs Bradley. "May I come with you and see the fun?"

"Then I needn't take the dog," said Felicity, laughing.

"Impudence," said Mrs Bradley severely, "is the weapon of the very young. Chastisement" — she seized Felicity in a grip of iron and smacked her hard — "is the reply of the extremely old."

She released her victim, and together they went out at the side gate into the lane which led to the Cottage on the Hill.

"You're horribly strong," said Felicity, "aren't you?"

"I am," replied Mrs Bradley with enormous complacence.

It was Lulu who opened the door. After a little delay, while he washed his hands and struggled into a collar, Wright joined them.

He was a short, thick-set, cheerful young man of twenty-eight, and looked more like a ploughboy than an artist. His hair was thick and dark and his eyes were bright blue with long lashes. He slid his arm familiarly through Felicity's and grinned at Mrs Bradley like an impudent faun. Felicity, hating him because he stirred her blood in some queer, exciting, vaguely improper way — or so she felt — released her arm and talked to Mrs Bradley all the way down the hill.

"It's a pity she doesn't like me," said Wright, when he could manage to interpolate a word. "I'm such a nice lad really."

As they passed Mrs Bradley's house, her dog came to the gate and greeted them. Maliciously, Felicity opened the gate and let him out. The Airedale sniffed suspiciously round Wright's grey-flannelled legs, and Felicity chuckled.

"Mind! He doesn't like strangers!" she said mockingly.

"Doesn't he?" Wright bent down, took the dog's muzzle between his hands, and stared into the clear brown eyes. "He's afraid of them, though."

The dog's stump of a tail drooped. Unable to meet the quizzically smiling gaze, he turned his head piteously aside.

Wright released him, wiped his hands on the seams of his trousers, and laughed.

When he saw the skull at the Vicarage he laughed again more joyously.

"Can I take it away with me?" he said. "I'll let you have it back to-morrow afternoon with any luck."

"Oh, can't you slap a bit of clay over it now?" asked the vicar.

"'Fraid not. All my stuff's up at the Cottage, you see. I'll bring it over to-morrow, sure as sure."

Mrs Bryce Harringay interposed.

"I feel that it would be the best thing to do, Reginald," she announced. "I shall have time to drive you home to Culminster if we start now. Otherwise I shall not be in time to do so. Will you come?"

The bishop, looking back longingly at the skull, which was lying in the crook of Wright's arm, followed her out to the waiting car. Wright chucked the skull affectionately under the chin, and walked home with it pressed between his elbow and his side. He carolled blithely as he went along.

True to his promise, he brought a complete head back next day. He had reconstructed in clay the features and lineaments of a man.

"Rather a curious resemblance, don't you think?" he said casually to the Reverend Stephen Broome, holding out the reconstructed head.

The vicar gasped. Low forehead, fleshy jowl, straight Norman nose, and sensual lips! — it was the head of Rupert Sethleigh.

CHAPTER
EIGHT

Second Instalment of the Same Tale

"That wretched policeman," complained Mrs Bryce Harringay petulantly, "is here again, and wants to see the car. I suppose he means the Bentley, but I don't know, and why he should want to see it I don't know, and why he should require to see it on Sunday of all days, I don't know, but I suppose he must be humoured. Take him round to the garage, Aubrey, will you?"

"Where is he, mater?" asked Aubrey, grinning.

"In the shrubbery, looking for footprints and cigarette ash," growled Jim Redsey, without glancing up from an old newspaper which he was pretending to read.

"Do not be foolish, James," said his aunt. "He is in the hall. And whatever happens, Aubrey, do not allow him to annoy Cooper. The only really reliable chauffeur," she observed as Aubrey went out, "that poor Rupert ever had."

Cooper, however, was breakfasting, so Aubrey returned for the keys and unlocked the garage door.

"Want her jacked up?" he enquired professionally of the inspector.

"No, Mr Harringay, I thank you."

Detective Inspector Grindy was large, like all policemen, good-natured, like most, and very fond of boys, but duty was duty. Very deliberately he turned his back upon Aubrey and made an entry in his note-book. Then he walked all round the car and wrote in his note-book again.

"Thank you, Mr Harringay. That's all," he said cheerfully.

"But you haven't looked at the tyres to see what sort of a track they'd leave. And you — and you haven't found out how much petrol there is in the tank and whether she's been filled up since the mater went out yesterday."

The inspector roared with laughter, and drew out a folding map.

"Never mind, Mr Harringay," he said. "Come here and point me out the route they took to get to Rams Cove yesterday."

"I say," remarked Aubrey, when the inspector had made a note of the route, "I wish I'd seen that skull that chap found. What was it like?"

"When we had duly admired the work of art with which Mr Wright had surrounded it, we packed same in the safe ready to peel off the clay which has dried rather hard. But I've no doubt that when we do peel it off we shall find that the skull underneath is exactly like any other skull, Mr Harringay." And the inspector winked solemnly. "We laughed quite a good bit, Superintendent Bidwell and me, over that skull."

"Oh, did you? Why?"

"Well, Mr Harringay" — the inspector coughed judiciously — "we know Mr Wright, you see. A very pleasant gentleman. Humorous, too! Must have his little joke, whatever happens, as you know. That's why we aren't in any hurry to peel off the clay. Won't help us much when we do."

"I don't know the fellow from Adam, except by sight," remarked Aubrey.

"No? Well, people round here know him well for his joking ways. It was him that dressed up as the ghost of Dicky Tell, who was hanged at the crossroads in chains for highway robbery way back a hundred years or more, and nearly frightened the folks into fits as they came home from Bossbury Fair one night. Oh, he's a rare funny chap, is Mr Wright."

"Yes, but what about the skull?"

"Well, Mr Harringay, a skull's a skull, isn't it?"

"How do you mean?"

The inspector grinned.

"Just what I say. I can't say any more. Even the police have to keep one or two things to themselves sometimes, you see. Now, before I go, I want a word with Mrs — with your mother, and then I suppose I must go over to Rams Cove and interview the young chap who actually found the damn thing."

The last words were addressed to himself rather than to Aubrey, for in concluding them he walked out of the garage and stepped briskly towards the house. Aubrey looked up and raced along to rejoin him.

"I say," he said eagerly. "I've got a bike. Couldn't I come with you to Rams Cove and — and sort of have a snoop round, you know?"

The inspector settled his cap.

"I don't think you'd better come with me, Mr Harringay," he said. "I shall be there kind of official, you see." Then, at sight of the boy's disappointed face, he added good-naturedly, "But, of course, if you should happen to be there quite accidental" — he paused and winked solemnly — "well, I couldn't hardly object, could I?"

Aubrey left him with Mrs Bryce Harringay and raced off to get his bicycle.

"I understand you were with his lordship the bishop when he found the skull, madam," said the inspector to a very frigid lady.

"You have been misinformed on two points, inspector. I was not with the bishop, and he did not find the skull."

"That's illuminating, madam." The inspector licked the point of his pencil and reflected comfortably that the more of a fool this type of woman thought him to be, the more information he could get out of her. "Will you kindly give me the facts? Begin at the beginning, if you please."

"Well, since you ask me, I suppose I must. Sit down, inspector, sit down. But you know it is all most upsetting and annoying, most! If I had had any idea that that wretched object would turn out to be Rupert's

98

skull, I would never have allowed the bishop to bring it home, never! What is it you wish to know?"

"First," said the inspector, glancing down at his notebook, "I want to know whether it is true that you accompanied the Bishop of Culminster to a spot called Rams Cove on the morning of Friday, June 27th?"

"It is correct to say that the bishop accompanied me. I ordered the car at nine-thirty, and Cooper, the chauffeur — my late nephew's chauffeur, I should say — drove me into Culminster, where I picked up the bishop at ten-fifteen. He kept the car waiting twenty minutes, I remember."

"Then you actually drove out of Culminster at ten-thirty-five, madam?"

"No, no! At ten-fifteen! I was waiting for him from five minutes to ten until a quarter past!" Her brow clouded at the recollection of that wasted twenty minutes. The inspector clicked his tongue sympathetically.

"Had you any special reason for choosing Rams Cove as the — er —"

"Object of our journey? None at all. The bishop insisted upon bringing his bathing things, and so, knowing from sad experience what babies men can be when they have set their minds upon some triviality of the kind, I instructed Cooper to take us to a seaside locality which was sufficiently safe and quiet for the purpose, because the bishop is a most mediocre swimmer, most! — and the spectacle of an Older Man in his bathing-costume is never, I feel, a particularly edifying spectacle. Well, very sensibly and suitably,

99

Cooper drove to Rams Cove, as I think you said the spot is called, and — much too soon after lunch, in my opinion! — the bishop bathed."

The inspector stared thoughtfully at the fireplace. Apparently the vision of the bishop bathing was too entrancing to be lightly dismissed from the mind.

"Then, it appears —" continued Mrs Bryce Harringay.

"Ah!" said the inspector, rousing himself. "The next bit of the story I shall have to get from his lordship, I think. Thank you, madam. Perhaps we could come now to the return journey."

"Very well. Although I can probably tell you the bishop's part of the story far more lucidly than he will. However — ! The bishop wrapped the Loathsome Object up in his towel and suggested leaving it at what he is pleased to call the Culminster Museum — you know it, I expect? The large room over Brown's antique shop at the corner of the High Street opposite the confectioner's? But on the way he changed his mind and determined to return by way of this village and show the skull to Mr Broome at the Vicarage."

"Why was that, madam?"

"I understand that Mr Broome is something of an authority upon Gruesome Relics of this type. The bishop wanted his opinion."

"I see. Whose suggestion was it that Mr Wright should build the rest of the head on to the skull?"

"Mr Broome suggested it. He disagreed with the bishop as to the probable antiquity of the Wretched Bone."

"Yes. Well, our own experts will tell us all about that. And Mr Wright brought the head back —?"

"Early yesterday morning, I understand."

"And the vicar has seen it, and yourself, and the bishop? Who else? We have it up at the station now, of course."

"The vicar's daughter may have seen it. I am not sure. The vicar's servant certainly saw it. I would not permit Aubrey to view it. I do not believe in Harrowing the Feelings of the young."

The inspector remembered Aubrey's disappointment, and hid a smile.

"Anyone else?" he enquired.

"To my knowledge, no. Oh," she added, after a second's thought, "a ridiculous woman called Bradley saw it. The vicar sent over to her house. And I imagine Mr Savile and his — er — and his companion must have seen it, as Wright shares their house. He would certainly have shown them the finished model, I should think."

"His companion?" said the inspector, puzzled.

"A Creature," observed Mrs Bryce Harringay, "who cohabits with Savile and Wright, but whose exact relationship to either or both of them will always, I imagine, remain veiled in mystery. Perhaps it is better so."

The inspector made rapid notes of the names, enquired the addresses, and took his leave. In accordance with previous arrangements, he met Superintendent Bidwell at the crossroads, and together they drove in the police car to Rams Cove. From the top of the cliffs the red-striped tent on the shore was easily visible. The inspector left the superintendent in the car and himself descended to the beach.

The big young man, still in shorts and a shirt, but this time barefooted, was having his dinner.

"Hullo," he said hospitably, "you're just in time. Bread and cheese and pickles and beer. Help yourself."

The inspector grinned.

"Food will have to wait," he said. "I wouldn't like to deceive you. I'm a police inspector."

"By Jove! I've got permission to be here, you know. You can't bung me off."

"No, nothing like that." The inspector drew out his note-book. "On the afternoon of Friday, June 27th," he announced, "you gave a skull — a human skull — into the possession of the Bishop of Culminster."

"Good old gaiters!" remarked the young man, with a glance at his own bare legs. "What about it?".

"How did you come to get hold of it?" asked the inspector.

"If you'll let me finish my grub, I'll come and show you the exact spot where I dug it out of the face of the cliff."

"What's your name? I might as well get the formalities over while I'm waiting."

"Look here, though!" cried the young man. "What's the game?"

"Nothing to do with you. I don't suppose that for a minute. So don't make a fuss about all the little things I shall have to ask as a matter of routine. Don't you read the papers?"

"Haven't seen one for ten days, thank heaven."

"Oh, well, it doesn't matter, Mr —?"

"Markham, John Ecclestone Markham, of Canby House, Slough, Bucks."

"Thank you, Mr Markham. Finished? Good. Now then, sir."

Markham led the way along the shore for about a quarter of a mile. Then he began to climb the cliffs. Twice the inspector's foothold crumbled away and he shot down to the beach again with a smother of loose earth and stones. The third time he managed to gain the place where Markham, who seemed to have a genius for avoiding loose places in the face of the cliff, sat astride a stunted bush which was leaning out over the thirty-foot drop to the shore.

"Here you are," he said, when at last Grindy reached him. "I had my brother and sister down here for the day on Friday, and my sister was very keen to take back one or two seaside plants with her to show her botany teacher, so Tim and I clambered about up here collecting things while she scouted on top of the cliffs and down on the beach. Well, Tim spotted a fine clump of seapinks — thrift, don't they call it? — and was going to jack up the whole lot when I yelled to him not to be a Hun, but only to take a bit of the stuff. I climbed across to him, opened my pocket knife, and tried to separate off a bit of the plant from the main clump. Unfortunately the soil was loose and up came the whole mass of it, and embedded next to it, but hidden until then by the spreading plant, was the skull. Of course, Tim was frightfully bucked. We clambered

103

down to the beach and washed the dirt out of the eye-sockets and took up a little plant which was growing merrily out of the jaws —"

"What?" said the inspector. He began to laugh. "All right," he said. "Thank you very much, Mr Markham. We shan't need to trouble you again. And you found the skull on Friday — in the morning, I suppose? — and handed it to the Bishop of Culminster the same afternoon."

"And we finished cleaning the thing by boiling it in the old saucepan," said Markham, grinning.

The ground gave way beneath the inspector once more, and in a shower of earth and stones he slid to the beach . . .

"Oh, well, the date is possible, but the plant in the mouth — jaws, I mean," said the superintendent when he heard the news, "is proof positive. It couldn't have been Sethleigh's skull. I never thought for an instant it was! Still, I suppose we must go and see what the bishop has to say."

"I suppose we can give him back the skull this young Markham found?"

"When we've pulled off the clay young Wright has modelled round it, the meddling young devil, and always supposing the bishop wants it back. It's no good to us. Our next job is to trace Sethleigh. Who saw him last, I wonder, apart from Mr Redsey, who went with him into the woods?"

"Mrs Bryce Harringay. Didn't she say she was watching them out of her bedroom window?"

"Yes, but that doesn't help us. I want somebody who saw them *after* they went into the woods."

"If Redsey would tell the truth about what happened in the woods that evening," said Grindy, "we might get somewhere. Something convinces me that the corpse was Rupert Sethleigh."

CHAPTER
NINE

Inspector Grindy
Learns a Few Facts

Preceded by Jim Redsey, the inspector entered the library.

"Now, sir," he said, "another word or two with you, if you don't mind."

"I don't promise to answer questions," said Jim at once.

"No, sir, no." The inspector's voice was soothing as he lowered himself into a chair and placed his cap on the carpet beside it. "There's no obligation at all. *Only*" — he stressed the word, with his eyes on Redsey's set face — "those that help the police in the execution of their duty are sometimes glad of it later."

"That's a threat, you know," said Jim, reddening.

"By no means, sir. Well now. I understand that you were the last person to see your cousin, Mr Sethleigh, before his" — he made a slight but suggestive pause — "his sudden disappearance."

"You can't prove that," said Jim. "And look here, inspector, there's no sense in going over all that ground again. You asked me that the last time you came."

"Very good. So I did. Well now. What was Mr Sethleigh wearing when you walked into the Manor Woods together at" — he consulted his note-book — "at five minutes to eight on the evening of Sunday, June 22nd?"

"I'm not swearing to the time, mind!" cried Jim jumpily. "I don't know what the time was. The date is all right. Rupert was in dark brown, I think."

"Plus fours, sir?"

"No. It was Sunday evening. A lounge suit."

"I see." He glanced at his note-book again. "The colour of the suit as given by Mrs Bryce Harringay is medium to light grey. And she says it was not a lounge suit nor plus fours, but a pair of grey flannel trousers supported by a silk scarf, and that he was also wearing a tennis shirt, owing to the heat of the day and the fact that a cold supper was to be served at ten o'clock instead of the usual dinner at a quarter to eight."

He glanced up keenly into Jim's angry face.

"Look here," said the young man, clenching his fists inside his blazer pockets, "I don't know what you mean by checking all my statements against those of my aunt. I'm telling the truth as far as I can remember it. I'm a man. I don't notice what people wear. My aunt's a woman. She does notice such things. And, anyway, what difference does it make what he was wearing?"

"Well, sir, if he's roaming about the countryside and we want to look for him, a good deal, I should say. And if that's his corpse which was found in Bossbury market, a good deal more, because" — he eyed Jim keenly again — "we haven't discovered the clothes belonging to that body yet. And we haven't been able to identify that body yet either."

"I thought you'd all made up your minds it was Rupert," said Jim. "Didn't Uncle Reggie find his skull or something? I heard some garbled yarn from Aunt Constance about it."

The inspector smiled.

"It's an interesting little story, that, sir. Care to hear it?"

Jim shrugged his shoulders and commenced filling his pipe.

"A skull was presented to your uncle, the Bishop of Culminster, by a man named Markham. The bishop showed the skull to the Reverend Stephen Broome, Vicar of Wandles here, and they had a bit of an argument about it. The upshot was that Mr Cleaver Wright, the artist chap up at the Cottage, took it to his studio with the idea of building up the head and face on to it. Well, I decided to take charge of Mr Wright's model, which was the image, I'm told, of your cousin Mr Sethleigh, and it's up at the station now. At least, the bits of it are, for when we broke up the clay in which Mr Wright had modelled the head and face there was no skull inside at all! Nothing but a coconut, sir."

"That's interesting," said Jim, offering his pouch to the inspector.

"No, thank you, sir. I don't smoke when I'm on duty. Well, I was somewhat knocked out, as you might imagine, especially as, between ourselves, the superintendent and I had come to the conclusion that the skull was a red-herring. Now we are not sure. Of

108

course, we've questioned Mr Wright on the matter, and he tells rather a funny tale which may or may not be true. He says that he dabbed clay all over the skull to make a kind of foundation to work on, and then he was called away to speak to someone at the door. When he came back he went on with his modelling, as he thought, exactly where he left off. But it almost seems as though somebody must have stolen the skull and substituted the coconut while he was gone. He was absent nearly three-quarters of an hour, you see."

Jim shrugged his shoulders, relighted his pipe, which had gone out, and tossed the match into the garden.

"I wish, sir, you would tell me what passed between your cousin and yourself in the woods that Sunday evening," said the inspector, after a pause.

"Well, I know it had no connection with his disappearance," replied Mr Redsey curtly.

"I suggest that it had, Mr Redsey. We've received an important letter from a firm of solicitors in London, signed by the senior partner, a Mr T. T. Grayling, which makes us rather anxious to know what happened in the Manor Woods that evening. Reading between the lines of that letter, Mr Redsey — for you know what lawyers are; always very guarded; never give themselves away — it almost seems as though you and your cousin quarrelled that night."

Jim shifted uneasily in his chair.

"What if we did?" he said. "I imagine it isn't an unknown thing for cousins to have a bit of an argument?"

"Bit of an argument hardly meets the case, Mr Redsey," said the inspector. He drummed with his fingers on the arm of his chair a moment, and then rose.

"Well, sir," he said, "I must say I think you'd do better to come across with what you know. Oh, don't tell me that!" And he held up a large square hand to stem the flood of angry denial which the young man commenced to pour forth. "I've had a good bit of experience, sir — not in cases of murder" — he lingered slightly over the dreadful word — "I must admit. But I know men pretty well, and I know when people are concealing something from me . . . It's no good going on like that, sir. The more you use language like that, the more certain I am that I'm right. And I say you'd do better to come clean. I'm speaking ex-official, and I'm giving you a friendly tip. So now, what about it?" And he sat down again.

"I'll tell you one thing," said Redsey dryly, "and that is, I think you are right about the body being that of my cousin. Rupert Sethleigh was more than a bit of a blackguard. I found that out when my aunt and I went through his private papers after his disappearance. Our idea was to find something to give us a lead in tracing him. We didn't get that, but we got plenty of evidence that at least six people had a splendid motive for murdering the beast."

The inspector nodded.

"Yes, sir. You're right. I came across the same evidence myself in his desk. I am glad you were not so foolish as to destroy it for the sake of the family name, or anything of that kind. Sethleigh was a moneylender at exorbitant rates of interest, and he was in possession of enough incriminating evidence against certainly four, perhaps five, and possibly six persons of recognized wealth to have allowed him to live in luxury on the proceeds of blackmail for the rest of his life."

"Yes. Well, there you are then! One of 'em has done in my precious cousin, and a good job too!"

"Well, sir, you may be right, but I don't think so. No, I fancy we shall have to get some other reason for Mr Sethleigh's disappearance or death. You see, sir, we've got on to all those six people, and the curious part of the matter is that, although Sethleigh knew enough to get one of 'em hanged and the others penal servitude or social Coventry for life or thereabouts, he doesn't seem to be known to a single one of them, and they are all living in peace and prosperity, and aren't even alive to the fact that there ever was such a fellow as Rupert Sethleigh. What do you make of that?"

"This," said Jim doggedly, removing his pipe and pointing the stem of it at the inspector. "The names of these six happen to have come to light. They know nothing of my cousin —"

"They will soon, when I've put Scotland Yard on their track," grunted the inspector. "You see if they don't!"

"Yes. My point is this, though. What about all his other victims, whose names have not yet come to light?"

"Ever go to the Picturedrome in Bossbury High Street, sir?" asked the inspector, grinning broadly. "I used to go regular when I was courting. We used to see headings on the films very like that mouthful you've just spoken. Mind you," he added, with lumbering tact, "I don't say there's nothing in the idea. I don't say that at all. All I do say is — it takes me back ten years at least, blowed if it don't. Victims! That's a good word, that is. Victims!"

He sat and bellowed with joy.

"Don't mind me," said Jim, furious. The inspector sat up and mopped his brow.

"No offence, sir," he remarked, rising and resuming the mantle of gravity. "Well, I'd better be off, unless, of course —?" He looked enquiringly at the young man.

"If you mean, will I make a voluntary statement, or some such rot as that, you can jolly well hop it out of here," said Jim savagely. "I'm not going to do your sneaking work for you!"

The inspector left him, and was walking down the drive towards the lodge gates when he met a perspiring and very dusty middle-aged gentleman in morning dress, who stopped to speak to him.

"Inspector Grindy? You received my letter? I ought to say that in justice to my client — perhaps I ought to say my late client — Mr Sethleigh, you should find out whether his cousin, Mr Redsey, was acquainted with the terms of his will."

"What about the terms of his will, sir? You suggested something about a will in your letter."

"Yes. Yes, I did. But one hardly likes to commit oneself on paper, you know, inspector. *Littera scripta manel!* Eh? Paper is so — so permanent at times. Yes.

112

Well, this is the point. It seems to me I ought, in fairness to my client, to mention it, especially if he has met with foul play. According to the terms of Mr Sethleigh's will, this Mr Redsey inherits the whole fortune and estate with the exception of about three thousand pounds. If the will were altered in accordance with a rough draft which Mr Sethleigh drew up less than three weeks ago, and which I have in my possession, Mr Redsey would find himself completely disinherited, as the result of a serious quarrel between the cousins."

"They did quarrel then?" cried the inspector. "What was the cause, sir? Do you know that?"

"Money. Mr Redsey wanted Mr Sethleigh to make him an advance — a loan, of course, not a gift — to enable him to buy a share in a Mexican ranch instead of going out there as a paid servant of the owner, a friend of his."

"And Mr Sethleigh refused?"

"In the roundest terms, inspector. Rather a pity, I think, as he could so easily have afforded the money."

"Redsey was angry, of course, sir?"

"Very angry. According to Sethleigh, he said, at the conclusion of one of the several acrimonious arguments which took place, 'Very well, you mingy devil! I suppose the stuff will be mine some day! Perhaps that day will come sooner than you think!'"

"And after that Mr Sethleigh decided to alter his will and leave Redsey out of it?"

"That's it. But, you see, he hasn't had the chance, apparently. I came down on Monday last and interviewed Mr Redsey, as Sethleigh was not there. A most unsatisfactory interview in every way. Oh, and a curious feature of the afternoon was Redsey's determination that Mrs Bryce Harringay and I should on no account approach the Vicarage by way of the Manor Woods. He went through the most extraordinary manoeuvres to prevent it."

"The Manor Woods?" said the inspector thoughtfully. "I wonder — ? We've exhausted the clues in Bossbury, I think, and in this house. In fact, I don't really know that there were any in Bossbury except fingerprints. Plenty of those! But who to fix 'em on to beats me, sir, blowed if it doesn't! But the Manor Woods! Tried to prevent your going in, did he? Did it come off?"

"I humoured him," confessed the lawyer. "I am sorry now that I gave way."

"Well, he won't prevent *me* going into them," said Inspector Grindy, "although, after all this time — a full week, you see — I doubt whether there will be anything much worth finding. Still, thanks for the tip, sir."

"A pleasure," said the lawyer. "Well, I might as well return to Town. You are the person I came to see, and I would just as soon not encounter Mrs Bryce Harringay," he added, as he saw the stately matron approaching them across the lawn, "as I am in haste to return to the station."

"There's just one thing," said the inspector, "and that is — could you give me any idea of a birthmark or other marks Mr Sethleigh might have had on his body, by which he could be identified?"

"No idea! No idea!" cried the lawyer, observing with dismay that Mrs Bryce Harringay was hastening towards them, and obviously had recognized him. "No idea at all! So sorry! I must really get that train!"

So saying, he gripped his neat attaché-case a trifle more firmly, snatched his silk hat from his head, and sprinted rapidly down the drive.

"Mr Grayling! Mr Gray-ling!" called Mrs Bryce Harringay behind him. The lawyer clenched his teeth and put a spurt on.

Mrs Bryce Harringay approached the inspector.

"Most unfortunate," she said, raising lorgnettes and glaring after the flying figure of the lawyer with an expression of intense annoyance upon her florid countenance. She objected strongly to calling loudly after people who took no notice of her cries.

"He was trying to catch a train, I believe, madam," said the inspector soothingly. "I suppose you can't offer any suggestion as to what became of that skull, madam, can you?"

"What information, exactly, are you attempting to extract from me, inspector?" enquired Mrs Bryce Harringay haughtily. "Pray ask your questions in a proper manner. I object to your attitude and your tone."

"Have you any reason for supposing that in a fit of absent-mindedness the bishop might have taken the skull away from Mr Wright's house?" enquired the inspector bluntly.

"The bishop is neither absent-minded nor mad," responded Mrs Bryce Harringay. "I do not know whether that is sufficient answer to what I can only hope and trust is not a fair sample of —"

"Oh, come now, madam," remonstrated the inspector. "I'll withdraw the question, if you like. The only point is this: if the bishop, who, in a sense, we might say, it belonged to, didn't move it from Mr Wright's house, who did?"

"I don't know why you are worrying about that skull at all," said Mrs Bryce Harringay petulantly. "You said yourself that you knew it couldn't be Rupert's skull, poor boy! If only the police would take a straight line to get to the heart of the mystery of my nephew's disappearance, instead of going off into these ridiculous side-tracks, it would be far more profitable, I consider. You should tackle James Redsey. He knows more than anybody! He must do! He was with him when he disappeared! Why don't you make him tell you what he knows?"

"All in good time, madam," said the inspector, more soothing than ever. "I don't want to make unpleasantness. There's no need at present. I know where Mr Redsey is, and I can get him when I want him."

"Yes, that's all very well," said Mrs Bryce Harringay aggrievedly. "And meanwhile poor Rupert is not being traced — no effort is being made to trace him — and James will slip through your fingers and go off to South America or somewhere before you know where you are!"

"That, madam, is certainly something to guard against," said the inspector, taking out his note-book. "And, talking of America, there is just one more point.

Why didn't anybody in the house worry about Mr Sethleigh's disappearance until Mr Redsey gave out that he had gone to America? See what I'm after, madam, don't you? None of you saw Mr Sethleigh after he walked into those woods over yonder with his cousin at about eight o'clock on Sunday night, but, so far as I can make out, nobody seems to have asked anything about him until nearly tea-time on Monday. A bit queer, that, to my way of thinking."

"Well, no, inspector," replied Mrs Bryce Harringay, opening her large protruding eyes very widely, "it was not in the least queer. Of course, when James was brought home on the Sunday night in such a horrible, hopeless, repulsive state of intoxication that I was obliged to have him carried up to bed and then to lock the door on him, I concluded that Rupert had returned to the house much earlier. I am a Slave to my Nerves, and I had retired to rest very early that evening. In fact, it was from my bedroom window that I perceived the two boys strolling towards the woods; it was not improbable, therefore, that Rupert should have returned to the house without my knowledge. As for our not being concerned about him the next day — well, the explanation is very simple. Rupert suffered from some kind of heart trouble — his doctor could tell you more about it — and often rested in his room all the morning. Sometimes he would appear at lunch, sometimes not. Therefore no one passed any comment that I can remember when we saw nothing of him on Monday, unless James's ridiculous behaviour in driving us out of the Manor Woods was a comment! As for

Rupert's going to America, the very idea was the height of absurdity. Rupert hated the sea too much ever to go to America."

"Didn't the servants inform you, madam, that their master was not in his room and could not be found? After all, they could not even supply him with his meals. Didn't they ask about that?"

"The servants," said Mrs Bryce Harringay majestically, "know better than to worry me with Trivialities!"

CHAPTER
TEN

He Puts Two and Two Together

I

"It all boils down to this," said Inspector Grindy to Superintendent Bidwell. "If the skull was an old affair which had lain buried for years and years, why did somebody think it worth while to steal it from Wright and stick some of his modelling clay on to that coconut to pretend it hadn't been pinched?"

"Well, we know Wright of old," grinned the superintendent.

"As a matter of fact, we don't, sir," observed the inspector. "He's lived in that house about three years, that's all."

"Long enough to make a name for himself as a practical joker, anyway," argued the superintendent. "Personally, I think he's pulling our legs about the skull. I propose we shelve the question of the skull for a bit, and go through the serious part of the business. What about young Redsey? To be frank, inspector, I'm assuming that the Bossbury body is that of Rupert

Sethleigh. After all, we must get some sort of a starting-point, and that's a very workable one."

"Redsey?" The inspector drew out his note-book, licked a spatulate finger, and rapidly turned the pages. "Looks rather bad, if you're going to take for granted that the body at Bossbury is Rupert Sethleigh. First of all, there's the question of motive. Well, it seems as though Redsey had a motive all right. Two motives, in fact. He would have been cut out of Sethleigh's will had Sethleigh lived, and, secondly, he hated his cousin pretty poisonously because Sethleigh wouldn't unbelt sufficiently to allow Redsey to buy a share in a ranch, so Redsey goes out there soon as a hand instead of a boss. Galling, that."

"I see. He doesn't seem to me a fellow who would kill out of revenge. But the will is a different matter. Who did you get the information from?"

"The family solicitor. A chap named Grayling."

"Oh, that's good enough. I know Grayling all right."

"Yes, sir. Well, next comes opportunity. So far as I can find out, Redsey was the last person to be in company with Sethleigh before the disappearance. Not only that, but he tried to establish an alibi, I should take it, by going into the 'Queen's Head' in Wandles Parva — landlord, William Albert Bondy — at about nine o'clock that night and getting dead drunk. Had to be took home by two labourers, Stanley Joseph Cummings and Henry Richards, both of Wandles Parva, who testify to the same, and were given sixpence apiece by Mrs Bryce Harringay for the job, which they thought could have been a shilling without exactly breaking the lady's heart. Now I figure it out like this. The two chaps, Sethleigh and Redsey, went into the woods talking, arguing, and, in the end, quarrelling. Then Sethleigh gets annoyed and hands Redsey the information about the will. Redsey gets properly shirty at that and kills his cousin. Then he hides the body in the bushes, and all next day he spends his time playing policeman and stopping people from going into the woods."

"Is that a fact?"

"I had it from Mrs Bryce Harringay first, and Mr Grayling confirmed it. Well, that's the case against Redsey, sir. Motive, opportunity, alibi, suspicious behaviour afterwards — it looks pretty bad."

"Yes, I grant that. But there's one thing — it puzzles me a good deal — how did he get the body from the woods into Bossbury market, and chop it up without somebody spotting him? I've had a lot of enquiries made in Bossbury while you've been working at the Wandles end of the affair, and I can't find anybody who saw him arrive or leave."

"It must have been done on the Monday night after dark, sir. Redsey can give a good account of his movements all day Monday, and the account is substantiated by his aunt, the lawyer, young Harringay, and the servants. I've gone into all that."

"But after dark, Grindy my lad, the market is shut and they drop steel doors over the entrances. I've been looking round it, and there's not a hole where a cat could squeeze in when that market is shut, let alone a chap carrying a dead body. No, that carving of the corpse was done in the daytime, and, if Redsey has got a complete alibi for Monday, you can give up your theories, because he *couldn't* have done that nice little job in the butcher's shop."

"Well, what about very early Tuesday morning, sir? The market opens at six, I suppose?"

"No, not until eight. And Binks the butcher was in his shop at half-past nine."

"An hour and a half. H'm! I see your point. Too risky. Binks might have turned up earlier, and caught him at the job."

"Yes. As a matter of fact, I fancy I may have stumbled on the method used by the — well, let's call him the murderer for a minute — to get into the shop without forcing the door. You remember we remarked it was curious that there were no signs of a forced entrance?"

"Yes, sir."

"Well, it seems that Binks usually reached the market shop at eight-thirty and opened it for business at nine. The odd half-hour was employed by him and his assistant in getting ready the stock for the day — bringing up carcasses from below, jointing up the stuff, sticking prices on it, and all that. Well, on that particular Tuesday morning the assistant, who had a key and generally turned up a bit earlier than Binks himself, came along and said he'd forgotten his key. It was the first time he had ever done such a thing, but Binks was rather annoyed, because, as it happened, he'd left his own key in his overall pocket, and his overall was locked up inside the shop. So he sent the lad home. Well, the chap was gone about twenty minutes, and then came back and said he couldn't find the key anywhere, so Binks sent him to his other shop, over which he lives, for a third key, which the lad brought. They then opened the shop and found the bits of the body, as we know."

"So either the assistant lost the key and the murderer found it —" began the inspector.

"Unlikely," demurred the superintendent.

"Or else the key was stolen from him —"

"More likely."

"Or perhaps he was bribed by the murderer to hand it over."

"That's quite possible, too. I've interviewed the fellow — as sawny a specimen as you'd wish to meet — and he swears he did lose it, but he can't say when or how. He had it on the previous Saturday, because he unlocked the shop with it. He thinks he may have left it sticking in the door, which has a patent lock. He has done that once or twice, and remembered it or seen it there later in the day. Personally, I got the impression he knows all about that key. I reckon he was bribed for it. Now, assuming that is what happened, you see, it means that the crime was not committed in a moment of sudden anger, but was premeditated."

"Yes," said the inspector, "that's a point, sir, in Redsey's favour, judging from what I can gather of his character. He might easily fly into a rage and hit somebody over the head, but a premeditated crime, all worked out and arranged beforehand — no, I can't see Redsey doing things that way. Hot-headed, sir, that's my opinion; but real vicious, no."

The superintendent nodded.

"But what I do think ought to be undertaken next," he said, "is a thorough search of those woods. After all, we don't *know* that the dismembered body is Sethleigh. He may still be lying hidden in some bushes, for all we can tell."

"An idea, sir," said the inspector. "I shall need some help to do a job like that thoroughly."

"You'd better take a couple of men and have a go at it this afternoon," remarked Bidwell.

"Very good, sir. And then there's the question of the Bossbury corpse's clothing. I suppose nothing's turned up?"

"Not a sign nor a stitch of it. I've still got men on the job, of course. Something's bound to turn up in connection with the clothes sooner or later. It is just a question of time."

"Then there are those fingerprints on the cleaver and knife at the butcher's shop. Luckily, Binks the butcher hadn't handled any of his tools that morning by the time we arrived on the scene."

"No. We took his prints, but of course they don't correspond with any that are on the implements. Luckily again for us, there was no confusion about the prints, because he always washes up his things, including the top of the chopping-block, before he leaves the shop each night."

"Of course the prints don't correspond with any that we know?" enquired the inspector gloomily. "That's the worst of murder. It isn't a profession, like burglary, where you can dig out the prints of all the old lags and check them up against the new stuff."

"Never mind," said the superintendent, whose self-appointed mission seemed to be the soothing of restless subordinates, "we've got the prints, and I dare say we shall find a use for them in time. They may be those of that sawny lout of a lad that serves in Binks's shop. I'll have another go at him to-morrow."

II

Jim Redsey sat moodily on the steps of the Club House at Culminster and chopped viciously at the turf with his putter. He was alone. Courteously, but quite definitely, three people he knew had cold-shouldered him. Even the pro. had looked at him with a kind of dubious curiosity and had kept out of his way.

A small shrivelled woman stood at the gate and watched him.

"Surely I've seen that large young man before?" she said.

Felicity Broome nodded.

"That's Jimsey," she said. "Rupert Sethleigh's cousin, you know."

"Indeed?" said Mrs Bradley. Then, after a pause, she added, "I am going over to speak to him, child. You stay here."

Felicity, who had discovered to her secret amusement that people always did as Mrs Bradley told them, remained at the gate.

"Young man," said Mrs Bradley.

Jim started.

"That's better. Put down that dangerous-looking thing and tell me why you are not playing golf to-day."

Jim, who, of course, knew Mrs Bradley by sight, as did everyone in Wandles Parva, grinned and stood up.

"Sit down again," commanded Mrs Bradley, "and I will sit beside you. Now answer the question."

Jim, who was prepared to like Mrs Bradley very much simply because his Aunt Constance hated and feared her, sat down again.

"All the cheery souls here have indicated pretty clearly that they prefer my room to my company," he said. "I believe there are rumours current that I murdered my cousin Sethleigh a short time ago."

"And did you?" enquired Mrs Bradley, in her devastatingly direct fashion.

"Well," said Jim slowly, "at one time I thought I had, but I'm glad to say that I was wrong."

"This," remarked Mrs Bradley, settling herself as for a pleasant chat, "sounds remarkably interesting. May I hear more about it?"

"Well," said Jim, "I've made up my mind to spill the yarn to the inspector and get it off my chest, so —"

"So I have come just in time for the dress rehearsal," said Mrs Bradley, with hideous laughter.

Jim took up the putter again and began digging at the turf with it while he talked.

126

"We had an argument on the Sunday night, Rupert and I," he said, "It was rather a stale argument. I wanted him to lend me some money, and he refused. Well, we started in the billiard-room, and were interrupted by the entrance of my aunt, Mrs Harringay, so we cleared out. We walked into the woods, still arguing. Rupert remained cool, like the silky devil he was, but I got a bit heated, and, to cut it short, I knocked him down."

"Ah, yes," murmured Mrs Bradley, nodding.

"I was very unlucky," pursued Jim. "The silly ass, instead of falling on the soft ground, as you or I would have done, had to go and smash his silly head against the trunk of a tree."

"Ah — ah!" said Mrs Bradley, interested.

"Yes," said Jim, in honest wrath, "it was exactly the sort of dashed annoying thing a silly fat-headed idiot like Sethleigh would do! No thought of other people's convenience! Never did have! Well, of course he lay so still and looked so white that I thought I'd killed him. I didn't know what to do! There he was, eyes shut, mouth wide open, looking like God-knows-what, and I was in the devil of a funk! I thought of rushing up to the house for some water. Then I decided I'd better not leave him, perhaps. Then I remembered he was supposed to have a weak heart. I knelt down and tried to feel it beating. Couldn't feel a thing! So with that I grabbed him by the armpits and lugged him into the middle of a thickish hazel copse and removed myself from the scene of operations as quickly as I could. Well, I pelted along to the 'Queen's Head' and went in. Then

I got beastly tight. Then two chaps carted me home. Then my aunt got scared to think of having a drunken man in the house, so she locked me in for the night. And that's all, except that I spent all next day in mooning about the house and keeping people out of the woods. Rupert had not returned, you see. I took jolly good care to find that out — strictly on the Q.T., of course. I *was* in a funk! That ass of a solicitor turned up and wanted to interview Sethleigh and everything! My hat! That was a day! Well, that night I went to bury Sethleigh's body in the middle of the woods. He wasn't there! So I know I didn't kill him. See what I mean?"

"And that's the story you intend telling to the inspector?" mused Mrs Bradley.

"Yes," said Redsey. He flung down the putter and stood up.

"Time to go home for lunch," he said. "Don't tell me to let the inspector go on guessing. I hate keeping secrets. Hullo! Is that Felicity Broome at the gate? You'll let me give you both a lift back to Wandles, won't you?"

"And when are you going to tell your little tale to Mr Grindy?" asked Mrs Bradley, as the Bentley spread her wings and glided along the Culminster road towards the village.

"This afternoon, if I can get hold of him. I don't think it will be difficult. He lives in our house from about nine-thirty until six these days."

"What's all this about?" asked Felicity.

Jim told her.

CHAPTER
ELEVEN

Further Discoveries

I

Anxious to search the Manor Woods now that he had heard Jim Redsey's story, the inspector, accompanied by Police-Sergeant Walls and Police-Constable Pearce, invited Aubrey Harringay to take them by the most direct path into the centre of the woodland. Pearce, who had come on his bicycle, left it propped against the trunk of a tree, on the outskirts of the wood, and in single file, silent, majestic, and heavy of tread, the police followed Aubrey along the leafy path which led directly to the circle of pines. In the middle of the circle stood the Stone of Sacrifice.

The inspector went up and scanned it closely.

"Come here, Walls," he said abruptly. Aubrey went up also, and the three heads bent over some dark stains on the greyish, glinting stone.

"Blood," said the inspector. "Bit of luck for us, I shouldn't wonder. Seen these marks before?" he added, turning to Aubrey.

"No," said Aubrey, excited. "Is it really blood?"

"That remains to be seen," said the inspector. "It looks like it, anyhow. Now, if Redsey spoke the truth — that's rather funny, because he distinctly said —" He broke off, cogitating. "Pearce," he said at last, "search about and see whether you can find any bushes that look as though they've been broken or disturbed in any way, or —"

"I say, inspector," broke in Aubrey. "I've got something I ought to tell you! Please tell me first, though; did Jim Redsey — Oh, half a second!"

Before either of the police officers could say a word, he had gone racing off along the narrow woodland path and was lost to sight among the trees. At the edge of the woods, leaning against one of the tree-trunks, was Constable Pearce's bicycle. Aubrey propelled it hastily over the short grass on to the path and, leaping into the saddle, pedalled swiftly across the park and on to the gravel drive. Arrived at the lodge, he shot through the great gates into the road, turned sharp to the right, and in a few minutes arrived at the Vicarage.

"I want Felicity! Quick!" he said to Mary Kate Maloney.

"Faith, is it a fire?" enquired Mary Kate, interested.

"No, no! It's urgent!" cried Aubrey, propping up the constable's bicycle and mopping his brow.

Mary Kate fled into the house, and Aubrey could hear her voice yodelling richly for her mistress.

"What is it?" cried Felicity, running down the garden path.

"I say, what did Jim tell the police when they interviewed him? Do you know?"

130

"Yes."

Felicity reported Jim's confession.

"That's what he told them?"

"Yes, Aubrey. Why, what's happened?"

"Nothing yet. You're sure that's all?"

"That's what Jimsey told Mrs Bradley and me he was going to say to them."

"Righto! Thanks. Tell you everything later!"

He leapt on to Constable Pearce's purloined and long-suffering bicycle once more, and raced back to the Manor Woods.

"I say, inspector."

"Look here, sir —"

"Yes, I know. The bike. Awfully sorry, but I had to hurry. Couldn't stop to ask permission. Police business, you know."

The inspector grinned tolerantly.

"Well, sir?"

"Yes, well, look here. On Monday night — after the Sunday when Jim and Rupert had that row — I scouted after old Jim to this place — these woods — and saw him snooping about in the bushes for the — well, I suppose I'd better say the body. Old Jim thought old Rupert had chucked in the towel, you see, and ought to have a decent burial or something."

"We've heard all this before, sir."

"Yes. Well, I watched him —"

"Where were you exactly?"

Aubrey considered.

"About here. Yes, here. You can see where my feet and legs scraped the leaves and things on the ground.

And old Jim was over there, just behind the sergeant and a bit to the left — my left, sergeant, and your right. That's it. He searched those bushes. He had a hurricane lamp. That's how I could see him."

The sergeant, who had been conning the ground near the bushes in question, straightened himself.

"Certainly seems feasible, sir," he remarked to the inspector. "Come and see for yourself. Twigs broken near the ground, soil and leaves scraped as though something has been dragged along — these ridges and grooves might as well be heel-marks as anything else — and the whole place looks disturbed and trampled."

"That's right," agreed the inspector. "Well, sir?"

"Yes, well, he was looking for old Rupert and old Rupert wasn't there!"

"Now, sir!" the inspector's voice rang out sharply.

"Well, I didn't go and look, of course," said Aubrey, "but it was pretty obvious. Old Jim looked properly flummoxed. Then he had another go."

"If there's anybody — no, of course there isn't —" began the inspector.

"Anybody to corroborate my yarn?" said Aubrey, guessing the inspector's thought. "Well, as it happens, there *is* somebody else who — who knows that Jim was in the woods on Monday night."

"Oh?"

"Yes. Miss Broome. You know, the vicar's daughter."

"The vicar's daughter?" repeated the inspector.

"Yes. She comes here whenever she wants to, of course. Gets in through the wicket gate that opens on to the road. Well, she wanted some fresh air or something, and came for a stroll, and saw me pinch old Jim's spade, and old Jim thought I was a poacher or something, and hounded me out. He fell down and tore chunks out of his Oxfords on the brambles, you know," added Aubrey, circumstantially, "and I got clear away while he was picking the thorns out of his eyebrows!"

"I see, sir."

At this moment Constable Pearce approached.

"Oh, I say, Pearce, you know," said the boy, "awfully sorry I pinched your bike. I don't think I damaged it."

"You're kindly welcome, sir," said the constable handsomely.

"Pearce," said the inspector, "you can get back to the station now, and tell the superintendent I'd like a word with him this evening. And I'd be obliged, sir," he went on, turning again to Aubrey, "if one of the gardeners would lend me a spade."

"I'll go and see about it," said Aubrey with alacrity. He grinned wickedly as he walked away, thinking of the trout he had buried.

"For of course they've spotted where the ground has been dug up," he said to himself, "and are going to have a look-see."

The inspector seated himself on a fallen log, invited the sergeant to sit beside him, and took out a packet of cigarettes.

"There's the hole Redsey dug that night," he said, pointing.

"I suppose you can believe the boy?" suggested the sergeant laconically.

"Don't know. Ought to be able to, at that age! And there's the young lady's evidence, you see, although we've still got to collect that."

"She's probably been got at," said the sergeant dourly.

"Oh, you can always frighten girls into telling the truth," said the inspector easily.

The sergeant, father of three daughters, laughed with sardonic amusement.

"*Frighten* them?" he said bitterly.

"Besides, she's the vicar's daughter," the inspector hastily interpolated.

"Caesar's wife, in fact," said a rich voice just behind them. Both men looked round in time to see Mrs Lestrange Bradley disappearing at a bend in the woodland path.

"Who's that?" asked the inspector, startled.

"Old party that's taken that place on the Bossbury road just the other side of Wandles," said the sergeant. "Queer old girl, by all accounts. Writes books about lunatics, or something."

"Doesn't look like a writer of comic stuff," said the inspector, frowning.

"No, not comic stuff, sir. The real thing. Finds out why they've gone dotty and tries to put 'em right again. Does it, too, sometimes, or so I've heard."

"She'd better not come nosing round where she's not wanted, anyway," said the inspector. "Looks suspicious."

Before they had finished the second cigarette, Aubrey returned with a spade, and the sergeant set to work.

134

The loose soil was soon thrown up, and a hole much the size and shape of that dug by Jim Redsey was made in the soft ground.

"Nothing here," grunted the inspector. "And, anyway, we know where the corpse is, although Mr Bidwell's got some idea there may be another body somewhere."

"Half a minute, sir." The sergeant thrust in the spade once more. "She's struck on something."

He dug away manfully. To Aubrey's amazement a darkish rectangular object was soon disclosed to view. The inspector and the sergeant finished off the job with their hands, and pulled up a suitcase.

Aubrey's eyes nearly started out of his head. He felt sick, and his heart thumped against his ribs. On the lid, plainly discernible, were Rupert Sethleigh's initials. It was the suitcase which someone had removed while he had gone for the fish that night.

"Well, I'm damned!" said the inspector. "What's this?"

He opened the lid. Inside the case was Aubrey's stuffed trout. It still looked affronted and resentful, and well it might, for stuck on to its back by the agency of a large pin was a legend written on a sheet of note-paper in pencil, and formed entirely of block capitals. Tersely it ran:

"A present from Grimsby."

II

Mrs Bradley was half-way across the lawn by the time the inspector had discovered the suitcase. She had spent about an hour and a half with pencil and paper after Jim Redsey had driven away from the gates of the Stone House, and Felicity, who had entirely forgotten her first unsatisfactory impression of the clever little old woman, sat on the step and affected to read. From time to time, however, her eyes strayed to the outrageously clad figure seated at the table, and what she saw did not encourage her to ask questions. At last Mrs Bradley raised her head and spoke.

"I don't see that they will have much choice in the matter, unless some fresh evidence turns up," she said.

"Who?" asked Felicity, laying down the book and turning round.

"The police, my dear. I have worked it all out, and, you see, Mr Redsey could have killed his cousin, hidden the body, and managed the alibi for Sunday night. Then, after you and Aubrey returned to your beds on Monday night, he could have dismembered the body in the woods and then taken the limbs and so on into Bossbury on Tuesday morning. He couldn't have dismembered the body on Tuesday morning, because there was not enough time for that, but he could have taken the remains in a car, unlocked the shop with the key which Binks's assistant lost, disposed the flesh of the corpse on the hooks in that charming way, and left the shop locked up again. No one would have noticed him particularly.

"Why wouldn't they?"

"Because I have a shrewd idea, child, that the man who performed that gruesome task would have had the sense to dress himself up to look like a person

136

delivering meat, if he —" She stopped short. "Good heavens!" she said suddenly, and paused. "Nobody in the market can remember having seen or heard anything untoward going on, you see," she continued in a few moments. "There was only the usual quantity of sawdust on the floor, too," she added irrelevantly.

"Where do you get all this information?" asked Felicity, divided between amusement and disgust. "And you don't really think the dead man was Rupert Sethleigh, and that — and that Jimsey did all that to the body, do you?"

"One question at a time, child. I obtain my information from two sources. My girl Phoebe, who, unhappily for me, is leaving in a day or two to get married, is own daughter to the sergeant at Bossbury police station. She tells me all that he tells the family. But do not divulge that fact to anyone. I should hate to get the man into trouble, and, besides, I do so love to know all there is to be known. My second source of information is the newspaper. It is quite informative to note the discrepancies between the two sources," she added, chuckling.

"But what about —?"

"The youthful James Redsey? I don't know whether he killed his cousin, but I don't believe he carved him up," said Mrs Bradley, with unqualified decision. "And I think we had better put our heads together to see if we can't prove it. Things appear dark for the young man. We may look forward confidently, I think, to his arrest within the next few days."

"It's that wretched will," groaned Felicity. "And Jimsey swears he didn't even know Rupert was going to alter it."

"I believe him. From what I can understand of Mr Sethleigh's character, I should say that he would prefer to let a thing like that fall in the form of a bombshell, rather than tell the person concerned of his intentions. He would love to gloat over the thought of his cousin's surprise and fury. A nasty person, Mr Rupert Sethleigh."

"Yes, he was," said Felicity, so briefly that Mrs Bradley stared at her keenly and interrogatively for several seconds. The girl flushed and shrugged her shoulders.

"He was odious. I never went up to the Manor House alone, unless Mrs Harringay and Aubrey were there," she said.

"I see," said Mrs Bradley. "And now," she added, with a complete change of tone, "I want to see young Mr Harringay. A charming boy! Is your father coming to lunch? Oh, there he is at the gate! Go and let him in, child, and this afternoon I will go over to the Manor House. I have one or two questions to ask the youth, and I want to see his mother also."

Thus it came about that Mrs Bradley took the path through the Manor Woods that afternoon and saw the police there.

Upon arriving at the house, she asked for Mrs Bryce Harringay.

"I see that the police are busy here again," said Mrs Bradley at the conclusion of ten minutes' desultory chitchat. Mrs Bryce Harringay stiffened.

"Indeed?" she said icily.

"I suppose they will arrest Mr Redsey as soon as they can prove the body in Bossbury was the body of Mr Sethleigh," Mrs Bradley went on calmly, in an easy, conversational tone. "You are prepared for that to happen, of course?"

"I suppose," said Mrs Bryce Harringay, throwing dignity to the winds and discovering herself to the other woman in her true guise of an exceedingly worried mother and aunt, "I suppose it is inevitable. I wonder whom we had better get for the defence?"

"If it comes to that," interpolated Mrs Bradley quickly, "you might do a great deal worse than try for Ferdinand Lestrange. I'll recommend you to his notice if you like," she added handsomely. "However, we shall hope that it will not be necessary. Your nephew is not arrested yet, you know. We must not lose heart."

Her sympathetic words were discounted by the malicious chuckle with which she concluded them. Mrs Bryce Harringay blinked rapidly, and produced a minute handkerchief.

"You are so clever," she moaned. "Can't you think of anything that will save him? I don't like James, of course. He was a rude, untruthful boy, and he has grown up an uncontrolled and vicious man, but it would be so awkward for Aubrey later on if it became known that his cousin had been hanged for murder. I want Aubrey to go into Parliament, you see, and you know yourself how very Blameless a man's antecedents must be if he is to succeed in political circles! Think of election meetings, for example. The horrible questions the hecklers would ask him! Most embarrassing for the poor boy — most!"

And she burst into tears.

Mrs Bradley dived into the pocket of her violently striped washing-silk frock and drew out a small notebook and pencil. Then she pulled off her mushroom hat (of a fashion long discarded) and dropped it on the floor.

"Now then," she said peremptorily tapping Mrs Bryce Harringay's wrist with her pencil to attract the lady's attention. "Sit up and attend to me. Who else hated Rupert Sethleigh besides" — she thought for a moment — "James Redsey, Felicity Broome, Lulu Hirst, Margery Barnes, and darling Aubrey? I include the girls because I understand girls were not attracted by your older nephew."

Mrs Bryce Harringay lowered the inadequate handkerchief and stared at her out of swimming, fishlike eyes.

"Rupert knew that Dr Barnes had an illegitimate son," she said with a gulp. "That's why I always have a Bossbury doctor when we are staying here. Most unpleasant, I think, to be attended by a man who has had Irregular Relationships — most!"

Mrs Bradley nodded solemnly.

"Most," she echoed in a sepulchral voice. "And the doctor knew that — er — that Rupert knew?"

"Oh, yes. It saved Rupert paying insurance money for the servants, you see. Dr Barnes used to treat them free of charge because Rupert knew and did not tell."

"Is Dr Barnes a surgeon?" asked Mrs Bradley keenly.

140

"He helped to amputate the major's brother's leg after a hunting accident, and he took out Margaret Somertoll's appendix," replied Mrs Bryce Harringay. "At least," she added darkly, "everybody *said* it was her appendix, but I drew my own conclusions. You see —" She lowered her unctuous voice to the note of the practised scandal-monger.

"Yes, I see," said Mrs Bradley at the end of a lengthy, complicated, and remarkably dull tale. "Most suspicious. I am so glad that you took up a Strong Moral Attitude about it." And she suddenly screamed with laughter.

"I fancy Rupert found out something about that too," Mrs Bryce Harringay concluded rather hastily, for Mrs Bradley's quite unnecessary mirth unnerved her.

"Yes? Well, all that you tell me is in James Redsey's favour," observed Mrs Bradley, shutting off her laughter with the abrupt efficiency of a person turning off a tap. "The more enemies we can prove Rupert Sethleigh to have had," she continued, "the more chance there is of showing that James Redsey's motive for accomplishing his cousin's death was less strong, perhaps, than the motive of some other person or persons."

"But the *doctor* did not kill Rupert!" exclaimed Mrs Bryce Harringay. "I'm sure I didn't intend *that* construction to be placed upon my remarks. I don't think extremely well of the man, it is true, but I should hesitate to accuse him of an Awful Deed!"

"Quite so," agreed Mrs Bradley. "But don't you see that our best line at present, if we wish to save James

Redsey from arrest, is to discredit the present findings of the police and so turn their attention to fresh channels of enquiry?"

"Yes, I see that, of course," said Mrs Bryce Harringay. "And the doctor, being a surgeon —" She shuddered with exaggerated horror. "Dreadful man! How glad I am that I refused to call him in when Aubrey contracted the chicken-pox two summers ago! Really, men are such monsters one scarcely knows why one married!"

CHAPTER
TWELVE

The Inspector Has His Doubts

The next thing to do, the inspector decided, was to discover the owner of the suitcase. This proved simple. Redsey, confronted by his cousin's initials, agreed that the case was Rupert Sethleigh's, but most emphatically denied all knowledge of how it came to be buried in the woods. Neither could he explain the bloodstained condition of its interior.

"The last I remember about that suitcase," he declared, "is getting Rupert to lend it to the vicar when he went for his holiday in May — that is — last month. It seems a long time ago, somehow."

The inspector went straight away to the Vicarage, where the Reverend Stephen, looking very foolish, agreed that the suitcase had probably been lent to him, but that he had forgotten all about it. He usually did forget all about things, he was sorry to say. Oh, here was his daughter. She would know more about it.

Felicity, appealed to, remembered perfectly well that her father had borrowed the suitcase, but thought he had returned it. However, he was so very absent-minded that it was more than possible he had forgotten all about it.

Then she told the inspector where she herself had found it, and of how she and Aubrey Harringay had decided to bury it in the Manor Woods.

"I wonder why you should think of doing that, miss," said the inspector, without finding it necessary to add that the police had found it.

Felicity shook her head.

"It just occurred to us," she said, with delightful vagueness.

The inspector went in search of Aubrey Harringay.

"Now, young man," he said sternly. "What made you decide to bury that suitcase?"

"But I didn't bury it, inspector."

"What's that?"

"I didn't bury it. I was going to, but while I had gone for the fish, you know, some blighter pinched the case and hopped off with it."

"The fish? Was that the fish we found inside the case?"

"Yes, it was. But I didn't put it there, I swear I didn't. I just buried the fish in the hole — for a lark, you know — and that's all. I had nothing to do with putting it in the case or — or — writing those words."

"H'm!" said the inspector non-committally, and went to the superintendent.

"I haven't tested Redsey's alibi for Sunday night," he said. "But this is what I've got against him so far:

144

"*First:* Had quarrelled with Sethleigh more than once. Plenty of witnesses to that.

"*Second:* Admits knocked Sethleigh down. Sethleigh's head struck trunk of tree. Redsey thought he had killed him, and confessed as much to me.

"*Third:* Redsey stood to gain the house, estate, and most of the money belonging to Sethleigh if the latter died before altering his will.

"*Fourth:* The bloodstained suitcase belonged to Sethleigh and has his initials on it. There is some evidence offered by Redsey to the effect that Sethleigh lent it this summer to the Reverend Stephen Broome. This statement is corroborated by the vicar and the vicar's daughter. Redsey swears case was never returned. Vicar uncertain on this point. Daughter thinks case *was* returned. Vicar absent-minded and forgetful. Daughter very much the reverse."

"Of course," the superintendent demurred, "the suitcase isn't important. There is nothing at all to connect it with the murder as far as we know at present. I think we might leave the suitcase out of it for a bit."

"The bloodstains, sir."

"Yes, well, we shall know more when we know whether it's human blood or whether they carried home the week-end joint without enough paper wrapped round it. Case of wait and see. Still, there's certainly a good deal of unexplained matter which could easily be worked into a case against the young fellow. He had the motive, you see. That's the big thing."

"Yes, sir. Still, his prints don't coincide with those on the butcher's knife and cleaver. Those prints were made by that daft assistant who apparently parted with the key, and there's nothing to connect *him* with the murder."

"No — but about James Redsey, now. You see, we can't prove he dismembered the body even if we think he did the murder. What about the prints on the suitcase?"

"Too confused to be trustworthy, sir. You see, at least four people have handled that case since somebody stowed it away on the Vicarage dust-heap."

"Four people?"

"Yes. Young Harringay, Miss Broome, the sergeant, and me. And then, you see, it had been buried. That makes a difference."

"Yes, I see. Still, as I say, even without the suitcase, the whole thing looks pretty clear to me."

"Yes. It's a darn sight too clear. That's what I think," said Grindy. "It's like picking apples off a tree. Too easy to be interesting. I don't like that kind of evidence. Murders aren't solved all that easy, sir, as you should know. That fellow Redsey is quite the sort of young chap as might do a murder — same as any of us — you don't have to be a criminal to up and kill a man when all's said and done. The feelings of that are in most of us, say what you please — but all the same, Mr Bidwell —"

"You come along to my place, and have a bit of supper, Tom," said the superintendent kindly. "And don't get highfalutin. You've got a bead on your man all right. I've thought so all along. You see, there have been nothing but family rows over that property since the grandfather's time. The brother, this young Harringay's father, was disinherited by the old man, and the two sisters had a lawsuit over the business — that's Sethleigh's mother and Redsey's mother, you know — and a lawsuit over property in a family means bad blood all round — it doesn't stop at a sisterly row between the two litigants. And now the trouble has worked downwards, and, in my opinion, young Redsey has just simply gone and cooked it. And, after all, dozens of men have been arrested on less than a quarter of the evidence you've got against him."

"Yes, I know." The inspector stared at the broad toes of his boots. "But it could all be explained away pretty easily. I mean, suppose Sethleigh *were* only stunned after all by that fall? Then, it seems pretty certain Redsey did not dismember the corpse — at least, we can't prove at present that he did cut it up, and we can't find an accomplice. Besides, on Monday night, and pretty late at that, it seems that Redsey was seen looking for the body."

"Eh?"

"Well, we can't *prove* that's what he was looking for, but it seems feasible."

"Well?"

"Well, don't you see, that shows he didn't know the body was dismembered and in Bossbury. He thought it was still in the bushes where he'd left it on the Sunday night."

"H'm! It's a point. But in view of what you've got against him —"

"Then the point about the will. He says he didn't know his cousin was going to disinherit him, and we can't prove that he did know."

"There's that, certainly. But I expect he knew all right. I bet that is what the final row was all about, as a matter of fact. After all, he admits it was about money. You've only got to go a step further. After all, to be disinherited —"

"Yes, I know, but *did* he know about the will? The alteration of the will, I mean. If he didn't, you see —"

"And if he *did*, Grindy — and I can't see why he *shouldn't* have known —"

"Yes, sir. It's a big point, of course. But proof, you see —"

"Proof! Why, you've got your proof! The murder of Sethleigh is the proof! What more do you want?"

"Somewhere," said Grindy slowly, shaking his head and laboriously working it out, "there's a flaw in that argument."

"You come and have some grub," said the superintendent kindly. "That bit of gardening's upset you!"

II

Aubrey himself, much mystified by the discovery of the suitcase containing his trout, wandered back to the

148

Manor House, and went up to his own room. He picked up his bat and was practising a few late cuts — the kind of stroke, he reflected, that looks so pretty at the nets, but which never seems to come off in a match — when the bell rang for tea.

Aubrey, always ready for his meals, hastily washed his hands and brushed his hair. Then he tore down the stairs, jumped the last eight, and nearly knocked Mrs Bradley flying. Before he could so much as apologize, she gripped his arm and hissed into his ear:

"Go upstairs again, and bring me the false teeth!"

Aubrey stared at her in stark amazement for a full minute. Then he bolted upstairs again, and shortly returned bearing a small cardboard box. This he handed to her.

"Thank you," said Mrs Bradley. "The trove of the dust-heap shall be paid for in — hard cash?"

Aubrey stuck his hands in his pockets and put his head on one side.

"No," he said. "Let me — let me have a bit of a look-in, will you, Mrs Bradley? There's going to be a lark, isn't there?"

"At six o'clock to-morrow night, so early in the morning, then," said Mrs Bradley, nodding and cackling and wagging a yellow forefinger at him. "Bring Felicity Broome and James Redsey. I *must* have James Redsey. Understand?"

"No," said Aubrey, laughing. "But it sounds the goods all right. I'll go and tell Felicity directly after tea."

"And I myself will invite James Redsey," observed Mrs Bradley, "and then he won't have the requisite amount of nerve to refuse the invitation. That young man is afraid of me! He darts behind potted palms at my approach! I've seen him do it! But this time he will not escape!"

She proved a true prophet. The spineless James fell an easy victim to an invitation which he spent the rest of the evening cursing and reviling, but which he had not found the courage to refuse when Mrs Bradley delivered it.

After tea, Aubrey went in search of Felicity Broome and found her lying on the grass in the orchard behind the Vicarage garden. She was weeping bitterly. He stood by her side for a moment and looked down upon her gravely, a tall, thin, brown-faced boy, sympathetic and diffident. At last he coughed.

Felicity raised herself and looked round. Slowly she sat up, and, with woman's instinct, began to tidy her rumpled hair. Her eyelashes were wet and her cheeks flushed with weeping. She was very lovely.

"I say," began Aubrey, abashed at the sight of woman's tears. He hesitated. "I suppose you know those police johnnies have been nosing round our place again?" he added awkwardly.

Felicity nodded. A sob escaped her, and she clenched her small teeth viciously. Absurd to let a kid like Aubrey see one cry, and all about a man whom one had only known about — about ten weeks!

"I'm sure they think — they think that Jimsey —" she managed to observe in a husky voice.

Aubrey nodded gloomily.

"Yes, I'm afraid so, too," he said. "And they found that bally suitcase, too, this afternoon."

"Found it?" Felicity stared at him. "The inspector was over here asking about it, but I had no idea they'd found it! Where?"

"Buried in old Jim's hole, where we had decided to put it ourselves. Comic, isn't it? But you don't want to worry, Felicity," he added hastily. "I mean, they can't prove anything, you know. Old Jim has been absolutely square with them. Confessed he knocked Rupert out and everything. That ought to count in his favour, you know. If only we could find out who bunked off with that bally suitcase that night, and then buried it like that!"

"Why?" Felicity gave her eyes a last dab and tossed back her hair.

"Well, don't you see! It must have been the — the real murderer. After all, if old Jim didn't carve up the corpse — and he swears he didn't, and the police don't believe he did, because I asked the inspector and he said they could check up Jim's alibi for Monday, when they are pretty sure it was done — unless it was done on the Sunday, when, again, Jim couldn't have done it — well then, it seems to me that Jim couldn't have killed Rupert, but only stunned him, as Jim himself said; and then Rupert got up, all woozy from the concussion or whatever it was, and somebody else stepped in and had a soft job finishing the poor blighter off."

Felicity shivered.

"Yes, but it's Jimsey they're after. I know it is! I can see it in that inspector's eye," she said with a gulp.

"Look here," said Aubrey, seating himself beside her, and grinning at two very young calves who came up to gaze at them, "let's get this straight. Do you or do you not believe that Jim Redsey killed Rupert?"

"Aubrey! You know I believe what Jim says! But, after all, what *does* he say? That he thought he'd killed his cousin! He himself thought so!"

Aubrey sighed.

"Well, anyway, I'm going to find the man who did the — what's that word the police always use? — yes, the dismembering of the corpse. You know, that stunt's often done, and people always think it's to cover up the crime by messing up the identity of the body. But I often think it must be because the murderer can't stick the sight of the victim when the deed's done."

"Be quiet," said Felicity sharply. "And look here, Aubrey, I know you're a clever boy. And brave, too. So, if you want any help, you know I'll do what I can."

"Good man," said Aubrey briskly. "Now the first job is one you can help me over right away. Will you come with me to see that old dame the mater hates so much?"

"Mrs Bradley?"

"Yes, she wants us to go there at six to-morrow."

"Yes, I'll come with you, of course. Did you know she gave Father five hundred pounds?"

"Five hundred? What for?"

"The Restoration Fund. But she won't come to church."

"Why not?"

Felicity giggled in spite of herself.

"She thinks the Church Catechism is immoral."

"So do I," said Aubrey feelingly. "I can't stick learning stuff by heart. But what's her objection?"

"The bit about your betters. She says the village children are led to believe it means the squire and the people who go fox-hunting and the factory owners who pay women about half what they would pay men for doing exactly the same work."

"Oh, I see."

"And the bit about our station in life. She says it's retrogressive to teach children ideas like that. They just think it means never try to get on and do anything with your life. She says the plutocrats made use of phrases like that to keep the workers down — what used to be called 'in their place', and made them put up with all sorts of bad conditions because it was the — the will of Heaven. She says she knows the Church doesn't interpret these things like that, but that the Victorians always did. She thinks it's a frightfully progressive sign that so few intelligent people go to church. She says, if people got up in a political meeting and made the sort of speech that the average clergyman 'dignifies by the name of sermon', most of the audience would walk out, and the vulgar ones would throw tomatoes and make rude noises."

"Has your pater heard all this?"

"Oh, yes. She and Father sit in the garden and argue for hours. I'm glad. It's a change for the poor darling and it keeps him out of my way. And she often has us

153

over there to meals and things. Dinner chiefly. She's got a French cook. Father loves going. So do I, really, although she scares me."

"Yes, you always feel as though she's getting at you," agreed Aubrey. "Have you ever played billiards with her?"

"No, I don't play."

"She's hot. Well, we'll go and see her to-morrow, then. Call for you at a quarter to six. That do?"

Felicity nodded.

"I shall be ready," she said. "And now I must go and wash my face. Do I look very horrible?"

She smiled up at him gloriously.

"You look all right," said Aubrey, fired by her loveliness, agonizingly conscious of the inadequacy of his words, but bashfully incapable of adding so much as a syllable to them. He put out a lean brown hand and helped her to her feet.

CHAPTER
THIRTEEN

Margery Barnes

I

At six o'clock on the following day, Aubrey and Jim called at the Vicarage for Felicity Broome, and the three of them walked over to the Stone House.

Mrs Bradley received them in the stone-flagged, oak-panelled hall, and without any preliminaries, except for the removal of Felicity's hat, she caused them to be seated at a large oak table, and presented each of them with a pencil and a pad of writing-paper.

"Plenty of paper, you see," said Mrs Bradley, cackling hideously but with obvious pleasure.

"Look here," said Jim Redsey, grinning. "Can't I be let off? Honestly, I'm not a scrap of good at these parlour games. I always make the most frightful fool of myself. You three play, and I'll be umpire and see you don't cheat."

"Oh, but this is a new game," objected Mrs Bradley. "And it doesn't need an umpire. Now, take up your pencils. Write your name and the date on top of the paper. Pencils down as soon as you have finished."

Aubrey giggled.

"It's like the kindergarten I went to as a small kid," he observed, scrawling the date in his curiously grown-up handwriting, and then laying his pencil on the table.

"Now listen to me," went on Mrs Bradley. "I want you all to make a long list of places where the skull which disappeared from Mr Wright's house may be hidden. Are you ready?" She smiled hideously around at the three hapless young people. "Then . . . go!"

At the end of twenty minutes she collected the papers and sent her visitors home. At seven o'clock another party of guests arrived. These were Lulu Hirst and Savile from the Cottage on the Hill. They had come to dinner. At a quarter past seven the vicar arrived with the major's two daughters. The two large, plain girls explained that their father's gout was troublesome, and so he would not come.

When dinner was over, Mrs Bradley went through the same performance with pencils and paper. The guests were uncertain whether to be amused or bored by the proceedings, but reflected that they had enjoyed an excellent dinner!

Next morning, Mrs Bradley walked over to the cottage where George Willows — in the act of commanding his wife to eat a second rasher of bacon — was having his breakfast, and asked him the same question.

Willows lowered a knife covered with yolk of egg into his mouth, while Mrs Bradley quickly averted her gaze, then he laid knife and fork down and turned in his chair.

"Take a seat, mum, if you please," said Mrs Willows, hastily but unnecessarily dusting a chair. Mrs Bradley sat down.

"Hide the skull?" said George Willows meditatively. He ruminated. "Happen I should bury un," he said at length, while a slow smile spread over his sun-tanned features. "Ah, that's what I should do meself, like. Bury un in the ground. And plant a big plant over un, like." he added, embroidering the idea richly.

"A helpful suggestion," observed Mrs Bradley.

"And if I knowed for certain sure it were the skull of that there Mr Sethleigh as turned me out with hard words and a blow too and all, I lay I'd stamp on un hard," concluded George Willows truculently.

Mrs Willows gazed at the bold fellow in terrified admiration. She had been a hero-worshipper for fifteen years.

"I think we might cross you out of the list of suspects, my friend," thought Mrs Bradley as she walked up the lane towards the house of Dr Barnes and turned in at the double gates. "Still, I am very glad I have had a look at you. Conclusive, I think. Exit Willows."

"I'm sorry," said Margery Barnes, straightening her back at Mrs Bradley's approach, for she had spent the previous twenty minutes in weeding the gravel path. "Father is out on his round. I'm expecting him home soon, though. He usually comes in at about ten, and goes out again at about eleven." She glanced at Mrs Bradley's face. "You don't look very ill," she remarked.

157

Mrs Bradley stretched out a claw-like hand and tweaked her short fair hair.

"I am not in the least ill, I am thankful to say," she observed. "I have come to consult your father about a different matter. Rather a serious matter, I am afraid."

Margery blanched.

"Not about that horrible murder? You're not going to ask Father anything about that?" she cried in consternation.

"Hoots toots!" cried Mrs Bradley, who professed an enormous admiration for the Scots people and occasionally expressed herself in what she fondly believed to be their native tongue. "And here *is* your father!"

"Oh, Father!" cried Margery. "Mrs Bradley has called to ask you —"

"To prescribe for old Martha Higgs down in the village," interpolated Mrs Bradley neatly. Margery gasped with relief, and subsided. "She is not an insured person, Mrs Bradley continued, "and she can't get a widow's pension because unfortunately she is a spinster. She has the old age pension and two shillings a week from her nephew — good luck to him for a dutiful and generous boy, for he has a wife and children of his own — and her rheumatism is really very bad. I think a time at Bath might help the poor dear. I suppose a cure, or anything approaching a cure, is hopeless at her age, but I think perhaps —"

Imagining that the discussion might probably last for some time, Margery slipped away to her own room, changed her shoes, put on a hat, and bicycled down to the Vicarage.

As soon as Margery had gone, Mrs Bradley propounded to the doctor her question as to the probable hiding-place of the skull.

"Of course," the doctor remarked, his fresh-coloured face flushing darkly, "if they had brought the thing to me instead of giving it to young Wright to monkey about with, I could soon have told them whether it was Sethleigh's skull or not. You had only to try his dental plate in the jaws and deduce whether it would fit."

"Quite so. I had thought of that myself," said Mrs Bradley. "But there were two objections to the plan at the time you mentioned."

"Oh, really?"

"Yes, doctor. For one thing, when the bishop handed the skull over to Cleaver Wright there was no idea of its being Sethleigh's skull. The bishop and the vicar had an argument to which historic or prehistoric period the skull belonged, and the vicar expressed some hope that a complete model in clay might help to settle the question. That was all. Secondly, the dental plate, I suppose, was in Sethleigh's mouth when he met his death, and so —"

"The police haven't found it, you mean," said the doctor. "H'm! I see. Still, it would have been an infallible proof, you know. Quite infallible! I mean, a man's dental plate, like his finger-prints, can't possibly belong to anyone else, you know."

Mrs Bradley shook her head slowly from side to side until she looked like some hideously leering idol from the East. "Is any proof ever infallible?" she asked sadly.

II

Felicity was out, and the Reverend Stephen Broome was preparing his sermon when Margery alighted at the Vicarage gate, propped up her bicycle against the untidy hedge, and walked up to the front door.

"The mistress is along by the village, and, sure, himself will have my life, Miss Margery, should I put the face of me inside his little room this day," exclaimed Mary Kate when Margery asked to see either the vicar or his daughter.

"I can't help it. If Felicity is out, I *must* see him! Tell him it's about the murder, Mary Kate. That ought to fetch him!"

"The murder! Oh, then, Miss Margery, what's come over you at all?"

"Nothing. Go and tell the vicar quickly, Mary Kate. Oh, do hurry up!"

Upon this, Mary Kate flung herself into the study, omitting even the formality of knocking at the door, and cried in a loud voice rich with direful woe:

"Glory be to God, your honour's reverence, Mr Broome! There's Mistress Margery from the doctor's house below does be after saying she's done the murder herself itself entirely!"

"Where is Miss Margery?" enquired the vicar.

"Sure, herself is below stairs waiting on your reverence."

"And don't call me your reverence! I've told you before that I am not of the Roman persuasion."

"More's the shame to you, then," retorted Mary Kate, recovering her wonted poise with speed and certainty, "that you wouldn't be an honest Christian man — and you to be baptizing the babes and burying the old people and all!"

The vicar, as usual, was left without the honours of war, and Mary Kate retired in triumph from the study. She returned in two minutes and ushered in a stammering and shame-flushed Margery Barnes.

"Please, may I shut the door?" she asked timidly when Mary Kate had departed. "I — what I have to say is absolutely private. I don't — nobody else — I couldn't let everybody know."

The Vicar of Wandles Parva laid down his pen and turned to face her. Without meeting his quizzical gaze, Margery went over to the door and closed it.

"Now then," said the Reverend Stephen. "What's all this? Some dark deed, or what?"

"It's partly about me and partly about somebody else," said Margery, looking past him and collecting her thoughts, and — or so it seemed to the vicar — her courage. He looked at her, half amused, and saw a red-faced, slightly perspiring, fair-haired, short-skirted, ingenuous maiden of eighteen, curiously like — who *was* she curiously like? He frowned. Margery caught his eye, and avoided it again.

161

"Mr Broome," she said at last, "do you think — I mean, there's no chance of Jim Redsey being arrested, is there? You hear such horrible rumours down in the village about him."

"I don't know." The vicar looked thoughtful. "I believe there's a good deal of evidence against him. He'll have to stand his trial if he is arrested, of course, unless anything turns up to point out the real murderer. It is a very nasty, puzzling business, this murder, isn't it? I shouldn't think too much about it, if I were you."

"You don't believe Jim Redsey did it, do you, Mr Broome? I can see you don't! Oh, I'm so glad!"

"Why, no, I don't believe he did it. And you don't believe it either, I see." The Reverend Stephen Broome picked up his pen and rustled some papers suggestively. But Margery refused to be turned out of the study by the feeble hints of work to be done. She crossed one thick, sturdy leg over the other and leaned forward confidentially.

"I *know* he didn't do it," she said unexpectedly.

"What?" The vicar looked startled.

Margery nodded her head emphatically.

"If I — if I tell you what I know, will you back me up with Father?" she demanded.

"What have you been up to, then?" The vicar laid down his pen and began to fill his pipe.

"I'll tell you."

She uncrossed her legs, leaned forward, with her elbows among the vicar's scattered sermon papers, and began.

162

"Rupert Sethleigh was supposed to have been killed on Sunday night, June 22nd, wasn't he? And, at about nine o'clock, Jim Redsey was in the 'Queen's Head'. Well, if anybody saw Rupert Sethleigh alive after Jim Redsey had knocked him down and gone off and left him for dead, would it prove that Jim was not — would they — I mean, they couldn't think Jim did it then, could they?"

"I couldn't say. It would make a difference, of course, because the police would then have to prove that Redsey returned and finished off the job, and, from what I understand of the matter, it would be impossible to prove that."

"Could they — would they try to prove that?"

"Well, I expect so. You see, the police seem to have a very strong case against Redsey. I'm afraid I don't read the papers, so I am not at all clear how far the police theories have gone, but one hears things. . . . Look here, why don't you go and tell what you know to the inspector? He'll be able to advise you far better than I can."

"But what about Father? He'll be furious when he knows what I've done!"

"Well, you'll have to face up to it. You didn't do anything desperate, I suppose?"

He surveyed her quizzically.

"I've brought up a daughter myself," he added, "so I know the sort of thing they get up to."

"I went into the Manor Woods to — to meet a man," confessed Margery, blushing furiously under her freckles and looking about ten years old.

"The dickens you did!" And the vicar grinned wickedly.

"Yes. I don't know what Father will say! He's frightfully particular about — about things like that." To Margery, obviously, it was no grinning matter.

"I see. Well, I'll try and cope with him; but, even if I can't mitigate his wrath, you must take comfort from the fact that you'll be doing the right thing, and the big thing, in owning up like a sportsman. See?"

"Yes," said Margery lugubriously. "What sort of view will the inspector take? I mean, will he be like you or — or pious and horrified, like Mother and Father?"

"You'd better trot along and see," said the vicar seriously. "Oh, half a minute! Here comes Felicity, I think."

He walked to the end of the passage, called her into the dining-room and said to her quite solemnly:

"Child, have you ever been to the Manor Woods by night to meet a man?"

Felicity stared at him.

"Well," pursued the vicar, "why did Margery Barnes go? She's in my study, by the way. Perhaps you'll go in to her."

"Margery? She never did! Little idiot! Who was the man?"

"I don't know who the man was," the vicar replied. "Will her father be very angry?"

"She's never going to tell Dr Barnes?" cried Felicity, horrified.

"Wouldn't you tell me?"

Felicity kissed the top of his nose.

"It's rather different, silly. Dr Barnes will *eat* her! And that idiotic Mrs Barnes, who can't pass a cow in the lane without wanting to squeal, will back him up when she returns from her holiday. But *why* is she going to tell him? I shouldn't, if I were his daughter!"

"She's going to tell the inspector first."

"The inspector? What for? You know, sweetest, it's rather morbid, I think — this passion for confessing one's sins to all and sundry. By the way, do you know Mrs Bradley's trying to find out all about — Oh, I *say!*"

Her grey eyes grew wide with surmise and fear. "It isn't anything to do with the murder that poor little Margery —!" Without staying to finish the sentence, she flew into the study. At the same instant, Mrs Bradley was announced at the front door. Felicity, who had had barely time to greet the doctor's daughter, left Margery alone and went down into the hall.

"Felicity," said Mrs Bradley, "don't you think it would be rather nice to take your Sunday-school class into Culminster and show them the cathedral? And the market cross? And the museum? So interesting for the dear children."

"Yes, I know," replied Felicity, puckering her brow. "It would be interesting, and I'd love to take them, but their parents can't afford the bus fare, and it's too far to walk. And *I* can't afford to pay for the dears," she added, "much as I'd like to do it."

Mrs Bradley fumbled in her skirt pocket and drew out a large practical purse.

"In the interests of their education," she said, opening it, "I hope I may be allowed to provide their fares." She pulled out a pound note. "And their teas." She pulled out another. "Sufficient? Good."

She waved aside Felicity's thanks.

"Don't encourage them to look at the case on the north wall of the museum. It contains, among other things, the model of a Roman shield, and, if you stand at the far end of the room opposite the door, half-close your eyes, and peer diligently behind that shield, you can see something extremely interesting. But do not show it to the children. I am very anxious for you to come, immediately upon your return, to my house and tell me what you have seen."

Felicity looked mystified, but promised to obey.

"And now," she said, "I've got Margery Barnes here with some tale or other which seems to be in connection with something which happened on the night of the murder. Shall I ask her whether she is willing for us both to hear it? She is in the next room."

Margery, blushing but valiant, was willing, and Felicity conducted Mrs Bradley into the study.

"You can all get out," said the vicar, who had returned to his den and wanted to get on with his sermon. "I'm busy. Go into the drawing-room. That's the place for visitors!"

Settled in the drawing-room, Felicity turned to the younger girl.

"Now then, Margery! What's all this about your wild oats?" she said lightly.

"It was all through Father saying 'Don't'," began Margery. She sighed wistfully. "Your father never says 'Don't'. I've noticed that. And, if my father never said it, what a lot of things in the world I should never ache and yearn to do!"

She sighed again, glanced down and became aware of very dusty shoes. She cleaned them surreptitiously on her brown stockings and continued hastily:

"The first time Father said 'Don't' about men was when Willie Bailey took me on the back of his motorcycle to Bossbury Fair. And we came home before it was anything like dark, so I don't see why Father need have been so sniffy. It wasn't as though Willie isn't a perfectly nice boy! Anyway, Father said I wasn't to meet Willie, or go with him anywhere ever any more. But, of course, I did. At school we were encouraged to be strong-minded and independent and to live our own lives, and I made up my mind that, if living my own life meant wanting to go out with perfectly decent or jolly clever men, I was going to do it! Well, it couldn't be by day, openly and above-board, because Father had forbidden that. So it had to be at night. Well, it came to that Sunday night. You know the one I mean! I'd arranged to be at the Manor Woods at a quarter to nine. That was to give the people a chance to clear away from the church, because I would have to pass it, and I didn't want to be seen. Well, it was all fairly easy that night, because Mother was on holiday — she'd gone away the day before, on the Saturday — and Father was going up to the major's — at least, he said something about it, and he wasn't at home when I came in from visiting old Mrs Hartley up at The Winnows — so, the coast being clear, I waited until twenty-five to nine and then I sneaked off. Well, I met him all right, although I felt rather scared. For one thing, I always had a dread that someone would see us, and tell Father, and then the Manor Woods always do frighten me, somehow — I think it's that horrible Stone — I dream about it sometimes, and it's always dripping with blood — and then, that night, *he* scared me too."

Felicity felt her heart beginning to beat faster.

"He would have us sit down with our backs against that horrible Stone," continued Margery with a shudder. "Said I was silly to be afraid of it, and the sooner I got over the feeling, the better. Well, I didn't feel so unsafe with him beside me, and he began to tell me stories — fairy tales, delightful things! — until his voice going on and on made me forget the Stone and everything. I just felt as though I must go to sleep. Suddenly he brought his hand down hard on my shoulder and pulled his face in close to mine, and glared into my eyes, and said in a horrible, blood-curdling voice, 'And then the ogre cried —!' I suppose he did it for a joke, but I was so terrified that I just tore myself free and jumped up and ran through the woods for all I was worth. I fell over things, and tore myself on brambles, and caught my feet in things, and it was getting quite dark in among the trees."

"What time was this?" Mrs Bradley rapped out the question from her corner.

"Time? Oh, just after nine o'clock. I remember hearing the church clock strike nine when I first began to feel drowsy. I was to meet him at a quarter to nine, you remember, so we had not been in the woods very long."

"Nine o'clock? I see. Please go on. I'm sorry I interrupted," said Mrs Bradley, sitting back in her chair.

"Yes, well, I don't know how I managed not to go crashing into tree-trunks, dashing about like that. Still, I was lucky, I suppose. Suddenly, what was my horror to come bursting out into a clearing! I knew there was only one clearing in the Manor Woods, and that was the pine ring with the Stone in the middle. And, sure enough, there it was — the great, sprawling, horrible toad-like thing! — but *he* was not sitting there. I suppose he went after me when I ran away. Anyway, I was so frightfully breathless that I felt, Stone or no Stone, I must sit down just for a minute, so I sat down, and bent my head to my knees, as our gym mistress taught us to do if we felt a bit faint.

"Well, just then I heard a slight sound quite close to me. Well, you know how it is when you hear a noise — you raise your head. Well, I raised mine, and, to my absolute horror, the first thing my eyes fell on was the figure of a man coming crawling out of the bushes like a great black slug!

"Ugh! Those awful woods! I'm afraid I shrieked. At any rate, I got up and ran. I stumbled by accident upon the main path to the wicket gate, and I simply tore along it, and fell through into the road, and raced home and went straight up to bed. Oh, Felicity, I wouldn't go out at night like that again for anything you could offer me!"

"Well, it's all very exciting," said Felicity gravely, "but what exactly is the point of it all?"

"Why, don't you see?" Margery gripped her arm in excitement. "That man crawling out of the bushes! After nine o'clock that night! It must have been Rupert Sethleigh, still funny in the head from concussion! Don't you see? And, if it was Rupert, then Jim Redsey didn't kill him, because he was in the 'Queen's Head' by that time!"

"But you don't *know* that the man was Rupert. You didn't really recognize him," Felicity objected.

"No, but I'd swear I did, if the police asked me," said Margery sturdily. "And, anyway, he did have a frightfully familiar sort of look, so I expect that's who it was."

"But you can't say you recognized him if you didn't!" Felicity stuck doggedly to her point. "It wouldn't be right, and, if you do say it, I shall contradict you."

"Anyone would think, Felicity Broome, that you *wanted* that poor boy to be hanged," said Margery, preparing to be tearful.

Felicity went white.

"Telling a lie to get people out of trouble doesn't help, and you are not going to do it," she said. "Besides, suppose it were found out that you hadn't spoken the truth? It would do Jim a lot of harm. You ought to see that for yourself. No, it's no use arguing, Margery. And look here. I don't want to seem like Paul Pry, but this

170

tale doesn't exactly connect up with Willie Bailey, you know. I mean, Willie is so very much an English Public School boy, isn't he? I'm sure he wouldn't think it at all the thing to meet girls in woods and then frighten them to death."

Margery's gloom perceptibly deepened.

"If it had been *that* baby kid, I wouldn't really be so scared of Father knowing," she said. "Although he said I wasn't to go out with him, I know. But still — I could wangle that. No, that's the whole point, Felicity. It was not Willie Bailey!"

CHAPTER
FOURTEEN

What Happened at the "Queen's Head"

I

Savile did not see her arrive. Clad in nothing but dark-grey flannel trousers and a pair of old shoes, he was standing in the middle of the back garden path between a gooseberry bush and a clump of lavender. His attitude, which might have graced a master of the ballet, seemed far from pleasing to Cleaver Wright, who, pipe in mouth and blue eyes narrowed into slits, was seated on the kitchen steps with a drawing-board on his knees and a scowl of intense ferocity on his brow.

"No, no!" he shouted. "It's no good like that, you ass!"

He took the pipe out of his mouth and pointed with the stem of it at Lulu Hirst, who was watching the proceedings from a hammock slung between two apple trees.

"Tip that girl out of there and hoist her up above your head. I want to see those back and shoulder muscles brought into play. You're supposed to be a

Japanese wrestler, damn you, not a tailor's dummy or a sinuous Salome! Come here, Lulu, and don't act the fool, or he'll drop you. Now then, Savile! Up with her!"

"Half a moment," demurred Savile, with his oily smirk. "These trousers. Too long. Inartistic, my dear fellow. If I am to be a Japanese wrestler I must look the part. My artistic conscience —"

"To hell with it!" said Wright resignedly. "Go on, then. Only buck up."

Savile stepped carefully over him and disappeared into the house. Lulu rolled gracefully back into the hammock and curled herself up like a sleek yellow cat. Mrs Bradley, smiling gently, advanced towards Cleaver Wright. Wright grinned.

"Take a seat," he said. "You ought to pay, really. Look. Isn't that beautiful?"

Mrs Bradley drew out a small reading-glass and surveyed the returning Savile. He was clad effectively and with great simplicity in a loin-cloth. His satin skin glistened with oil. Without a look or a word he trotted across to the hammock, gathered up the recumbent form of Lulu with as much ease as he would have handled a kitten, and carried her across the garden to his former position in the centre of the path.

"Now then," said Wright. "Up with her. That's the ticket. Can you keep her there a second?"

"Oh, yes," said Savile, who, to Mrs Bradley's surprise, appeared to find little difficulty in holding Lulu clear above his head on outstretched arms. The muscles of his back and shoulders stood out like cords under the beautiful, creamy skin. It was a delight to look upon such perfect muscular development.

Wright picked up a piece of charcoal.

II

"Well," said Mrs Bradley, "I never would have believed it!"

"No," agreed Wright, putting finishing touches to his sketch. "A bit startling, isn't it? He looks such a worm in his clothes. But take them away, and, damn it, the chap's a pocket Hercules. Most surprising fellow."

He held the drawing at arm's length and studied it thoughtfully.

"Not too bad," he said at last. "Two guineas. Want it?"

"Yes, if you'll take me in and show me the other things you have done, young man," said Mrs Bradley. "I have never seen a studio. It will be an experience for me. And at my age" — she glanced at him out of the corner of a beady black eye — "one embraces new experiences with avidity, because there will come a time —" She broke off and cackled — a harsh, unlovely sound. Wright looked pained. His bright, intensely blue eyes sought hers sombrely.

"Oh, come now, auntie —"

"Beatrice," supplied Mrs Bradley promptly.

"Thank you, Beatrice. Ah, come now, Auntie Beatrice! Don't talk like that. Come in quick, before

174

you cause me to burst into tears. Look see! This is my dear little room."

Mrs Bradley followed him into his studio. The first thing which took her eye was a large plan of a human skeleton, carefully annotated in small neat script and covered with red-ink dotted lines. She examined this plan with great interest.

"Most informative," she said at last, after giving it a prolonged scrutiny.

"Yes. Old Savile stuck that up and wrote the book of words. Thinks it helps him to draw pictures of gods and wood-nymphs! Heaven knows why. I find the thing rather revolting."

He turned the elaborate chart with its face to the wall, and led her over to a stack of canvases.

"And the model of Rupert Sethleigh's head," said Mrs Bradley, when she had examined several oil-paintings and Wright had directed her attention to a small clay figure of a Roman gladiator. "Did you model that in here?"

"That? Oh, yes. Funny business, that, you know. Deuce knows what happened to that skull. You heard, I suppose, that when the police johnnies broke up my model to get the skull out, they found a bally coconut inside? Most astounding! Well, it astounded me, anyhow! Most extraordinary thing. I couldn't believe it. Thought the inspector was pulling my leg at first. But no!"

"The silly part was," said Savile, who had entered behind them, and was once again the sleek-haired, sallow-complexioned, rather unpleasant person Mrs

175

Bradley had met at Felicity's tennis-party, "that the coconut itself was the one which our young friend —"

A sudden crash drowned the rest of his sentence.

"Damn!" said Cleaver Wright, picking up a dummy figure which had been seated in a rakish attitude on top of a tall pedestal. "I beg your pardon, Mrs Bradley, for the wicked word, but I've broked my poor dolly." He stroked the head of the repulsive object tenderly.

Mrs Bradley smiled, and involuntarily Cleaver Wright squirmed. He had seen the same gentle, anticipatory, patient smile on the face of an alligator in the London Zoological Gardens. It was a smile of quiet relish. It was the smile of the Chinese executioner. In spite of the afternoon's warmth, Wright found himself shivering. He changed the subject hastily, and laid the dummy down.

"I suppose the police have pretty well made up their minds that poor old Redsey killed his brute of a cousin?" he asked.

Mrs Bradley raised her sparse, black brows.

"Really?" she said. "I don't know why you should think that."

"Oh, one reads the papers," said Wright carelessly. "That's all. Still, one is very glad one has a complete alibi, of course," he added, grinning wickedly, "as one is known to have disliked the chap oneself."

"A complete alibi?" Mrs Bradley grimaced. "Then you've more than I have, young man. If the police came and asked me where I was on the evening of Sunday, June 22nd, I should be compelled to tell them that I was alone in the house from four-thirty until five minutes past eleven; that nobody called during that time; and that, had the spirit so moved me — which, in confidence, young man, I may inform you it did *not!* — I could have gone out and killed Rupert Sethleigh without a soul being any the wiser!"

She hooted with owl-like amusement. Cleaver Wright grinned.

"Well, I'm better off than you," he said. "I went to the 'Queen's Head' for a nightcap, and got embroiled in a row with a great oaf of a farmer called Galloway. Didn't finish the scrap until nearly closing-time. Choice, wasn't it?"

"Did you get hurt?" asked Mrs Bradley.

"Got pretty badly knocked about," said Wright carelessly. "Never mind." He grinned again.

"And you bear Mr Galloway no malice?" said Mrs Bradley musingly. "That is so nice, I think. It is what they call the true sporting feeling, isn't it? They teach it at the Public Schools now, don't they?"

Wright glared at her suspiciously. Women, especially ancient dames like this one, were fools, he knew. Yet was it possible — ? But Mrs Bradley's wrinkled yellow face was mild and sweet as that of a grandmother — which, owing to the extreme distaste displayed by her only son for the whole female sex, she certainly was not! — and Wright was forced to the conclusion that — alas for the progress of feminism! — it *was* possible! The woman was an idiot. Why had he shivered when she smiled?

He grunted and moved towards the door. Mrs Bradley followed him, but on the way she paused at some shelves of books. On top of the bookcase was a fine array of silver sports trophies.

"Old Savile's, mostly," said Wright.

Mrs Bradley drew out her reading-glass and scanned the engraved inscriptions closely.

"But you have two," she said, with a beam of senile futility. "How very nice! What did you do to win such lovely cups? Oh, and there's a belt! How extremely amusing. *What* are they for?"

Wright shrugged his shoulders.

"Oh, for boxing," he said carelessly. "About the only thing I'm any good at in the sports line."

"They *are* pretty things," said Mrs Bradley, even more fatuously than before. "You *must* be clever!"

When she had gone, Wright pulled on an old pair of boxing-gloves, made one or two preliminary sparring movements, and then, by way of relieving his feelings, measured the distance with his left hand and then with his powerful right he split a panel of the studio door from top to bottom.

III

Mrs Bradley entered the bar of the "Queen's Head" in some trepidation. It is not often that respectable elderly ladies, expensively, albeit hideously, clad in magenta silk dress, summer coat to match, large black picture hat (quite ludicrously unbecoming, the last-named, to Mrs Bradley's beaky bird-like profile and sharp black eyes), walk into the bar of a public house. At the

"Queen's Head" such an occurrence was absolutely unknown.

Wandles Parva (or those three-quarters of it which could command the entrance to the house of refreshment from the cover and vantage-point of the upstairs bedroom window) was keenly interested.

"Be going to ask Billy Bondy for a subscription for the church, like?"

"What, she? Never you need think so! Her don't never go into church without it might be on a weekday like any of they heathenish Catholics, and then her only goes there-along to gape at the old door and the windies, like silly folks in they charries from London do come and do!"

Mrs Bradley addressed herself to the landlord, a small, alert, bright-eyed Cockney.

"Kindly call to mind," she said, "the evening of Sunday, June 22nd."

The landlord looked perplexed. Would there be any special reason — "Oh, ah! Of course! That there murder!"

"No, not the murder. I heard rumours down in the village of a fight between —"

"Alfred Owen Galloway, of this town, and what's-his-name Wright, late of Somewhere Else," supplied the landlord humorously. "Quite right, mum. So there were. 'Ere they stood, right in this very bar. We pushes back the old table to give 'em room. On my right, Mr Galloway. On my left, Mr Wright — only 'e 'appened to be all wrong that evening. There was no seconds as you'd notice, and the rules was 'ardly Queensberry, nor yet N.S.C. I acts as timekeeper, referee, stooards, manager and permoter, and *Evening Star* special reporter all at once. And at twenty past nine, mum, I starts 'em 'orf by me watch — Greenwich time.

"It wasn't too bad, mum, for about a round and a 'arf. Mr Wright was nicely inside 'imself, and looked to me to 'ave the style and the science in 'itting. But at the end of Round Two 'e lets Galloway put 'im to the ropes — which is to say this 'ere counter — with a nasty left 'ook, and only the call of time saved 'im from punishment. Well, when the fight was resoomed in the third round, Wright was seen to be weakening. 'E stopped a left-'anded wallop to the jaw, but Galloway's right found 'is claret, which began to flow 'eavy. A sharp exchange o' blows follered, but Galloway, gettin' excited, steps in and mixes it as nice as I ever see. It weren't science, mind you, but it was real meaty! A nice two-'anded scrapper only wants a bit o' training to be a world-beater, mum, as you know. Well, Wright took some nasty body-blows, and we 'ears 'im grunt as they got 'ome on the short ribs. Suddenly Galloway gets 'im in the stummick — a foul blow, by boxin' law, but we was bein' broad-minded that evenin' — and as the pore feller comes forward — doubled-up, you know — Galloway gets 'im under the jaw with a cosh what made the glasses rattle on this 'ere tray.

"Well, I counts Wright out, and we brings 'im round and 'elps 'im on with 'is coat, and some of the fellers would 'ave 'elped 'im 'ome, but 'e preferred to go orf on 'is own. Well, the chaps stands Galloway a pint or two as the winner, and we shakes 'ands with 'im all round, and 'e goes 'ome."

"I have to thank you, Mr Bondy," observed Mrs Bradley, "for a most exceptionally concise, clear, and interesting account of the proceedings. You are not a Wandles man, I take it?"

"Wandles?" The landlord found the spittoon in the corner with unerring aim. "King's Road, 'Ammersmith — that's me. Used ter be a perfessional footballer, I did. Played for Fulham. Unlucky team, Fulham is. Still, me benefit was all right. After I collected it, I retires, and buys this 'ere little 'ouse. It's a nice little 'ouse, but sometimes I finds myself thinkin' wistful-like of the lights and the trams and the drunks and the gals and the Pally Dee Danse where we went when we was flush, and the little 'all orf the Bridge Road — billiards and pool and snooker — where we went when we wasn't — and takin' the old lady to the 'Ammersmith Palace or the Shepherd's Bush Empire to see 'Etty King and them — I tell you, mum, it's an 'orrible thing to be 'omesick. There's bin nights in Bossbury when I could 'a' sit and cried just with the stink of the fried fish shops remindin' me of the old Grey'ound Road!"

Mrs Bradley paid his homesickness the tribute of a few moments' unbroken silence. Then she said:

"And how did this quarrel between Mr Wright and Mr Galloway begin?"

"It began," said the landlord, with a reminiscent grin, "it began, mum, with Mr Wright taking an 'og-pudden and 'itting Mr Galloway over the napper with it. It would a-bin a lovely fight if only Wright 'ad

181

stood up to 'im," he went on regretfully. "But 'e give in, and Galloway fair et 'im. I'd give a pound note 'ere and now to see a match between Galloway, if 'e'd 'ad a bit of trainin', and Battlin' Kid Stoner of Parsons Green. Of course, if young Mr Redsey, what there's some nasty rumours about down in the village on account of the murder of 'is cousin Squire Sethleigh — if only 'e'd bin 'isself 'stead of sitting there as screwed as an owl or a bookie's tout on Derby Day from about 'arf-past eight till closing time, we might 'ave put '*im* up against Galloway. I see 'im in an exhibition bout at a charity fair down in Culminster a week or two back. Nice style, mum, but too much of the gentleman to suit me. Ever see Bombardier Wells fight, mum? Ain't yer? Well, if you 'ad, you'd know more what I mean. Afraid to 'urt the other chap's feelings, like. Plucky as they make 'em — so's this Mr Redsey — but don't seem to go in and mix it like the rough-necks do. I remember a little Sheeny as used to doss orf the Gold'awk Road — regular lovely little two-'anded fighter, 'e was. Take on an elephant and make it look sick, 'e would, if the boys 'ud trot out the dough. 'Ad to give 'im the purse first, though, we did. 'e wouldn't fight without. No charity matinées for '*im!* But 'e'd come up grinnin' at the end of fifteen rounds like the bloomin' little thoroughbred 'e was! Reminded me of a fox-terrier dawg I used to 'ave. Game as game! And, as I say, carried a two-'anded punch as wouldn't do no discredit to a middle-weight champion. No temper, y'know, mum! 'Eart of gold! But 'e'd fight with 'is 'ead and 'e'd fight with 'is guts and 'e knowed when a bit of rough stuff was the goods, and

182

would 'and it out liberal! Cut and come again, like! But this 'ere Mr Redsey — 'e was more like a dancin'-master. You know — tap and prance, tap and side-step — it were more like the Russian bally than anythink *I* ever see. 'E'd be a stretcher-case in a rough-'ouse, 'e would. And that's why," said the landlord, very earnestly, "when I 'ears silly ginks in this 'ere bar talking about 'im doin' this 'ere murder, I says to 'em that they 'ave no business to think the young gent done it, no matter what anybody says. I says so to Constable Pearce me own self. I says to 'im, 'Pearce,' I says, 'you oughter know more about charicter,' I says, 'than to try and get evidence agin' a young gent,' I says, 'what I've seen — yes, me, with these 'ere eyes,' I says, 'with a chap's guard right down and 'is jaw just askin' for the count of ten,' I says, 'just flick it with 'is open 'and and then grin silly-like. ''Tain't likely,' I says to 'im, 'as a chap that can't bring 'imself to slosh a jaw what's 'anded 'im on a plate, is goin' for to do a murder,' I says. 'Especially *this* murder which is by way of being what I calls a very nasty murder indeed. It ain't in nature, Mr Pearce,' I says to 'im. And in my experience, which is wide and deep, what's not in nature, mum, don't 'appen!"

Mrs Bradley was about to reply when she observed that two labourers had entered the bar. So she thanked the landlord and departed, leaving the astonished villagers with half a crown apiece and an admonition to spend at least a portion of it in drinking the health of Battling Kid Stoner of Parsons Green.

Outside the door a new thought struck her. She re-entered the place, and, having waited near the door until the labourers had been served and were seated, she again approached the landlord.

"By the way, Mr Bondy," she said casually, "where did Wright obtain the — er — the hog-pudding with which he struck Galloway on the head?"

"Where? Why, mum, 'e pulled it out of Galloway's coat-pocket, Galloway 'avin' been give it by 'is grandmother over by Short Woodcombe for 'is Monday morning breakfast. Galloway wouldn't a-minded so much if it 'adn't bin 'is own 'og-pudden, you see. Sort of add insult to injury, that were. They tied the 'og-pudden round Mr Wright's neck arterwards," he concluded, with hearty relish, "and told 'im 'e was born to be 'anged! It was a good length 'og-pudden, and the ends just met nice at the back."

CHAPTER
FIFTEEN

The Culminster Collection Acquires a New Specimen

I

Twelve little girls and three little boys lined themselves up at the crossroads and waited for Felicity Broome.

"Now don't forget to look behind the Roman shield," was Mrs Bradley's parting injunction, "and not a single word to anybody about what you see. Good-bye, my dear. I should like to come with you, but there are several little jobs I must attend to this morning. Give the dear children my kind regards, and see that they all have something they like for tea. That's the main part of an outing to children — that and the ride in the bus."

She waved to the party until the bus turned a corner, and on the way back to her house she encountered the inspector. Grindy looked warm and felt worried. He was making no appreciable headway with the case, and he was resolute in refusing to arrest James Redsey

185

without some proof either that he had dismembered the body or else that he had found an accomplice to carry out that part of the crime. Failing to prove either of these things, and irritably conscious that the chief constable of the county had already been twice to talk matters over with the superintendent at Bossbury, his deputy, the inspector was a moody and disgruntled man. Scotland Yard had been mentioned, and Grindy had all the provincial police officer's dislike of handing his cases over to the Yard for solution. The public, however, was becoming restless. Local magnates were writing letters to the *County Times* and the *Bossbury Herald*. The superintendent had given up clicking his tongue sympathetically every time Grindy reported his complete lack of progress, and was beginning to avoid his comrade's eye and mutter remarks concerning "lack of initiative in making an arrest", and "doing something to shut the mouths of fatheads who didn't realize what the police were up against", and — even less encouraging to a conscientious police officer who had won his present position through efficiency, keenness, hard work, and scrupulously just dealing — "no good being a thin-skinned sissy when it came to a clear case of murder. Make an arrest and stick to your guns!"

Grindy, however, was staunch to his own opinion. In his heart of hearts he felt that the case against James Redsey had broken down. A man of few words, he contented himself with grunts of disagreement with the superintendent's opinions, and occasionally by the terse statement that he was damned if he would arrest a man on assumptions that could be blown to bits before they ever reached the ears of a grand jury. Assumptions were not facts. It was facts he was after.

The superintendent lost his temper, and said some hard things. It was when Grindy was walking from Bossbury into Wandles Parva to relieve his feelings by some brisk physical exercise, and, incidentally, to find out whether the gardener Willows had a good and sufficient alibi for the evening and night in question, that he encountered Mrs Bradley.

"Ah, inspector," she said. "If you will come to my house — you know it, don't you? — the Stone House, just along the road there — I will give you a list of persons, one of whom is the murderer of Rupert Sethleigh — that is, supposing always that Rupert Sethleigh is dead. The last is a theory not yet proved satisfactorily, I believe."

The inspector treated her to a wintry smile.

"If you're pulling my leg, madam," he said, "my advice is for you to leave off. I don't feel much like joking about this murder, and that's a fact."

"Why don't you arrest James Redsey? Everybody thinks he killed his cousin, you know."

"Then everybody is a fool, even if it includes yourself, madam," retorted the inspector rudely.

Mrs Bradley put out her hand and grasped the inspector's massive paw.

"A Daniel come to judgment!" she observed, with a little squeal of laughter which made the stolid officer stare at her in perplexity.

"Have you really got hold of anything, madam?" he asked.

"Not yet. But I have hopes! Such hopes!" She cackled happily.

The inspector saluted and strode on. He then shook his head sadly. Poor old girl! She looked like being a case for a mental home before long. Harmless, though, he supposed. He came to the wicket gate leading into the mazes of the Manor Woods, and took the main path which led to the clearing. He thought he might as well have one more look at that damned Stone! . . . And there was that skull. Funny it should have disappeared. Wright must have moved it himself for a joke . . .

Mrs Bradley had barely turned into the lane which led to her own front gate when she heard footsteps behind her. It was Aubrey Harringay, taking his mother's darlings, the stout Marie and the snuffling Antoinette, out for a short walk.

"I refuse," said Mrs Bradley with great decision, "to be pestered with those abortions. Take them away, little boy."

Aubrey grinned, and promptly hitched the end of the lead to Mrs Bradley's front gate. "They'll be all right there for a minute," he said. "Loathsome little brutes! Old Jim hoofed Antoinette this morning. He's in the mater's black books in consequence. I wish she'd buy a decent dog — or let me have one. I had the offer of a four-months' Great Dane puppy for eight and six last year, and she jolly well turned the deal down. Said it would probably eat these two hog-puddings by mistake." He cast a jaundiced look at the apples of his mother's eyes as they sprawled obscenely in the dust and lolled their tongues out.

188

"Hog-puddings," said Mrs Bradley thoughtfully, "reminds me of something. Did Rupert Sethleigh have his flannels made by a tailor or did he buy them ready-made?"

"His whites would be tailored, of course, but I daresay he bought a couple of pairs of grey ones from an outfitter's."

"You don't know for certain, do you? Would your mother know?"

"I could find out. I'll go and dig into his wardrobe. Will that do?"

"I don't know. I can tell you that when you bring me the result of your findings."

"It's a queer thing," said Aubrey thoughtfully, "about grey flannel bags. A chap can almost always wear another chap's greys. I suppose they are built a bit slackly or something. I've worn old Rupert's, which are too big in the seat; I've worn old Jim's, which are too big everywhere; I've bagged chaps' at school when I couldn't find my own; and chaps have bagged mine and worn 'em. And yet, somehow, they seem to look much about the same when you've got 'em on."

"A point," said Mrs Bradley, "which I had imagined might possibly be raised by someone other than myself, a point which I had hoped might be raised and a point which I intend to bring to the immediate notice of Inspector Grindy, who is a peculiarly worthy man and deserves a little preferential treatment."

"A good chap," said Aubrey earnestly. "Hundreds of chaps in his place would have arrested old Jim ages ago, but old Grindy hangs on. A dashed noble fellow, if you ask me."

"To-morrow," said Mrs Bradley, "I want you to take me up to the top of the old Observation Tower. I want to have a look round. Take the Armenian atrocities away now. I'm going to pay a call on the Saviles, and another on Dr Barnes. No, you can't come, but I shall enjoy your company to-morrow, dear child. Oh, and I want to see the vicar. Go round that way home, there's a sweet fellow, and ask him to spare me five minutes in three-quarters of an hour's time. Thank you so much."

Savile was in the back garden again when Mrs Bradley arrived. To her amazement, he was standing at the head of a small hole with an open book in his hand, an expression of unctuous piety upon his sallow face and a clerical collar round his neck.

Wright put his head out of the kitchen door just as Mrs Bradley approached. He gazed at his friend in amazement.

"What the devil are you doing now?" he cried.

Savile gazed at him benignly.

"I am interring Lulu's canary," he said solemnly. "It has passed away."

"You're a blasphemous idiot!" said Wright, half angry at the mockery, half tickled by the absurdity of the scene. "What's that book?"

Savile glanced at the volume in his hand.

"It is called *Hints to Bird-Lovers*," he replied.

Mrs Bradley pursed up her lips until she looked like a bird herself. Then she turned on her heel and retraced her steps. Wright waved his hand in a semi-derisive farewell. Savile, absorbed in his task, had not known of her approach, and did not hear the latch of the garden gate announcing her departure.

Mrs Bradley clicked her tongue.

Dr Barnes was dressing the wound of a farm labourer who had cut himself on a scythe, and Mrs Bradley was obliged to wait in the outer room until he had finished.

"Well, what is it this time?" asked the doctor, in his full-bodied, loud-voiced, robustly cheerful way.

"Nothing much," said Mrs Bradley. "Can you give me something for a slight attack of indigestion?"

"You haven't got indigestion!"

"No, I haven't, I am thankful to say. But my new girl has — or else it's homesickness. I do hope and trust," she continued piously, "that it *is* indigestion, for she really is rather a treasure. But perhaps it is homesickness, because she read me bits out of one of the family letters yesterday. Her sister has a new baby and she hasn't seen it, and the grandfather already plays bears on the floor to amuse it, and the baby really seems pleased. Isn't that charming?" And she grinned hideously at him.

The doctor shot some bismuth tablets into a piece of paper, sealed up the ends, and scribbled on the outside with his fountain-pen.

"Well, I can safely say I shall never play bears on the floor to delight *my* grandchildren," he said, handing her the small neat package. "Tell her to take them as the directions suggest, and to drink some hot water every morning. I never amused Margery in any such ponderously inane fashion — I don't believe in pampering children by allowing them to see me make a fool of myself."

"Personally, I think that's a pity," said Mrs Bradley brightly. "But still, no two people ever did agree on how to bring up children, and I don't suppose they ever will. Thank you so much. Good-bye."

She slipped the white packet into her capacious skirt pocket, and tramped briskly along to the Vicarage.

Mary Kate Maloney was preparing lunch.

"To-day being Saturday," observed Mrs Bradley, "you would like to go into Bossbury with my new girl, who is rather homesick, and show her the sights of the town."

"Is it me to be going into Bossbury of a Saturday, Mrs Bradley, ma'am?" cried the scandalized Mary Kate. "Sure, I won't be allowed to do that same while the vicar has his health, which is more than I thought he would have when he come home to us that Sunday night all sopping wet and nearly drowned, through walking into the river near Culminster Bridge and himself deep in his thoughts and not heeding where he was walking at all."

"What?" said Mrs Bradley, so sharply that Mary Kate started and almost cut her hand with the potato-knife. "When was this?"

"'Tis the queer thing that I'm able to remember it," said Mary Kate, who was that mine of information, a keen gossip, "but it was the same Sunday night as that murder, so I wouldn't forget the day in a hurry. Yes, right up to his neck he walked, and himself the sight for

192

Mother Ruickeen herself to be gaping at, so he was! I declare to God entirely," pronounced Mary Kate, in an ecstasy of horrified recollection, "never have I seen such a sight as himself since they pulled poor Johnny Doran out of the river at Ballymocar, the same being smothered with the green water-weeds and his hair black with the wetness of it, poor boy."

"Very sad," agreed Mrs Bradley. "And you'd like to go to Bossbury with my girl Jane, wouldn't you? All right. You shall. Go and tell the vicar I'm here, and I will see to the rest . . ."

The vicar pushed back his chair and smiled at her.

"So you've robbed me of my housekeeper for the day," he said, "and now you want Mary Kate also! Woe is me!"

"Yes," said Mrs Bradley decisively. "What are you going to do when Felicity marries?"

"Marries?" The vicar looked blank. "But Felicity won't marry for years! She's only a child."

"She's twenty. Nearly twenty-one. And she's in love with James Redsey."

The vicar blinked.

"I like Felicity," Mrs Bradley went on. "And before I leave this neighbourhood, which I expect to do very shortly, I want to make certain that the young man will not be charged with this murder."

The vicar blinked again.

"And that you get married," said Mrs Bradley firmly. "It's time all this pathological nonsense was ended. Here you are — a youngish, perfectly healthy man, just going to seed. Look about you, and see whether you

193

can't find a nice wife! Isn't there anyone you fancy? Someone who is a bit of a bully would suit you best, I think. She would improve your memory for you."

The vicar chuckled.

"Do you really think it would be a good thing?" he asked, half seriously.

"Excellent. What about Mrs Bryce Harringay?"

The vicar shuddered. Mrs Bradley laughed.

"Did you really walk into the Cullen on the evening of Sunday, June 22nd?" she asked, changing the subject.

The vicar grinned shamefacedly.

"And do you ever wear flannel trousers — grey ones?" Mrs Bradley continued unexpectedly.

The vicar rang the bell.

"Mary Kate, do I ever wear grey flannel trousers?" he asked.

Mary Kate glared at him, suspecting a jest.

"And I to be wearing myself to the bone trying to get the stains out of them where you went shopping for the meat and dripped the blood all down yourself!" she retorted angrily. "Sure, some man, they say, is born to be the heart's bane of every woman, and it's yourself is the heart's bane of me — God help you for a poor, forgetful, moithering, foolish thing!"

"Blood?" said Mrs Bradley.

"Out of the best English beef," said the vicar, gently nodding his head. "I remember now."

"And when was this?" asked Mrs Bradley.

Mary Kate, appealed to, was unable to say. Her attention had not been drawn to the ruined trousers until the vicar wanted to put them on again to go for a tramp with his Boys' Club — "and that was only last Thursday, as ever was, ma'am. How long they had been like it I couldn't say, for I'll not be calling to mind when last he put them on."

"I want those trousers," said Mrs Bradley firmly. "Where are they? And do try to remember when it was that you brought the meat home. It may be important."

Mary Kate produced the trousers. Between the original stains themselves and her original methods of cleaning the stains off, the garment seemed in a sad state. Mrs Bradley inspected the maker's label, and then turned to the Reverend Stephen.

"Well?" she said. "Have you remembered?"

The vicar frowned thoughtfully, and then shook his head.

"It must have been before I went for my holiday," he said, "because I took those trousers out of the case Sethleigh lent me. And yet Felicity wouldn't have packed them if they had been in that condition, would she? I feel sure she would not. Of course" — he brightened — "it may not have been the meat at all. There seems rather a lot of blood for a pound or so of topside of beef, doesn't there? We always have topside, because Felicity likes it lean."

Mrs Bradley felt irritated, but did not betray the fact. Instead she said:

"I suppose I may take them with me? I will let you have them back."

"Is one permitted to enquire the reason of this curious whim?" asked the vicar, smiling.

195

"Yes," replied Mrs Bradley. She gazed at him much as a scientist might gaze at a museum specimen of interesting appearance but doubtful authenticity. "I fancy these stains are not the mark of the beast," she said at last. "They appear to be more like the brand of Cain. I shall be surprised, my dear friend, if these turn out to be your trousers. I rather fancy that they once belonged to Rupert Sethleigh. And as I propose to hand them straight over to Inspector Grindy, you had better try to remember a little more about them."

The vicar stared helplessly after her as she walked out of the house with the trousers slung gracefully over her arm.

II

At eight o'clock in the evening, Felicity returned. She helped the last child off the bus, delivered each of the fifteen to a waiting parent, returned the courtesies of the whole band — parents and children too — and walked straight in at Mrs Bradley's front door, which was standing wide open.

"Well?" said Mrs Bradley, appearing abruptly from the kitchen, where she had been superintending the dishing up of dinner.

Felicity seized her arm.

"I've seen it!" she said.

"Seen what, my dear?"

"Behind the model of a Roman shield. How did you know? Had you seen it, or did you guess? Oh, but you must have seen it! But how did it get there? Nobody has a key to those cases except Father and the curator — oh, and the bishop, of course! Mrs Bradley" — she shook the old woman's arm — "do explain! What is it?"

Mrs Bradley led her into the dining-room and pushed her into a chair.

"To the best of my knowledge and belief," she said, "it is Rupert Sethleigh's skull."

"But how did it get there?" Felicity pulled off her hat and pushed a hand through her hair.

"That is something which I would give a good deal to know for certain," said Mrs Bradley. "I suppose it would be too much to ask you to take another party of children to-morrow and look to see if it's still there? I would go myself, but I am particularly anxious not to appear in this little comedy. My part shall be that of stage-manager. Oh, and tell your father the inspector refuses to be parted from those trousers! I am awfully sorry. I feared something of the kind might be the case. However" — she chuckled ghoulishly and bared her tigerish teeth — "they are *not* the nether garments of the late lamented Sethleigh. I can't think why I ever thought they would be, but of that some more anon. Never mind! The skull is his if the trousers are not! Half a loaf is better than no bread. Go up and wash, child, and stay here to dinner."

The last thing Felicity saw as she turned to go up the stairs was Mrs Bradley's grin. She began to understand how Alice in Wonderland must have felt upon first beholding the Cheshire Cat.

CHAPTER SIXTEEN

Mrs Bradley Takes a Hand

I

"I want to hear more about that suitcase," said Mrs Bradley to Felicity Broome. "Can you spare ten minutes?"

"I should be glad to get away from this for a little while." Felicity waved her arms expressively at sixteen yards of curtaining which she was cutting up and machining ready for the Vicarage windows. "It's ages since we had some new curtains, and I simply had to have these. Not that we can afford them," she added frankly, "but the unspeakable Lulu scorched the last lot nearly to bits, so I simply *had* to get some more." She pushed the billows of material aside and stood up.

"Lulu? You don't mean —?"

"Lulu Hirst, otherwise Savile. Yes, I do. She took a fancy to Father and offered to do anything we liked in the way of washing and ironing. She used to work in a laundry before she became an artist's model. She does all Father's and the choristers' surplices, and things like that. We daren't trust Mary Kate with anything which really matters, so when Lulu offered to wash and iron the curtains I didn't like to refuse. But you should have seen the state in which she brought them home! She was frightfully upset about it, of course, and offered to provide new ones, but we could not let her do that, especially as she had always done everything so beautifully and so carefully before."

"Well, come along," said Mrs Bradley briskly. "In here? All right. Now, first I want to know who found this suitcase."

"I did."

"Where?"

"On our dust-heap."

"Do you often have occasion to visit the dust-heap?"

"Yes. You see, Mary Kate is so frightfully wasteful that the only way I can keep her in check is to visit the dust-heap daily and make myself frightfully nasty if she has thrown away anything unnecessarily."

"I see. And you thought it was unnecessary to throw away a suitcase?"

"Well, I picked it up and at once noticed Rupert Sethleigh's initials. I knew Father had borrowed it for our holiday in May, but I was under the impression that he had returned it."

"Now think very carefully for a minute," said Mrs Bradley, "and then tell me what gave you that impression."

Felicity's grey eyes, lovely in their sweet seriousness, gazed unseeingly into the blue haze of the July morning. She had seated herself on the broad step which led into the garden and her hands were clasped round her knees. Mrs Bradley, looking at her, sighed inaudibly.

After some moments, Felicity looked up at the old woman and answered slowly:

"After we came back from Hastings, Father put it on the landing outside his bedroom door, because he knows how absent-minded and forgetful he is, and so he said that seeing it would remind him to return it. Well, now. We went to Hastings in early May — I've got the date somewhere. Excuse me a minute. I'll go upstairs and find it."

She soon returned with a small blue diary.

"Here we are."

She turned over the pages.

"We went down there on May 2nd, and we came home on May 12th. Short, but quite sweet, you see. The suitcase would have been put on the landing — Now, let me see, Father did not unpack it until the Monday, when I reminded him that his collars and things must be washed. The 12th was a Wednesday, so that makes it the 17th when it was put on the landing. I last saw it —" She screwed up her charming nose in a gallant effort to remember, but at last was compelled to shake her head. "I am awfully sorry," she confessed, "but I can't remember. It couldn't have been more than a fortnight ago, I think, that I noticed it there, but I can't remember the actual day. I know I continually badgered Father to return it, but he kept forgetting. I would have returned it myself, except that I hated going up to the Manor House alone when Rupert Sethleigh was there. I don't mind now."

The Reverend Stephen Broome came in just as she finished speaking.

"Oh, I say, Felicity," he began. Mrs Bradley cut him short ruthlessly.

"Be quiet, my dear," she said.

The vicar stopped short, and stared at her as a man might who had been wakened suddenly from sleep.

"And let me think," Mrs Bradley went on. "Felicity, did Lulu Hirst ever wash and iron your father's clerical collars?"

"Always," replied Felicity. "Why? Oh, and one is missing, by the way. I must ask her about it."

"Do, my dear. And now, where is my friend Mary Kate?"

Felicity went to the door and called her by name. Mary Kate entered, wiping her hands on her apron.

"And what will you be after this time, ma'am?" she enquired, with a deference she would have scorned to display towards weaker and meeker women than Mrs Bradley.

"First, I will be after suggesting that you do not come into my presence and that of your mistress fingering your apron in that distressingly fidgety fashion," replied Mrs Bradley. "Secondly, I want a piece of string and a sheet — a very large sheet — of brown paper."

"Is it a string and brown paper you're expecting to get the loan of in this house!" cried Mary Kate, lifting her hands in horror. "Sure, Saint Michael and all his

201

angels couldn't be finding string and brown paper hereabouts, without they would be bringing it with them! Sure, I'm telling you, the only bit of string that was fit to hang a cat I ever saw in this house was the same that was holding up the trousers of his reverence on him, the way he wouldn't be knowing which way to look for the buttons that were off them when the bishop and Herself came here for a wet of tea that day. And myself baking the face off me with the scones they ate and the dog over the way snatching the cold meat from under me very nose and I grasping it from his jaws before himself could be ating it entirely, bad cess to him for a slavering brute of a great rascally thief!" cried Mary Kate, in an inspired burst of rhetoric.

"Oh, I see. So you just pushed the laundry into the suitcase and handed the case to Lulu Hirst as it was,' said Mrs Bradley, nodding her head.

"To Lulu Hirst indeed!" said Mary Kate indignantly. "Indeed, then, and I did not! But to an impudent bit of a snubby-nosed gossoon of a boy that's had the rough side of me tongue more than once, and will be feeling the weight of me hand if he's after asking me again did I go on me holidays to the Isle of Man!"

The obscure but apparently lasting significance of spending one's holiday in the Isle of Man was lost on Mrs Bradley, but the circumstantial evidence that Rupert Sethleigh's suitcase had been handed to the boy was not. She left the Vicarage, went in search of Aubrey Harringay, sent him upon a quest, and learned that the boy had safely delivered the suitcase to Lulu. He was a bright boy. Closely questioned, he remembered the date. It was the day his father had given him fourpence to go on an outing on the following Saturday.

"It would have been the Thursday, missus. And the Saturday would have been the Saturday before that there Bossbury murder. Yes, the day before, missus. Thank you kindly, missus. Yes, missus. Good day."

II

Mrs Bradley, closely followed by Aubrey Harringay, climbed the apparently innumerable steps of the old Observation Tower, and at last emerged triumphantly upon the platform at the top. Slung across her shoulders was a pair of powerful field-glasses, and in her right hand she carried a roughly sketched plan of the Manor House and its grounds, including a little of the surrounding country.

"Now, I've killed Sethleigh — here," she said to Aubrey, spreading the plan on top of a stout iron post which helped to carry the safety railing around the platform on which they stood. She pointed a yellow talon at the Stone of Sacrifice, which was indicated on the plan by a black blob. "Now, it is necessary to hide the body during the night. Where can I hide it?"

She glanced down at the plan and then gazed narrow-eyed at the country below.

"Ha!" she ejaculated at last. "Aubrey! What is that shed arrangement over there to the left? The hockey club's dressing-shed? Oh, that's interesting, I used to play hockey once."

"Old Jim's good," said Aubrey. "Plays centre half. Played for Southern Counties against the Rest once. Only just missed being picked for England the year before last. Don't suppose he'll get hockey in Mexico."

"If he ever gets to Mexico," said Mrs Bradley dryly. "Hockey is a winter game, isn't it?" she added inconsequently.

Aubrey, who had begun to look sober at the reference to the murder, now grinned.

"Yes," he said. "Why?"

"A very important reason," returned Mrs Bradley. "Is the shed ever used for other purposes? I mean, does any club use it for summer games — cricket, for instance?"

"No, I don't think so. But I say! Old Willows will know all about it. He acts as groundsman to the hockey club during the season. There he goes by the shrubbery. Shall I hail him? You knew the mater had reinstated him, didn't you?"

He split the air with a war-whoop which shook even Mrs Bradley's iron nerves. Willows looked up.

"Come up here!" yelled Aubrey, wildly signalling in case his words should not be heard.

They could hear Willows come tramping up the stone steps.

After regaining his wind, he answered Mrs Bradley's curt questions.

No, the hockey club's dressing-shed was not used for any other purpose so far as he knew. He did not know whether it was kept locked. Probably not. There was no one to interfere with it. No, it was not exactly a local club. It was composed of a few gentlemen from Culminster and the old boys of Bossbury Grammar School. They played once a week, on Saturday afternoons. No, nobody ever went near the hut except during the season. It was across two fields and stuck in the middle of nowhere, you might say.

"I think, Aubrey," said Mrs Bradley, "that we ought to go and look at this hut. Will you accompany me?" She dismissed Willows with a nod and a smile, and a promise to come and see his sweet peas.

A little-used footpath, baked hard by the summer sun, led them across the first meadow, and, after diving through a gap in a hawthorn hedge between two ancient wooden stakes, they found another path which ended at the hockey shed. It was a mere lean-to, not even locked on the outside. Aubrey pushed open the badly fitting door, and Mrs Bradley walked in. The one small window was heavily covered in cobwebs, but the wide-open door flooded the little place with light. Ominous dark stains on the boarded floor immediately attracted the eye.

"It is for the police to determine whether these are bloodstains," said Mrs Bradley impersonally. "You're not going to be sick, are you?" she added anxiously.

"No," said Aubrey, rather pale. "This is where he killed him, then."

"What do you mean, child?"

"Well, he hid the body here during Sunday night, I suppose. Jolly risky, lugging a dead body across these fields, even in the half-light of ten p.m. or thereabouts. I bet he wangled him here while Sethleigh was still feeling woozy from that bash on the head. Got him here, and then did him in. Besides, the chap wouldn't have bled like this if he was dead when the other chap lugged him in. The other chap then collected some of his victim's blood in — in — in what? — we shall have to find out — and poured it upon the Stone of Sacrifice. You know. Devil worship stunt! That accounts for the blood on the Stone."

"But then," mused Mrs Bradley, "if he killed him here, and not in the Manor Woods as I first assumed he did, what on earth was that young man in such a stew about? Am I wrong? *Have* I picked out the right person? I *can't* be wrong. Shut the door, boy, and go for the inspector. Bring him along here and make him a present of the spot where the murder was committed." She cackled sardonically, and then added, "I *thought* there was not enough blood on that Stone. Don't say anything. Just go! I'm going to walk a little way — and think."

Aubrey left her.

Mrs Bradley crossed the hockey-field and sat down in the adjoining meadow. She rested her sharp bony chin on her hands, and stared into the distance. Suddenly she began to chuckle. Then she stood up, and the sheep, looking up startled from their peaceful grazing, saw a small elderly lady, clad in rainbow-coloured jumper and check tweed skirt, sprinting gallantly across two fields back to the little wooden shed.

Aubrey and the inspector, whom he had met as though by prearrangement at the lodge gates of the

Manor House, were walking towards her. She waved to them, and disappeared inside the hut. In about half a minute she reappeared with equal suddenness and walked out to meet them. The inspector grinned cheerfully at her, and winked to himself.

"We ourselves thought there wasn't enough blood on the Stone for the murder to have been done there," he observed cautiously as she came up. "But I wonder —"

"The first point I want to make clear, inspector," interpolated Mrs Bradley, "is that, if the murder was committed here, and not in the woods, then James Redsey was not the murderer."

"How do you make that out, Mrs Bradley?"

"The time. Mrs Bryce Harringay saw the two cousins disappearing into the Manor Woods at five minutes to eight. At about five and twenty minutes to nine, James Redsey was in the 'Queen's Head' drinking himself fuddled. That means in forty minutes he argued with his cousin, knocked him down, hid him in the bushes, gave him time to come to, inveigled him up here across that field and alongside this one, stabbed him in the throat, collected his blood in Sethleigh's own silver tobacco-case, carried this case gingerly back to the Manor Woods, emptied it over the Stone of Sacrifice, disposed of it among the bushes, went to the 'Queen's Head' without a single visible mark of blood on his clothes or hands, and was seated there drinking hard at twenty-five minutes to nine."

The inspector scratched his head.

"I'd like to put that down," he said dubiously. "You're leading me up the garden somewhere, Mrs

207

Bradley, and I can't just see where for the moment. There's a catch in that explanation of yours. Just give me that idea again, if you don't mind."

Mrs Bradley cackled.

"Inspector, you should go far," she said. "There *is* a flaw in that reconstruction. A big flaw. Tell me when you find it. But do me the justice to look for that silver tobacco-case, won't you? Oh, and do have another good hunt for those clothes," she added brightly. "Oh, and there is poor James Redsey's wicked accomplice to be found, who so obligingly carved up the body for James, since we can prove the boy did not perform that nasty job for himself. That accomplice, unwept and unhonoured, has been sung for by all the newspapers in the country. I really think you must find him, inspector, you know."

The inspector grinned good-humouredly.

"You've got me there, all right," he admitted. "The clothing and that accomplice would down any case against James Redsey, in the hands of a clever defending counsel. I keep on telling the superintendent so. We can't prove that the boy cut up the body. He *didn't* cut it up. And that's where the thing hangs fire."

III

"The worst of amateurs who think they can teach the police their job," remarked Inspector Grindy sententiously to the superintendent, "is that they don't even give us credit for a bit of ordinary gumption such as

208

you would think even a baby would have. Now, look at that hockey-shed business! Interfering old busybody! And look here, sir, I got on to Wright again about that skull which disappeared from his studio, but I can't get hold of anything. Of course, I'm not worrying overmuch. Don't believe it has anything to do with Sethleigh. I searched the Manor House. Nothing, except notes of those people Rupert Sethleigh did *not* blackmail. I searched the park and the woods. Nothing again, except freshly dug earth, which turns out to be a practical joke on the part of the boy, although he denies it —"

"Does he?" said the chief constable who had been called into the case in a consultative capacity, and was now standing with them on the Manor House lawn. "Then, you know, inspector, I should almost feel inclined to believe him."

The inspector grinned.

"Would you, sir," he said noncommittally. "Well, never mind about that. Whoever did it, it didn't help us. Next there was blood on the Stone. Now it seems to have occurred to this Mrs Bradley — although who gave her permission to wander over the grounds at will, I don't know — but, anyway, she has decided there was not enough blood on that Stone to indicate that the murder was done there. Well, we had been inclined to think that from the beginning. We looked about to give ourselves other ideas. Spotted the hockey shed over Kerslake's field. Investigated. Floor covered with blood. Quite promising! Took samples for testing. Turns out it's a regular poachers' rendezvous, and the blood is rabbits' blood. Then, after days and days of picking up dead matches, and coughing like Sherlock Holmes, and finding me pairs of the vicars' trousers that don't mean anything, but are simply where he leaned over a newly painted fence to get a kid's ball, this Mrs Bradley also finds the shed, and spots the blood. Sends the boy chasing off to find me, and hands me her Important Discovery" — the inspector's voice was harsh with emotion — "of the spot where the murder was committed! When, after a consultation with the super here, I tell her the truth about the bloodstains, instead of giving her the tip to keep her nose out of things which don't concern her, what does she do?" He glared ferociously, kicked an inoffensive buttercup out of existence, and answered his own question with a belligerent scowl. "Grins in my face and thanks me so much for saving her the time and trouble of testing the bloodstains for herself. Had the infernal damned cheek to tell me she herself had thought it couldn't be Sethleigh's blood, and got off a bright bit about — now, what was it she said? — oh, ah! — 'the elimination of unnecessary, and, in fact, dangerous matter' — and, after telling me things about my inside that makes me go all hot to remember, she goes off cackling to herself as though she'd made a joke or laid an egg or something!"

CHAPTER
SEVENTEEN

The Stone of Sacrifice

"Heads!" shrieked Aubrey Harringay, lifting a full toss from George Willows high into the deep blue of the summer sky.

Mrs Bradley smiled serenely, and, timing it nicely, brought off a neat catch. She flicked the ball back to Willows and walked up to the nets.

"Come out of that a moment," she said, addressing the batsman. "I want you to accompany me into the woods."

It was early in the afternoon. Mrs Bradley, having ascertained, without trouble or waste of time, that the bloodstains on the floor of the hockey shed were not connected with the murder, had gone home to lunch in a contented frame of mind. Aubrey had returned to the Manor House. The police had gone back to Bossbury, for they were still exploring various avenues of research from that end of the case by assuming that the dismembered body was not that of Rupert Sethleigh. So far, they had had little fortune with either of their assumptions, and, to all intents and purposes, the body which they had discovered in the butcher's shop remained unidentified. The fact that both Grindy and

Superintendent Bidwell felt certain that the murdered man *was* Rupert Sethleigh availed little without actual proof, and some person or persons unknown had gone so cleverly to work that proof of such kind seemed as difficult as ever to obtain.

At two-thirty, Felicity Broome, groaning but obedient, had met ten old ladies of the parish and followed the two boldest on to the top of the Culminster bus. They were to go over the cathedral, have a short river excursion, tea in the riverside gardens of the Temperance Hotel, and then were to fill in the last quarter of an hour or so before the departure of the seven o'clock bus by looking at the exhibits in the Culminster Museum.

"Do what you like. Pay what you like. Give the dears a good time," said Mrs Bradley generously, "but whatever happens you must take them to see the Culminster Collection."

"But why?" asked the puzzled Felicity. "I could understand going there yesterday to see the skull, but what is the point of going there to-day?"

Mrs Bradley grimaced.

"If you don't go, I must," she said. "If you go in with all these old ladies, nobody will take any notice. If *I* go, I shall probably be murdered to-night. Don't ask me why. I'll tell you more about it later. That's all. Will you take them?"

Felicity went white.

"Then — what is it? The skull — what do you mean?" she said.

212

"Nothing," replied Mrs Bradley with brusque finality, and left her. This was at nine of the church clock that morning. It was now a quarter to three, and the bus with its cargo of pleased old ladies had bucketed round the corner and was well upon its way. Having watched it out of sight, Mrs Bradley now sought out Aubrey Harringay.

"First of all, I want James Redsey," she said. "Do you think he will come with us?"

Aubrey went to enquire, and found Jim in the billiard-room, listlessly knocking the balls about. He looked tired and worn. It had been an anxious fortnight. At any moment, he felt, the inspector might have him arrested for the murder of his cousin, and he knew just enough about the law to realize that it is easier to get caught in its gigantic and terrifying machinery than to get clear again. He slept badly, ate little, brooded, and loafed. Even Felicity, who loved him, had scolded and poured scorn on him.

"You *look* like a murderer!" she said one day, in complete but helpless exasperation. "Why don't you buck up and look as though you don't care?"

"Well, I don't," grunted Jim. "It isn't much use caring, old thing. But if you caught that inspector's eye boring holes in the back of your neck as often as I do, and if you never opened a door but he was behind it, and if you couldn't even have a bath without seeing his ugly face come goggling against the frosted glass of the window or hearing his silly voice asking you idiotic questions through the ventilator shaft, perhaps you'd feel much as I do — that the Third Degree and the

213

Spanish Inquisition were bedroom farces compared to the hunted-cat life I lead while he's conducting his damned investigations. Why, I even took my aunt's pet bow-wows to my bosom the other day because Marie bit a piece out of the lad Grindy's trousers, and he fell over Antoinette into the water-lily tank! And you know my general opinion of those galvanized sugar-pigs of hers!"

His voice was surcharged with emotion. Felicity pressed his hand.

And now, to add to his trials, here was this frightful dame named Bradley coming and invading the place and sending him idiotic invitations to play silly party games with pencils and paper at her house, and wanting him to take her into the woods, and show her the exact spot where he'd punched the blighter Rupert's fatheaded jaw for him! It was a bit thick. He was damned if he'd go! Damned, he went.

Mrs Bradley grinned evilly. He thought he had never seen such a wicked old woman. She reminded him of some dreadful bald-headed bird he had seen in a picture at some time. Not that she was bald-headed, of course — but you got the same sort of sick feeling when you looked at her. And yet, on second thoughts, wasn't she more like one of those reptiles — no, not reptiles! What was that word? — saurians! When she was amusing herself at your expense, which was ninety per cent of the time — and the other ten per cent was when she didn't even seem aware that you were on the map at all! — her little smile was like that he had seen on the face of a newt — no, a sand lizard! — no, one of

214

those repulsive-looking giant frogs. But when the woman really got in a nasty one and grinned a bit wider, why, then you could see what she must have been in a former existence! Those reincarnation johnnies were right! The bally woman had been on the earth before — as an alligator! Ugh! Man-eating! Ugh! He was jolly glad he *hadn't* cut up old Rupert and hung him on hooks! He felt certain that, if he had done so, Mrs Bradley would not only have been perfectly aware of the fact, but was quite capable of thinking out a better way of doing it, and of disclosing the same with her hideously sinister cackle. He shuddered.

The three of them walked silently across the park.

At the edge of the Manor Woods, Mrs Bradley halted.

"You first," she said to Aubrey. "Mr Redsey next. I will come last. Forward, children. Straight to the Stone of Sacrifice."

A comparatively short walk in single file, along the narrow winding path by which Aubrey led them, brought them to the circle of pines. Even on this brilliant summer afternoon the place was eerie, gloomy, and chill. A faint wind moaned in the tops of the trees, although Jim Redsey felt certain that when he crossed the park the air had been hot and still.

Mrs Bradley walked up to the Stone of Sacrifice and laid a claw-like yellow hand upon its surface. The stone was reptile-harsh and curiously cold to the touch. She drew her hand away and gazed benignly at the strange old rock.

215

"It reeks of evil," she said solemnly. "What blood was shed; what wicked deeds were done; what screams, what torture, and what agony this ancient monument has heard and seen, by great good fortune we shall never know."

She turned abruptly to Jim Redsey.

"Take the child over to the spot where you knocked your cousin down," she said.

Jim touched Aubrey's arm and they walked about twelve paces.

"Here," he said laconically. (Easier to humour the old girl. What was the game, anyway?)

"Very well. Lie down, boy." Aubrey extended his thin form on the ground. "Like that, Mr Redsey?"

"No. Get your head round to the left a bit more. Stick. That's right."

"Thank you, Mr Redsey. Now haul him into the bushes. Oh, by the arms, was it? I don't think your clothes will hurt, child. You must pick out the pine needles afterwards. Now, Mr Redsey, come out again and go off in the direction of the 'Queen's Head' at the pace which you took on the night of June 22nd."

Jim leapt away to the right, crashing through bushes and leaping over brambles, and was lost to sight in less than three seconds.

"Thank you!" called Mrs Bradley. But the opportunity for flight thus offered him was too good to be missed, thought Jim. He affected not to hear her, ran swiftly down the path, and vaulted the wicket gate. He then walked at a swinging pace down the

216

Bossbury-London road towards Culminster and re-entered the Manor grounds through the lodge gates.

Mrs Bradley chuckled gently.

"Never mind. He's done all that I wanted him to do," she said. "Now I want you to crawl out of those bushes where you are and advance into the clearing. Come slowly. You're not feeling very well or very happy after that crack on the head you received when you struck your head against a tree in falling. Hands and knees. That's right. And you are wearing a white shirt and light-grey flannel trousers." She stared unseeingly at his navy-blue blazer and white flannels. "At eight o'clock on a fine summer evening. At a quarter to nine on a fine summer evening. Yes, quite so. Get up, child. A great black slug. Indeed?"

She shook her head and wrinkled her brow.

"Well, well," she said, "all these things are sent to try us. I'll buy you some new flannels, boy, if you've spoilt those. Come and have another look at the Stone. Where are those bloodstains? H'm!"

She produced a reading-glass and examined them closely.

"They haven't found the weapon yet," said Aubrey unexpectedly, "with which old Rupert was done in. Wonder what it was?"

"The weapon," responded Mrs Bradley, lowering her voice and almost hissing the words into his ear, "is washed and inspected so often that, if we saw it, the inspector wouldn't know and I wouldn't know and you wouldn't know whether it was verily used to murder Rupert Sethleigh or not."

"Oh, you mean one of those butcher's tools! Of course," agreed Aubrey, edging away from her.

Mrs Bradley cackled softly.

"Perhaps I do mean that. And perhaps I don't," she observed helpfully. "Go back into the bushes and lie down as you did before. Do you mind removing your blazer first? Thank you so much. That's right. Hang it over that little branch over there."

Aubrey walked off and was soon lost to sight in the hazel-copse.

"Now we will try again," said Mrs Bradley. "Redsey has run away. You are unconscious. I am the person for whom the police are looking. I have seen Redsey knock you down. I conceal myself behind a tree."

She did this, and then went on, in her rich, slightly drawling voice:

"I have seen him drag you into the bushes. It occurs to me that he thinks you are dead. I have seen him dash away. I wait. I listen. Yes, he has gone for good. I emerge. I search the bushes."

She did so.

"I discover you lying prone upon the ground."

She drew aside the hazel boughs and grinned fiendishly down upon the prostrate Aubrey.

"Keep still. You are unconscious, remember. I seize you by the heels. (Yes, I really must provide you with some new flannels, child.) I drag you out into the clearing. I examine you. It occurs to me that I hate and fear you; that James Redsey believes he has accidentally killed you; that it is a golden opportunity to be rid of you for ever. I gag you with your own shirt, in case you

218

should commence to recover consciousness before I decapitate you. Yes, it does seem a little indelicate on my part, but I'm afraid it must be done!"

She jerked at the buckle of his suède belt, and with incredible swiftness pulled his shirt over his head — ("Here, I say, though!" protested Aubrey, through two thicknesses of cream flannel) — and with a deftness born of nursing-experience in mental hospitals she turned him over and pulled the shirt off.

"You won't be cold. You've your vest," she observed thoughtfully. Aubrey was unable to reply, for in Mrs Bradley's steel fingers the shirt made a clumsy but effective gag. She secured it in place by a clever use of the sleeves. The tail hung like a beard over his breast until she flung it up over his face, almost suffocating him.

"I secure your wrists with your own belt," she continued. "Kick out hard if that shirt hurts too much. Then I put my foot against the soles of your shoes, seize your bound wrists and jerk you into a sitting position. Then I slip your bound wrists over my head so that you are clinging to my neck. Then I straighten myself (Heavens! What a length you are, child!) and carry you over to the Stone of Sacrifice. I lay you out flat on the top of it, face uppermost. Then I hack off your head! . . . No, not really. Cheer up! Some blood runs down the Stone. Poor boy! You are rather uncomfortable."

She released his mouth and his wrists, and Aubrey swung himself to the ground. Mrs Bradley carefully unrolled the shirt, and shook it out. Aubrey disappeared modestly behind the Stone and put it on.

He reappeared grinning and chafing his wrists, obviously not at all impressed by her version of how Sethleigh had been treated.

"You're hefty," he said admiringly, "but really —"

Mrs Bradley shrugged her thin shoulders.

"Are you willing to conclude the little drama?" she asked. "Good. Well, I wonder what to do next. Suddenly I hear voices. A man and a girl are approaching the Stone. I have little time to think or to act. I lay the body on the ground a little way from the Stone" — her eyes, assisted by the reading-glass, searched the grass — "here, I think, but the exact spot is not important. I take up the gag — that is, your shirt . . . (Yes, I know I have, but the murderer had less consideration. Besides, Sethleigh was dead — you're not!), and take the head away with me. Also I release the wrists and take away the belt also."

"Old Rupert generally wore a silk scarf on grey bags," observed Aubrey helpfully, but still refusing to take her seriously.

"Indeed? Easier to tie him up, then. I now conceal myself near at hand. The next bit of the proceedings is still rather obscure. You see, undoubtedly Margery Barnes and the man — whoever it was — I think I know, but I haven't proved it yet — came upon the scene very soon after the head was hacked off. Now, I do not fancy the man saw Rupert Sethleigh's dead body immediately they entered the clearing, and Margery Barnes undoubtedly did not see it at all. I don't think it is outside the bounds of probability to suppose that she saw the Stone from the opposite side as they emerged from the path into the clearing and so did not spot the body. Just go over to the path down which James Redsey disappeared a little while ago, and tell me whether you can see me from there."

She lay full length on the spot where she supposed the dead body of Sethleigh had been placed.

"You cannot see me? Very well," she called. "Walk towards the Stone and sit down. Now get up and bear away to your left. Now glance this way and stand still the minute you can see any part of me."

Aubrey walked on, round the immense Stone. This was rather a rag. He espied one of Mrs Bradley's shoes, and halted.

"Your foot!" he called out promptly.

"Very well. Walk on, and stop the moment you can see the whole of me."

Aubrey obeyed.

"Very well. Now run over to Dr Barnes's house and bring Margery here, when you have marked the spot where you are standing. Here's my penknife." She sat up, delved in her pocket, and tossed the knife with unerring aim. "Open the big blade and stick it in the ground."

Aubrey was about to ask what excuse he should make to Margery for hauling her up to the Manor Woods on a hot and tiring afternoon, when Mrs Bradley stood up.

"And when Margery has shown us exactly where she sat while the young man told her those tales of his, and I have told her the name of the said young man, I think

221

we shall begin to find matters moving towards the detection of the murderer," she said. "*Did* Rupert buy his grey flannels ready made?" she continued abruptly. "Oh, and do you know whether he was wearing a vest that Sunday night?"

"No. Had 'em tailored by the chaps who made all his other clothes — Roundway & Down. Yes, always wore cellular trunks and vest — you know the things?"

"Oh, thank you! That simplifies matters," said Mrs Bradley. Aubrey turned to go for Margery Barnes, but his movement was suddenly arrested. With a sharp sound, a yard-long arrow stuck quivering in the trunk of a tree. It had missed Mrs Bradley's head by less than three inches.

"Good Lord!" said Aubrey, rather pale.

Mrs Bradley cackled with genuine gratification.

Before she could make any remark, however, the sallow-visaged Savile came bounding into the clearing past the white-faced, startled boy, and ran swiftly up to her. In his right hand he carried a six-foot long-bow. He was clad in a drab-coloured waterproof, and had a quiver of arrows slung over his shoulder. On his head was a green cap decorated with a startlingly tall pheasant's feather. He raised this extraordinary headgear as he approached.

"Dear me!" he exclaimed in tones of consternation. "How terribly careless of me! I almost killed you! My dear Mrs Bradley, I scarcely dare hope that you will accept my apologies! This is what comes of practising for amateur theatricals!"

He opened his waterproof with the hand which was not holding the bow, and displayed a suit of Lincoln green.

"How very charming!" exclaimed Mrs Bradley. "Do let me hold your long-bow whilst you remove this outer husk."

She seized the bow, and Savile, smiling in his suave, deferential, deprecating way, delicately removed the sad-coloured garment and stood displayed in all the beauty of Robin Hood tunic and hose. The reason for the feathered cap was now made apparent. A bulge they had noticed beneath the waterpoof transformed itself into a handsome hunting-horn, and, round his waist, Savile was wearing a leather belt on which a deer-skin wallet was gallantly and nattily slung.

It was an attractive costume, and Savile's perfect figure set it off to great advantage.

"Jolly fine," said Aubrey politely, with a boy's instinctive aversion to fancy dress. Savile glanced down at slender legs shapely as an actor's, struck an attitude, and smirked unpleasantly.

"And what part do you play?" Mrs Bradley enquired with great interest. "And have you to shoot an arrow at somebody?"

"I think I will collect the one in the tree," remarked Savile, without attempting to answer either question. "A pity to lose it, don't you think?"

"Let me get it whilst you resume your waterproof," said Mrs Bradley, and before Savile could protest she had stepped nimbly up to the great tree and was wrenching at the arrow with both hands.

"I am quite pleased to think that you *did* miss me, young man," she observed, as, after the fourth successive pull, she jerked it out.

"I was actually in the public woods on the other side of the Bossbury road," said Savile, taking the arrow from her and placing it carefully in his quiver. "But when I observed that the arrow had flown over here into the Manor Woods, I hurried across at once to make certain no damage had been done."

"Liar," said Aubrey under his breath. "That arrow never flew from the other side of the Bossbury road," he thought to himself.

"Are you also acting a play?" Savile went on.

"Yes," said Mrs Bradley unblushingly. "A very modern play," she added circumstantially. "I am sorry the full cast is not here. Aubrey and I were carrying out our respective roles of villain" — she pointed dramatically to the thin, brown-faced boy — "and innocent victim." She simpered idiotically and then leered with horrible effect. Savile stepped back a pace.

"Oh, you must go? Good-bye, then," said Mrs Bradley, extending her repulsive-looking claw and giving Savile's olive-hued hand a grasp which made all the bones grate together.

She waited until he had disappeared, and then hooted joyously.

"It's nothing to laugh at, you know," said Aubrey, the stern young male. "He nearly killed you."

"Ah, well! Boys will be boys," said Mrs Bradley philosophically. "And I don't think I'll bother about Margery Barnes, after all. I'll walk over and see the doctor myself."

CHAPTER
EIGHTEEN

The Man in the Woods

"Consanguinity is a queer thing," remarked Mrs Bradley.

Dr Barnes filled up a medicine bottle with water, corked it carefully, dried it, labelled and directed it, laid it aside for his boy to deliver, screwed the top on his fountain-pen, and then turned round. Against his white dispenser's overall his florid face looked even larger and more ruddy than usual. He grunted. He disliked and mistrusted Mrs Bradley to a singularly flattering extent (at least, she thought his attitude flattering, for she had a habit of taking anybody's dislike of her person and character as a compliment of the highest order!), and made no attempt to conceal his aversion from the object of it. After all, the woman was never ill! Boasted of the fact!

Mrs Bradley, who had watched his professional manoeuvres with detached interest, smiled unpleasantly.

"Don't you think so?" she went on conversationally.

The doctor washed and dried his hands, removed his overall, and hung it carefully upon its appointed hook.

"Never thought about it," he replied briefly. He stretched out his large, shapely hands and turned them

226

over. He was proud of them. "Of whom are you thinking? Somebody in particular, of course?" he said, with perfunctory politeness but complete lack of interest.

"Yes. My son, Ferdinand Lestrange. And — *your* son."

The doctor shrugged his great shoulders.

"Oh, is he your son? I didn't know that. Brilliant man," he remarked casually. Mrs Bradley's sharp black eyes, quick and bright and callous as those of a bird, watched him beadily, steadily, as he took his morning coat from a hanger and put it on.

"Yes, Ferdinand is my son," she repeated. "A clever boy! Takes after his mother."

She smirked self-consciously, and the doctor scowled. He hated to see any woman making a fool of herself, but when it came to old women! Of course, the unlovely creature was famous in her way, he remembered! He supposed it had gone to her head!

"Defended you in a murder trial, didn't he?" he remarked, pleasantly conscious that he was saying, socially and humanely speaking, quite the wrong thing.

"And got me off," said Mrs Bradley succinctly. "Excuse me! A slight crease across the shoulders. A well-fitting coat, but a little formal, surely, for the time of year?"

"We have to suffer in order to maintain the dignity of the profession," said the doctor, a slightly sardonic smile lifting his dark neat moustache. "If it is Margery you came to see," he continued abruptly, "she went to shop in the village. After that she was going to take on the vicar at tennis! Wish *I'd* gone into the Church. Lazy lot, these parsons."

"But the vicar is not good at tennis," Mrs Bradley observed as she followed the doctor out into the garden, "whereas Margery is quite a star performer, according to Aubrey Harringay. I should think she would require a more expert opponent."

"She's gone there to practise her service," the doctor said carelessly. "The vicar is the only person who doesn't care when people knock the heads off his flowers and things, you see. I won't have a court marked out on this lawn here. Spoils the grass."

Mrs Bradley walked to the front gate, leaving the doctor to proceed towards the garage.

"Hats off to the National Health Insurance!" she said to herself, looking back at the wide-open doors of the shed where the doctor's gleaming chariot was housed. "If the Medical Council don't make all their members vote Liberal — well, they're an ungrateful lot! That's all I can say."

She began walking briskly in the direction of the Vicarage, but half-way there she changed her mind and went up to the Cottage on the Hill instead.

II

Lulu was at home. Almost as much to the point, Savile and Wright were not.

"I'm sorry," said Lulu, leading the way into the drawing-room, which was immediately underneath

228

the room Wright and Savile used as a studio. "Did you want 'em particular?"

"I called on behalf of the Restoration Fund," lied Mrs Bradley glibly.

"Oh, that. Yes, it wants doing up bad, don't it? Lovely I think them old churches is, but law! the draught. I give up going. I couldn't stick it. Not as I ever was one for religion much." She giggled and slid a glance sideways at Mrs Bradley from under her eyelashes. She was a lovely creature — one of those women sometimes to be seen in East End Thames-side localities; women with something of the Orient in their ancestry, something of its mystery and allure beneath the crudeness of Cockney speech and the hearty freshness of English laughter.

Mrs Bradley nodded.

"But you thought sufficiently kindly of the vicar and his daughter to do the church laundry-work and wash the vicar's own clothes," she said quietly.

"Oh, that!"

Lulu tossed back a permanently-waved lock of lustrous hair and laughed, displaying fine teeth.

"Brought up to the wash-tub, I was. No 'ardship to put a few bits of things through a drop of water. And that gal of theirs — Shin Finer or somethink I should say by the look of the washing she 'angs out. I couldn't stand seeing them bits of boys and the parson in them dirty-lookin' yaller chimmies of theirn Sunday after Sunday. 'Disgraceful, I calls it,' I said to Clef. That was before the draughts got too much of a good thing, and I used to go to 'ear Clef sing. Lovely 'e sings. 'Aven't you never 'eard 'im? Bit of all right, I tell you. So I washes 'em now. It ain't nothink, but I may get a good mark for it one of these days when my number goes up. Never know, do you?"

"No, you never do," agreed Mrs Bradley gravely. "But all the same, child, how did you come to scorch the things so badly about a month ago?"

"'Ow did *I*?" said Lulu, flushing with anger. "I never did! It was that pop-eyed swine I goes with done that! 'I'll 'elp you for once, my gal,' 'e says and wi' that 'e snatches the iron and dabs it on a couple of 'ankerchiefs of' is own I'd just put there ready for ironin'. I swore at 'im, but it wasn't no good, and grabbed at the iron, but there! 'E'd 'ave dabbed it on me face for two pins, the vicious 'ound, so I snatched up the parson's things and ran off, all except the collars and the curtings. I couldn't grab them up with all the chimmies."

"Surplices?" enquired Mrs Bradley.

"That's right. I done them when 'e was gorn — next day it was. One collar what 'e done and all the curtings was good as spoilt, the collar 'specially. Nothink but a bit of black charcoal, it wasn't, and I 'ad to chuck it away. There was a tie of his own ditto, and a pair of sort of little short drawers and a vest of 'is what 'e give me to wash that week. Like 'is sauce! Still, I done 'em! And then 'e went and scorched 'em so they 'ad to be throwed away, and who'd washed 'em that week, blowed if I know, for *I* never! Nor the curtings neither. Been 'aving a gime, some of 'em."

230

"What shape was the collar?" asked Mrs Bradley keenly.

"Oh, one of them sorft collars like they wears on tennis shirts. I suppose even parsons leaves orf their dog-collars sometimes."

"I don't know. Are you sure it was not one of Mr Wright's collars? — Or one belonging to Mr Savile?"

Lulu turned and stared at her. Surprise, suspicion, apprehension, chased each other across her face like clouds of storm across a lowering summer sky.

"Look 'ere," she said thickly, "what's all this? I said it was the parson's collar, didn't I?"

Mrs Bradley rose, walked to the fireplace, and stood with her back against the mantelpiece.

"Won't you answer the question?" she asked, very gently.

"I will." The blustering alarm of the frightened London urchin changed Lulu's whole attitude and expression. "It wasn't Clef's collar, and it wasn't George's. See?"

"So clearly," said Mrs Bradley, in the same gentle, almost melancholy voice she had used before, "that I think you had better tell me a little more."

Lulu's lips drew back in a sneer. Her eyes gleamed hard. Her bosom rose and fell — a certain sign of agitation. Her harsh breathing was disquietingly audible in the small room.

"You better get out of this," she said between clenched teeth. "Go on. You're only little, and I'm damn' big. And if you come 'ere nosin' about, I'll do for you, see? *See?*"

She walked up to Mrs Bradley until her red mouth was on a level with Mrs Bradley's shrewd, humorous black eyes. She was in a dangerous mood, and was obviously careless of consequences.

"Onions," said Mrs Bradley, distinctly and with repugnance. "If I've said it once, I've said it one hundred times to you girls — do not come into my presence when you have been eating ONIONS. A repulsive, disgusting, sickening, malodorous, anti-social vegetable!"

Decidedly taken aback, Lulu retreated a step.

"I — I —" she began haltingly.

Mrs Bradley swiftly followed up the advantage.

"Yes, you have," she said, grinning. "How do you expect your husband to kiss you when —"

"'Im!" The monosyllable was expressive. "'Im kiss me! Huh! I'd like to see 'im! Be a change, that would."

She laughed, a short, hard, incredibly bitter sound, and swung herself up on to the table, where she sat kicking her legs and sulking — an out-generalled, pouting, rebellious child.

"Well," went on Mrs Bradley smoothly, "never mind that. What I want —"

"Oh, I don't mind it!" said Lulu, flinging back her hair and sniffing indomitably. "There's others can do 'is share of kissing and their own too. And they don't live far away, neither!"

She laughed recklessly. Mrs Bradley straightened her unbecoming hat before the mirror above the mantelpiece. Then she turned, looked at Lulu, and shook her head sadly.

"My poor child," she said, with real sincerity.

"Don't you dare pity the likes of me!" cried Lulu passionately. "You nasty dried-up old crow, you! You leave me alone, do you 'ear? There's one man dead for me already, and —"

Mrs Bradley ruthlessly cut short this epic of a second Helen.

"And another will be hanged for you if you don't keep silent," she said emphatically.

Footsteps at the front of the house heralded the approach of Savile. His head was bare, his shirt grimy, and his shoes were covered in dust. He entered the room like a tornado.

"So I've caught you out at last!" he shouted. "You dirty little —" Then he caught sight of Mrs Bradley.

"Oh, I — er — oh, it's you?" he said helplessly. "I thought — I mean —"

Mrs Bradley smiled.

III

By the time the old woman reached the Vicarage it was eight o'clock, and Felicity had just arrived home. Margery Barnes was still there, and Felicity was entertaining her and the vicar with a description of the afternoon's proceedings. She stopped when Mrs Bradley was announced, but, being pressed by Margery to continue what appeared to be an entertaining narrative, she installed Mrs Bradley in the most comfortable chair and concluded a lively account of the old ladies and their outing to Culminster.

"And what do you think?" she cried, turning to Mrs Bradley. "I —"

Mrs Bradley suddenly began to cough. She coughed and coughed; she gasped, wheezed, croaked, gurgled, panted, and clutched her breast. Paroxysm after paroxysm seized her, and held her in dreadful thraldom. She was speechless for several minutes, for after the spasm of coughing had passed she seemed breathless and exhausted.

"Do have some water," cried Felicity, returning from the kitchen with a tumbler.

"Thank you, my dear," the old lady wheezed, as Felicity held the glass to her lips. "Old age and the night air! Time to go home to bed! So sorry to be a disturbance!"

"I'll come with you," said Felicity readily.

"I must go, too," said Margery, getting up. "Father will think I'm lost."

"Shall I join the party?" asked the vicar. "It is a perfect evening for a stroll."

The four of them left the house together, and in the narrow lane which led to the Bossbury road they separated into couples, the vicar and Margery in advance, Mrs Bradley and Felicity behind.

"I am sorry to have engaged your sympathy under false pretences," observed Mrs Bradley, gazing up at the tall elms.

"What do you mean? You certainly had a terrible fit of coughing, you poor dear," said Felicity.

"Yes. A useful gift. I have employed it more than once," said Mrs Bradley, with a sigh at the recollection of her own duplicity. "The great advantage of it is the awful noise it makes. You were within an ace of giving away a little piece of information which had better be reserved for my private ear, I think. What were you going to tell them about the skull?"

"Oh — it has gone from behind the Roman shield," replied Felicity. "It was stupid of me to begin blurting it out like that, but I thought Father —"

"Yes, yes, of course," Mrs Bradley hastily agreed. "Still, perhaps the fewer the better when it comes to sharing news about a murder. So the skull has gone? I thought it would. The question is — where?"

Felicity laughed.

"You'd better look up all our answers to that question," she said. "Don't you remember that game we played at your house? And you haven't told us yet who won!" she added.

"No, I haven't, have I?" said Mrs Bradley. "Wait a minute." She bent down and fidgeted with her shoe. The two in front stopped, looked round, and then strolled back.

"Go on slowly with your father, I want to talk to Margery," Mrs Bradley said in a low tone. This small manoeuvre was accomplished, and Margery and Felicity changed partners.

"Now, young woman," said Mrs Bradley sternly, "I want a plain answer to a plain question, and no ridiculous quibbling in the name of honesty or honour.

Who was the man who met you in the Manor Woods that night?"

"Which night?" The girl's voice was defiant. Mrs Bradley sighed.

"Very well," she said. "You met Cleaver Wright, didn't you?"

Margery stalked on without a word.

Mrs Bradley clutched her arm, and caused her to moderate her pace.

"Don't be foolish, child," she said, cackling gently. "It doesn't make a scrap of difference to me whether you answer the question or not. You see — I know."

Margery looked straight ahead at the figures of the vicar and his daughter. They were turning on to the main Bossbury road, and in less than a second she lost sight of them. She was alone in the world — or so it seemed — with this terrible little old woman. She stopped short and faced her.

"I promised I wouldn't tell," she said, "and I'm jolly well not going to tell! So there!"

"You haven't told; I have guessed," said Mrs Bradley briefly. "Margery, whereabouts in the clearing did the two of you sit? No, my dear! Don't repeat that lie you told us before. You and Cleaver Wright did *not* sit your backs against the Stone — I know that! Oh, wait a minute, though. I beg your pardon. You may have done so. I wish you would be quite frank with me about the whole business."

Margery stiffened, and set the large obstinate jaw she had inherited from her mother.

"I won't tell you anything. And if you want to know, it *was* Cleaver Wright I met, and we *did* sit with our backs against the Stone. We sat on the side of it facing the path which leads to the wicket gate, because I told Clef that if anything in those woods scared me, I should bolt like a rabbit down that path."

"I don't know why," said Mrs Bradley, beginning to walk on again, "but when you were telling the tale to Felicity Broome and me, you managed to give me a distinct impression that the two of you sat on the other side of the Stone — the side facing the Manor House. I learned this afternoon that you could not possibly have done so."

"Mrs Bradley" — the defiance had gone from Margery's tone, and only trouble was left in her young harsh voice — "there's something I don't understand behind all this. Clef told me to *think* of us as sitting on the side of the Stone which faces the Manor House, so that if I *did* let out where we had been it might not matter so much. Mrs Bradley, what is all this mystery? It isn't — oh, it isn't anything to do with that terrible murder, is it?"

Mrs Bradley shrugged her shoulders. "Only this much," she said, "that your Cleaver Wright is a very foolish young man, to say the very least of it. He walked round the Stone after you ran away, and saw the dead body of Rupert Sethleigh. He bent down to examine it, and got blood on his hands. Dirty, careless, thoughtless, and lazy, like nearly all painters, he wiped his hands on his clothes. What can you expect of people who habitually wear overalls which other people have to wash? Then he felt rather bad. A young man of deplorable habits, as I say, he made immediate tracks for the nearest public house. Before he arrived there, however, some grain of common sense was vouchsafed him, and he realized that to walk into a public house on a Sunday evening with blood on one's clothing and a murdered man lying in the woods close at hand is asking for trouble. So, mother-wit coming to his aid, he picked a quarrel with the young farmer named Galloway and got himself so badly knocked about that it would be impossible for anyone later on to detect his own bloodstains among those he had acquired from contact with the murdered man. You see, it is a little too much to expect that even a foolish old woman like me will believe that a young man who has won beautiful cups and belts for boxing is going to allow a great clumsy ox like Galloway to punch him on the nose and knock him about as he chooses. No, no! Cleaver Wright knew that Sethleigh had been murdered! He had seen his dead body in the Manor Woods that night!"

"But how *could* he have seen Rupert Sethleigh's dead body? Because when I came running back into the clearing I saw Rupert Sethleigh *alive!* He came crawling out of the bushes! I said so! I told you that!" Margery's harsh tones rose higher and higher in her excitement.

"A great black slug," said Mrs Bradley appreciatively. "A great black slug! Most apt, dear child! Most apt!"

And she chuckled ghoulishly all the way to the doctor's house.

CHAPTER
NINETEEN

The Skull

I

"I do wish," said Mrs Bryce Harringay petulantly, "I do wish, James, that you would get rid of that policeman! Heaven knows what he thinks he is looking for! And he worries my poor darlings almost to death!"

She fondled the obese Marie and smiled tenderly upon the corpulent Antoinette. Jim glowered. The expression had become habitual upon his beforetime ingenuous features.

"He wanted to know the address of Rupert's dentist," he growled.

"It is in Rupert's memorandum-book. Did you give it to him?"

"Yes. Can't think why Rupert went to that fellow in Bossbury High Street. Always have my teeth seen to in Town."

"The Bossbury man is cheaper. And he is a very good dentist. There is far too much nonsense talked about dentists," observed Mrs Bryce Harringay austerely. "If a man is qualified, he is qualified. If he is not qualified, no reasonable person would dream of

239

attending him. There is not the slightest necessity for harping upon these somewhat depressing subjects."

"I am not harping on them," her nephew responded morosely. "It's you."

"Really, James, you are most trying lately — most! Do please refrain from direct contradiction of my remarks! Direct contradiction," continued Mrs Bryce Harringay, warming to her subject, "is, of all breaches of manners, the most embarrassing with which to deal, and I consider it most unkind of you, James — most! — to nonplus me in this way. I cannot argue with you without sacrificing my personal dignity. This," she proclaimed vigorously (inadvertently upsetting the personal equilibrium of Antoinette, who had chosen an ill-advised perch on her mistress's ample but precipitous lap), "I refuse to do! I am dumb. I suffer your discourtesy in silence. In wounded silence, James; nevertheless, in silence."

James groaned and turned to go out of the room. He was prevented from taking his leave by the appearance of the butler.

"Mrs Lestrange Bradley is here, sir, and would be glad of a word with you in private."

"I am just going," said Mrs Bryce Harringay frigidly. She rose and swept out of the room. A moment later Mrs Bradley came in.

She looked more like a bird of prey than ever, thought Jim. He waited for her to speak.

"I thought the inspector was here," she said. Jim glowered darkly.

"He has gone into Bossbury to see Rupert Sethleigh's dentist," he said.

"At my suggestion. How long has he been gone?"

Jim glanced at the clock.

"Two hours — just over," he replied. "Looks like his car coming up the drive now."

"Good." Mrs Bradley seated herself in an armchair, and drew out a small loose-leaf note-book.

"Such a clever idea," she observed, waving the tiny pad expressively. "A page is used. It will be needed again. Good. It can be preserved. But — it is dangerous to keep it? The wrong eyes may see it? The wrong interpretation may be placed upon it? Good. It shall be destroyed."

The inspector tapped on the French windows, coughed, and walked in.

"Well, Mrs Bradley," he said, "you've won the first round, madam. The teeth are certainly Mr Sethleigh's. The dentist swears to them. Now what, madam?"

"I should say — produce the skull, inspector, and find out whether the teeth ever fitted its jaws."

"The skull!" The inspector laughed harshly. "We've looked everywhere for that blessed head, but it's gone."

"Oh, yes." Mrs Bradley grinned. "You policemen! You drag the ponds and search the hedges and beat down the nettles and walk in the ditches, and risk your necks climbing trees — and all to find a thing which a little thought and a little common sense would have produced for you in five minutes!"

"You mean you've found it?" The inspector was almost excited. "Where?"

"No, I haven't found it," Mrs Bradley coolly replied. "But I know where it was, and I think I know where it is now."

"Where, madam? Come on, please! We've lost too much time already about that skull! I knew there was something fishy the minute I heard it had been stolen from young Wright's studio."

"Well," Mrs Bradley languidly drawled, "it *was* in the Culminster Museum behind the model of a Roman shield. I saw it there, and sent Felicity Broome to look at it. She saw it too!"

"When was this?"

"During the last fortnight, inspector."

"But — dammit all," roared Inspector Grindy. "During the last fortnight! Why ever didn't you let us know?"

"Sit down, inspector," said the little old woman quietly, "and I'll tell you. If I had shown you the skull, what would you have done?"

"Had it outside that museum damn quick!" replied the inspector forcefully.

"Exactly. And what good do you think that would have done, pray?"

"I could have proved, with the help of this dental plate of Sethleigh's, whether the skull was his!"

"Yes. And that is all."

"Well, what else?" The inspector's tone was blustering.

"This." Mrs Bradley leaned forward and tapped him upon the chest with a yellow talon.

242

"By waiting for somebody — *not* the police — to move the skull out of the Culminster Museum, I have been able to do much more than prove the identity of the Bossbury corpse. As a matter of fact, you can't prove that the Bossbury corpse belongs to the skull merely by using this dental plate which the child Harringay discovered upon the Vicarage dust-heap."

"I shall assume it belongs to it," grunted the inspector, "and I shan't expect to be contradicted."

"Yes, well said. Well said," murmured Mrs Bradley. "When in doubt, the tactics of a bull at a gate do occasionally answer rather well. Now, as I said, the skull has been removed from the Culminster Collection —"

"Eh?" The inspector leapt from his seat as though he had been stung. "Removed?"

"I said so," replied Mrs Bradley in a pained tone. "And I don't know where it is."

"The devil you don't!" The inspector had had a trying fortnight. "Then what in hell —"

"Look here, you!"

Jim Redsey had got up from the small table on which he had seated himself and advanced in menacing fashion upon the police officer. "I've put up with a lot from you in what you have the damned impudence to call the execution of your beastly duty, but I'm hanged if I'll stand any more of it! I don't like Mrs Bradley, but if you can't speak to her civilly, out you go! I've been spoiling for a chance to push your face into the flowerbeds for a damned long time now, so you'd better look out for your manly beauty! That's all!"

He sat down again.

"Mild but fairly well-sustained applause then rippled over the vast hall," said Mrs Bradley sweetly, waving the incensed inspector back into his chair, "and a cordial vote of thanks was returned to the speaker for his inspiring address. Never mind, Mr Grindy. You have my utmost sympathy. Believe me, I understand your point of view. But listen."

She put her head on one side and grinned hideously up at him.

"Suppose I can give you a list of eight persons, one of whom most probably moved the skull and so may know something about the death of Sethleigh — always supposing that the skull proves to be his skull and not the skull of somebody else! — wouldn't that narrow the enquiry down beautifully for you?"

The inspector looked dubious.

"I reckon it would be more to the point, madam, if you told me where they've put it," he said lugubriously. "But I expect that's more than you can do! I'm afraid you've hampered me proper not letting on about the skull being in Culminster."

"If you are anxious for the skull, I dare say we can make up our minds where it is to be found," said Mrs Bradley calmly. "Where is the very best place to hide a thing, James Redsey?"

Redsey grinned.

"Where it has been looked for already," he responded.

Mrs Bradley beamed royally upon him.

"Clever boy," she said. "Now then, inspector."

But Grindy merely looked resentful.

244

"You're wasting my time, madam," he growled.

Mrs Bradley sighed.

"Such a pity to be peevish, old dear," said Jim, beginning to enjoy himself at sight of the inspector's angry discomfiture. "Try the old butcher's shop again."

"Really, James!" said Mrs Bryce Harringay at the French doors, "considering that we all supposed the unfortunate remains in the butcher's shop to be those of your late cousin, I should imagine that you might find it possible to refer to the dreadful place a little less flippantly."

"He's right, anyway," said Mrs Bradley briefly. "So come. Will the car carry three, inspector?"

"Look here," said the inspector, gloomily barring the way, "is this a joke, or what?"

"Man and brother," said Mrs Bradley, raising her skinny claw as though in benediction, "it is not a joke. You have a key to the butcher's shop? And you do not desire my company? Very well."

"Oh, come if you want to," said the inspector ungraciously. "I've got to pick up the superintendent, though, at Bossbury police station."

Mrs Bradley was seated in the back of the car before he had finished speaking, and with a very bad grace the inspector climbed into the driver's seat and started the engine.

The little shop was still locked and shuttered. The inspector produced a key and opened the door. He lit the gas.

"Nothing doing," he grunted in the tone of a man who had never expected to find anything doing.

"Wait a moment. Where do butchers throw all the odd bits and bones?" asked Mrs Bradley, peering ghoulishly over the threshold of the little shop.

"In the drawer under the chopping-block or the counter," grinned the superintendent, whom they had picked up at the police station. He jerked at a brass handle.

"Here we — By gum! It is, too! What about this, Grindy?"

The inspector leapt to his side as he drew out a skull.

II

"But how did you *know?*" asked Aubrey, later.

"By taking thought, child, and by musing on the vagaries of human nature. Consider. This affair was so neat. Now murder is not usually a neat crime. Theft can be neat. So can forgery. Seduction and even arson can be classed among the finer arts. But murder — no. Your murderer is a person of greed or passion. He is in the grip of the primitive. And the primitive is invariably untidy. I considered that a man who would disjoint a body so efficiently, and clear up the mess after himself, and dispose of the human joints upon meat-hooks in that passionate tidy way, was no ordinary person. That was why I immediately dismissed James Redsey from my mind. I don't say that James could not commit a murder. Most of us could. Most of us would, too, but for some natural fear of the consequences, or some unnatural inhibition which frustrates our desires. But

246

James did not dismember the corpse, and James is not tidy — no, not even when he digs a hole in which to bury a body! And he is extraordinarily true to type. There isn't an original streak in the whole of the young man's mentality. I have ceased to consider him as a carver of bodies and a person who runs about the countryside conveying skulls from place to place. Never mind! We have quite a number of extraordinarily constituted persons living among us. I made a list of them. First there is the Reverend Stephen Broome."

"The vicar?" Aubrey's voice was shrill.

"Yes, my dear. A man who takes the clock to bed with him, and thrusts other people's vases and cut glass preserve jars into his pockets, and is as appallingly absent-minded and forgetful as that poor dear man, is a very pretty study for a psycho-analyst."

"Oh — that," said Aubrey, disappointed. "I thought you meant old Broome had done the murder."

"Then," continued Mrs Bradley, ignoring the remark, "there is your own mother. Mrs Bryce Harringay is a remarkable woman, and — a point which everybody seems to have overlooked — she had a very good motive for getting both Sethleigh and Redsey out of the way."

Aubrey giggled.

"Hang it all!" he said. "I mean to say — the mater! She couldn't cut short the life of a blackbeetle!"

Mrs Bradley smiled sympathetically, but shook her head.

"Your mother is very fond of you," she said. "And fond mothers will do the most curious things in an

247

attempt to achieve material welfare for their children. If Sethleigh and Redsey were out of the way, you, young man, would be the heir to the whole of the family property."

"Yes — if Sethleigh and Redsey were out of the way," said Aubrey.

"Well" — Mrs Bradley rapped out the word like a shot — "who first turned the attention of the police to Sethleigh's disappearance? Who informed them that she had seen the two cousins disappearing into the woods at seven fifty-five that Sunday evening? Nobody else saw them go there together! Nobody else swears positively to the time! If Sethleigh were murdered and Redsey hanged, they *would* both be out of the way!" She concluded this extraordinary exposition with hooting laughter.

Aubrey straightened himself. He had been lying back in Mrs Bradley's most comfortable deck-chair, arms behind head, feet up, listening with tremendous amusement to Mrs Bradley's theories. This last one, however, was a direct challenge. He sat up, put his feet to the ground, one on either side of the footrest, and leaned forward.

"Yes, but the mater — she isn't that sort of person. I mean — well, she just wouldn't! And as for cutting up the body —"

"Exactly." Mrs Bradley nodded. "So much so that I almost think we might leave her out of a list of possible suspects. Character, habits of mind, social customs — these things are of boundless importance in a case of this kind. And your mother would not have moved the skull from Culminster to Bossbury."

"Why wouldn't she?" asked Aubrey curiously. "Of course, I know she didn't because she wasn't the murderer, but what makes you say —"

"Then there are the two young men and the one young woman who live in the Cottage on the Hill," Mrs Bradley went on serenely. "Wright — an artist. That is, in the popular conception, a man without morals, personal decency, or legal obligations. A pariah, an outcast, an unscrupulous dodger of debts. A promiscuous sitter on other people's unmade beds, a habitant of yet other people's made ones. A sipper of absinthe and imbiber of cocoa. A creature long-haired, filthy, depraved, and mentally unbalanced. A cocaine fiend, a dram drinker, an apostle of obscenity, lust, and freedom."

"Thanks," said Aubrey gratefully. "I've got all that down in shorthand. Stafford Major called *me* a bug-hunting stinker last term!"

"Wright," went on Mrs Bradley, relinquishing her platform voice for something a little less forceful, "is just the sort of person who would think it funny to hang human joints on hooks. He is certainly capable of murder. He could have stolen the skull from his own studio most convincingly, and he could have substituted the coconut for it. He is capable of thinking out that clever touch of inserting a tiny living plant in the skull's jaws to make it appear that it had been buried in the cliff far longer than was actually the case, and he would have had the forethought to plant the big clump of thrift over it to conceal the spot. He is stupid enough to have picked out the largest and most attractive clump of thrift he could find, too."

"How do you mean?" asked Aubrey, who had finished transcribing Mrs Bradley's remarks about artists into long-hand and now felt that he possessed sufficient verbal ammunition to account for three or four Staffords Major at the beginning of the next school term.

"He picked out a clump of flowering plant which immediately attracted the attention of those young people who came to camp on the shore," said Mrs Bradley. "Shortsighted, that. He should have picked out a less noticeable clump of thrift."

"Yes. Yes, it was shortsighted, wasn't it? Still, jolly difficult to see how old Wright could have done the actual murder," said Aubrey, weighing it up. "He had a pretty sound alibi, you see."

"How do you know that?" Mrs Bradley's voice was sharper than usual.

"Church until a quarter to eight."

"Granted and proved." Mrs Bradley nodded.

"Met Margery Barnes at a quarter to nine."

"Who told you that, child? I thought nobody knew that he was the man she met in the woods! She told *me*, of course, but —"

"Well, she told me too. Only yesterday, though. Said she'd told you, and so she supposed it didn't matter about telling other people. Made me swear to keep mum when the doctor was about, though."

"The doctor?"

"Yes. Margery's pater. I say, I suppose *he* wasn't Jack the Ripper?"

"Jack the —?"

"The jolly old murderer, you know."

"I was coming to him. Doctors have been known to commit these crimes. There was Dr Crippen."

"Oh, yes. Old Cora asked for it, though, didn't she?"

"I dare say Rupert Sethleigh asked for it, too," said Mrs Bradley tartly. "That is the worst of a crime like murder. One's sympathies are so often with the murderer. One can see so many reasons why the murdered person was — well, murdered. The chief fault I have to find with most murderers is that they lack a sense of humour."

"But you just said that Cleaver Wright —"

"I know, child. I know. And it almost, but not quite, persuades me to leave him out of the list of suspects. He *has* a sense of humour — morbid, perhaps, but real. I almost think I must acquit him."

"But what has a sense of humour to do with it?" Aubrey asked, lying back in his chair again.

"Everything, child. Lack of humour means lack of balance. Lack of balance implies mental instability. Mental instability is, logically, madness. All murders are committed by lunatics. I am referring to premeditated murders, of course."

"Really? Do you mean all murderers are mad?"

"Except me. And my outrageous sanity is in itself a kind of mental defect, I sometimes think."

She chuckled. Aubrey grinned lazily.

"But you haven't told me yet about moving the skull," he said.

"You remember playing a little game at my house?"

"Oh, yes. We all played it, didn't we? Go on."

"That's all," said Mrs Bradley. "Think it out, child."

"We all wrote down where we thought the skull was hidden," said Aubrey slowly. "And — I've got it! Think so, anyway! Somebody who played that game thought you were getting a bit too hot on the subject of the skull, so they moved it. Idiots! Much better have left it alone."

"Well, I don't know," said Mrs Bradley, frowning thoughtfully. "It wasn't the murderer who played this game of Hunt the Thimble with the skull, you see."

"Oh, you know who — you know — I mean, how do you know that? Do you know who the murderer is?"

"I know that the man who moved that skull from Culminster to Bossbury was a man in a panic," said Mrs Bradley, "and that the murderer is not in a panic. He feels perfectly secure. And upon my word," she concluded vigorously, "if I didn't feel certain that the police will sooner or later make out a case against some innocent person, I would leave him in peace. Rupert Sethleigh —" She stopped. After all, this charming, serious boy was related to the murdered man.

Aubrey nodded.

"Asked for it," he continued. "Yes, he did, didn't he? 'Rupert Sethleigh — Bounder' ought to be on his tombstone."

"Still, I fancy that when we come to the end of these complicated affairs we may discover that it was a case of diamond cut diamond," amended Mrs Bradley, completely serious for once.

CHAPTER
TWENTY

The Story of a Crime

"The policy of *laissez faire*, exemplified by some of our leading statesmen during the eighteenth century," observed Mrs Bradley, fixing a beady, bird-like, sharp black eye upon the Vicar of Wandles Parva, who, absent-minded as usual, was endeavouring to insert a small but valuable silver vase, happily empty of water, into the right-hand pocket of his best alpaca jacket, "has its application even at the present day."

"My dear man!" exclaimed Mrs Bryce Harringay in horror, grasping the charming little receptacle very hastily and rising to restore it to its former position on Mrs Bradley's drawing-room mantelpiece. "It can't be kleptomania in a gentleman of his profession," she confided in a sibilant aside to the owner of the vase, "so it must be pure absent-mindedness."

"Not kleptomania, no," replied Mrs Bradley composedly, but turning suddenly and terrifyingly serious. "That has become a mere police-court term to account for the astonishing vagaries of the idle rich." Her mirthless cackle added ironic corollary to the theorem.

"I believe the young people have concluded their game," said Mrs Bryce Harringay. "It sounds like it."

"Then I expect they would like some tea," said the hostess, rising to ring the bell. "Shall we go into the garden?"

The young people, consisting of Felicity Broome, Margery Barnes, Aubrey, and Jim, had been playing croquet on the lawn. It was a beautiful lawn, admirably kept, but none of the four cared for playing croquet upon any lawn whatsoever. However, their hostess, with a determined frown upon her forehead and a vinegary grin upon her lips, had insisted upon pressing mallets and balls upon them, and herself had placed the hoops ready for play. It was impossible to refuse to fall in with the arrangements. Mrs Bryce Harringay beamed approval.

"A most delightful pastime, most!" she observed largely, waving her plump white hands in a kind of careless benediction upon the incensed Aubrey, the embarrassed James, the giggling Margery, and the shrugging philosophical Miss Broome. "So good for the manners! So suitable for a summer day! A most attractive game, most!"

"There," said Mrs Bradley to Aubrey, who promptly smacked his ball through the open gate into the road, where it trickled merrily downhill for a hundred yards or more, "now you can squabble and fight and lose your tempers and accuse each other of cheating for at least an hour, while we old, decrepit persons engage one another in gentle conversation punctuated by snatches of sleep."

She waved a skinny claw at them, watched Aubrey stalk moodily off to recover his ball, and then she went into the house.

At tea the conversation turned inevitably upon the murder. "I wonder who on earth it can be? The inspector is getting absolute wind-up. I should think the police will be compelled to make some sort of a move soon, with all the newspapers shouting at them like this," said Aubrey to Mrs Bradley.

She shrugged her shoulders.

"I wonder they don't pay more attention to Mr Savile," said Felicity. "He can't show an alibi for the evening of June 22nd. He attempted to kill you in the Manor Woods —"

Mrs Bradley chuckled.

"Aubrey here told the inspector so," she said, "and there is no doubt that Sethleigh used to meet Lulu Hirst in the Cottage and also in the Manor Woods. And Mr Wright did some curious things on the night of the murder. So did Mr Broome," she added, grinning.

"Attempted to kill you?" exclaimed Mrs Bryce Harringay. "Good gracious! When was this?"

"Aubrey will remember, I dare say," replied Mrs Bradley comfortably. She selected a piece of cake with careful discrimination. "He was with me at the time, as I said. We were in the Manor Woods, and I was attempting to reconstruct the crime from the data which we had at our disposal at that time. I imagine that I was speaking in a loud voice. Suddenly an arrow — a cloth-yard, goose-feathered, Battle of Agincourt affair with a great iron barb and a most professionally

Robin Hood flight, came whizzing past my ear and stuck in the trunk of a tree on the farther side of the clearing. The police theory seems to agree with Aubrey's idea that the arrow was shot with the deliberate intention of putting an end to my quiet and harmless existence. All the same. Savile came forward immediately and apologized quite nicely for his carelessness."

The vicar laughed.

"Depends what meaning you attach to the word 'carelessness'," said Jim Redsey. "He probably meant he was sorry he'd made such a boss-eyed shot."

Mrs Bradley shook her head, and Felicity Broome broke in.

"I should think he would have run away if he really attempted your life," she said. "I mean, he wouldn't have wanted to advertise his presence exactly, would he?"

"Intent to deceive," said Aubrey, eating raspberries and cream with aplomb. He scooped up a delicious spoonful.

"Greedy pig," said Margery Barnes indulgently. "Pass the cream."

"No, honestly," continued Aubrey, passing it, "I expect he thought somebody might have seen the shot, and wanted to lull their suspicions — and Mrs Bradley's, too."

"Well, I certainly accepted his apology in the spirit which appeared to inspire it," said Mrs Bradley.

"I wonder someone doesn't confess to the murder and have done with it," said Margery. "I mean, if I had committed a murder I should be in such a funk that I should throw in my hand and get the hanging over, I think." And she shivered at the thought.

"Oh, I don't know why one should confess," protested the vicar, passing his cup for more tea. Mrs Bradley took the cup from his hand, and he began to drum on the table with his long fingers. "After all, there is no need for a fellow to queer his own pitch, is there? It's up to the police to prove he did it."

"You know," said Felicity, when the servants had cleared away the remains of the meal, and all were lounging comfortably in garden chairs, "I can't quite see anybody doing all that."

"All what?" Margery Barnes looked across at her.

"Well, all the horrid part. I mean, well, *take* Mr Savile, for instance. He always seemed to me such a feeble specimen, somehow."

"Psychologically it would be possible for such a man to commit such a murder," pronounced Mrs Bradley, "and I told the inspector so! Not that it seemed to carry much weight, I must say. He could have done it; so could Cleaver Wright, I think. Dr Barnes would be capable of dismembering the body, owing, of course, to his training as a surgeon rather than, let us say, to his natural gifts!"

"The police don't worry about psychology," said Jim, grinning lazily, "and yet they seem to catch a good many murderers."

"And hang 'em, too," said the vicar, puffing contentedly at his pipe as he applied a match to the bowl.

Mrs Bradley sat up, and looked from one to the other of them.

"Is that a challenge?" she asked. Out from between her two rows of small, even teeth came a little red tongue. She passed it very slowly over her top lip. Her smile did not alter very much while she did it, and yet Jim Redsey wriggled uneasily in the long, well-cushioned, comfortable chair, and averted his eyes. The vicar was busily applying another match to his pipe, so that he saw neither the smile nor the tiny movement of the tongue, both so suggestive of a cruel beast of prey in lazy contemplation of a meal he is in no hungry haste to devour . . .

Mrs Bradley lay back again.

"The police are usually guided by what is known as circumstantial evidence," she said. "After all, there can seldom be any eye-witness of a crime like murder, and therefore direct evidence of guilt is difficult to obtain. Circumstantial evidence is the next best thing. That is about all which can be said for it. Sometimes it leads the police aright, and sometimes it leads them entirely wrong. Take this murder of Rupert Sethleigh. Let us work it out this way:

"At seven fifty-five on the evening of Sunday, June 22nd, Rupert Sethleigh and his cousin, James Redsey, went into the Manor Woods to continue an argument which had degenerated into a bitter quarrel.

"They had not been in the woods very long — put it that they walked to the Stone of Sacrifice, probably by devious ways, and that it took them ten minutes — when, in that rather sinister place, the quarrel became so bitter that Redsey turned upon Sethleigh and knocked him down. As he fell, Sethleigh struck his head, probably pretty hard. At any rate, his cousin firmly believed that he had killed him. He was panic-stricken at what he thought he had done, and, instead of going for assistance or doing any of the sensible, level-headed, humane things which ought to have suggested themselves to his mind under the circumstances, he took fright, hid what he supposed was the dead body of Sethleigh in a hazel copse, and made for the 'Queen's Head', where he intended to perform for himself the double service of proving as plausible an alibi as the circumstances would permit, and of drinking himself into incoherence, helplessness, and forgetfulness."

Jim writhed. Felicity gazed at him reproachfully, and Margery giggled nervously.

"Well, it was not a very plausible alibi, because, unluckily for Redsey, it was known to Mrs Bryce Harringay that he had accompanied his cousin into the Manor Woods, and no one could be found who would swear to having seen Sethleigh alive after the woodland had swallowed them both up.

"Now it seems practically certain from the police point of view that Sethleigh was not dead when Redsey fled from the woods to the public house. They think he was stunned. The evidence offered in support of this contention is that Redsey would have found it difficult, if not impossible, to dismember the body. He could prove satisfactorily where he was all that Sunday night, and that he was in and about the Manor House all day

Monday, and it seems certain that he could not have transported the body into Bossbury, introduced it into Binks's shop, and dismembered it between the hours of eight a.m., when the market opened, and nine-thirty a.m., when Binks and his assistant entered the shop on Tuesday morning. For these reasons the police assumed that he was not the murderer, unless he had an accomplice who performed the more gruesome part of the task for him. As no such accomplice could be traced, the police assumed, as I say, that Redsey's blow had stunned his cousin, and had not caused his death.

"That disposes of Redsey's part in the matter. That he spent part of the Monday night in digging a grave in the woods for the reception of the body, and searched, without success, in the bushes near the clearing for the corpse which had disappeared, is further evidence in support of the theory that he had nothing to do with dismembering the body.

"Now I come to a peculiar circumstance which has been allowed to waste its full significance upon the desert air until this moment. An axiom among historians and great detectives is to beware of the bit of evidence which refuses to fit. These little awkward facts are keys to mysteries. Now, in this case, we have such an awkward fact in a remark made by Margery Barnes to —"

Margery sat up with a jerk, consternation written all over her ingenuous countenance.

"Me?" she exclaimed. "Oh, but I'm sure —"

"To Felicity Broome, in my presence," continued Mrs Bradley, proceeding serenely with her argument.

"The remark was to the effect that at about nine o'clock or just after, on that fateful Sunday evening, being in the Manor Woods for a purpose which had nothing to do with us or with the murder of Sethleigh, she saw a man come crawling out of some bushes behind the circle of pines which mark the clearing. Now, rather naturally, I think, considering the circumstances, afterwards she assumed that this crawling man must have been Rupert Sethleigh, and that, through having seen him alive after nine o'clock, she was in a position to prove positively that James Redsey could not have killed him at about five minutes past eight.

"Now, I refused to have anything to do with that part of Margery's tale for two reasons. First, she did not actually recognize the man as Sethleigh; she merely assumed, after she had heard that James Redsey might be accused of the murder, that a man crawling out of the bushes in the Manor Woods on the evening of Sunday, June 22nd, must necessarily have been the man James Redsey knocked down and whose body he hid. The second point is a good deal more important because, after all, although the idea that this man must have been Sethleigh was mere auto-suggestion on Margery's part, yet the notion was far from improbable. It might very well have been Sethleigh whom she saw, except for one strikingly important fact.

"The human eye, in moments of terror, acts like the snapshot attachment of a camera. There is no long exposure, as, to speak fancifully, we get when we calmly admire a fine view. No! The mind clicks a shutter —

down and up! I am terrified! I cry out! I run! And one distinct impression of the thing which terrified me remains upon my mind. Margery retained such an impression. When you were telling us the tale, your words, Margery, my dear, were these: 'And a man came slowly crawling out of the bushes *like a great black slug!*

"Now, at nine o'clock on a midsummer night it is very far from dark. It might have been dark in those woods under the trees and among the bushes at that time, but Margery saw this man in the large circular clearing where the Stone of Sacrifice stands. It would have been as light there as in any other open space — light enough to play tennis, for example. Well, I took particular care to find out what Rupert Sethleigh was wearing that night. So did the police. But my reason was not theirs. Never mind. I will come back to that, perhaps, in a moment. The point is this: instead of the dinner-suit one might suppose that Rupert Sethleigh would be wearing, he had on that evening a white tennis shirt and light-grey flannel trousers."

"Aha!" said Aubrey Harringay. "If Margery had really seen old Rupert, you mean she couldn't have thought he looked black?"

"Exactly," said Mrs Bradley, beaming upon him fondly and causing him to feel exactly three and a half years old.

There was a long pause.

"Then *who was it* I saw?" asked Margery at last, in a queer, frightened tone. She glanced hastily behind her, and then sat up and checked off the names on her fingers.

"It wasn't Rupert Sethleigh. You've proved that. It wasn't Jim Redsey, because we know he was in the 'Queen's Head' at that time. It wasn't Cleaver Wright, because he was there too, I suppose, or on his way, at any rate; and, anyway, I feel sure the man was bigger than Mr Wright —"

"A good point, but it doesn't do to feel too sure about a thing like that. You didn't allow yourself much time to look, remember. Personally, I think you would have had no difficulty in recognising Mr Wright, had it been he."

Margery blushed.

"It might have been Mr Savile, mightn't it?" she suggested.

"It might." Mrs Bradley put her head on one side and half closed her eyes. "And it might have been your father —"

"Father? Oh, but —"

"Do you know where your father was at nine o'clock that night?"

"I understand he was at the major's."

"Very well. That's a thing that can be proved. Go on. We'll assume for the moment that he *was* at the major's."

"I can't think of anybody else! Oh, yes!" She glanced mischievously at the Reverend Stephen Broome. His pipe was well alight now. He was sprawling back in a deck-chair with his black shining alpaca jacket wide open, showing his black clerical vest and the little gold crucifix he wore. His long, black-trousered legs were

264

stretched out in front of him, and his large, strong, long-fingered hands were clasped behind his head.

Mrs Bradley chuckled.

"Well," she said, "his clothes are certainly black enough, and he asked for it just now! He shall have it, too! We will assume that it was the Vicar of Wandles Parva whom you saw crawling out of the bushes, and we will try our circumstantial evidence on him. Mr Broome!" She prodded him in the stomach with her mauve and white parasol. "Wake up!"

"Eh?" said the vicar, who had been far away, as usual. "I beg your pardon?" He raised himself and blinked at her with his heavily lidded blue-grey eyes.

"Where were you on the evening of Sunday, June 22nd?" asked Mrs Bradley keenly.

"At church, I expect."

"Yes. And after church?"

"Went for a walk, I expect. I generally do, while Felicity gets the supper."

"Where did you go?"

"Haven't the least idea. Round and about, you know." He lay back in his chair again, and puffed away at his pipe.

"We'll assume he went for his walk in the Manor Woods," said Mrs Bradley to Margery, disregarding the vicar's shake of the head. "Now, then."

"*You* must go on," said Margery. "I can't get any farther."

"Very well. At five minutes past eight we see Rupert Sethleigh stretched senseless on the ground. James Redsey catches hold of him under the arms and drags

265

him into the bushes. James disappears in the direction of the Bossbury road, *en route* for the public house. In a few minutes Rupert regains consciousness. The church service of Evening Prayer is concluded at a quarter to eight. The vicar leaves the building at eight o'clock perhaps —"

"Five to," came in lazy tones from behind the pipe.

"Very well, Mr Broome. It makes it all the worse for you. Gives you five more minutes for the murder. At five minutes to eight he goes off for his walk. He enters the Manor Woods by the wicket gate. He walks along the path which leads to the clearing. He is just in time to see the cousins quarrel, and he witnesses the blow which stretched Sethleigh senseless on the ground. He marks the spot where Redsey hides the body. Influenced unconsciously by Redsey's action in dragging his cousin in among the bushes, he concludes that Sethleigh is dead. He hates Sethleigh. When Redsey has fled from the woods, the vicar parts the bushes and has a look at the man he loathes."

"The man he loathes?" said two voices.

"Of course," replied Mrs Bradley, surprised. "Everybody who met him seems to have detested Rupert Sethleigh. Why should the vicar be any exception?"

"His cloth," suggested Mrs Bryce Harringay in honeyed tones, directing a languishing glance at the sprawling figure of the Reverend Stephen Broome. "The feelings of an ordained priest —"

"Oh, rubbish!" said Mrs Bradley brusquely. "An ordained priest feels like any other father of a charming daughter, I suppose? Why shouldn't he?"

Felicity turned her nose up.

The vicar went on smoking — less placidly. A slight frown gathered between his contemplative eyes.

Margery Barnes held up a shapely bare arm and eyed its contours with artless satisfaction.

"Yes," said Mrs Bradley, under her breath. "No," she added immediately.

"Go on," said the vicar. "Don't mind me. I shall go to sleep as soon as I've finished this pipe."

"By the way," said Mrs Bradley, "do you carry your tobacco in a pouch?"

"Used to," replied the Reverend Stephen Broome.

"What do you use now?"

The vicar looked embarrassed.

"Well — er — as a matter of fact, you see —" he began confusedly.

The company sat up and began to look interested. Felicity scowled, and glared at Jim Redsey, who was grinning broadly.

The half-amused tone in Mrs Bradley's voice had gone when next she spoke. Her words seemed almost unwilling to issue forth.

"When the vicar found Sethleigh he had an unpleasant shock," she said.

The vicar's unhappy expression changed to one of thoughtful serenity at the resumption of the tale. He lay comfortably back in his chair and closed his eyes.

"He found that Sethleigh was not dead," contributed Aubrey.

"Thereupon, although he was disappointed and furious to think that this man had escaped," continued Mrs Bradley, "he helped him out of the bushes, and Sethleigh lay down on the Stone of Sacrifice to recover. The sight of his prostrate form incensed the vicar to the point of madness. He drew out his penknife —"

"Never carry one," came in muffled tones from behind the pipe.

"And stabbed Sethleigh in the throat."

Margery Barnes glanced fearfully behind her. Felicity said crossly:

"What nonsense!"

"Then he heard voices," pursued Mrs Bradley, unperturbed by this frank comment, "the voices of Margery Barnes and Cleaver Wright. Hastily he lowered the body of Sethleigh to the ground on the side of the Stone which faces the Manor House. Then, stooping low so that the Stone would cover him, he entered the woods on the house side, and gradually worked his way among the trees and bushes until he had partially compassed a circular course, and was hidden in the bushes — where, Margery?"

Margery sat up, blushing hotly. She opened her mouth to speak, closed it again, met Mrs Bradley's basilisk gaze, and was prompted to reply:

"Do you mean where did I see that man come crawling out? Oh — er — well, it was about opposite the right-hand side of the Stone if you had your back to the Bossbury road."

"Yes, thank you," said Mrs Bradley, with a courteous inclination of the head. "Well," she continued abruptly, "when Margery fled from Cleaver Wright, that young man, finding no pleasure, but rather a somewhat ludicrous dismay, in finding himself left seated upon the pine-needles, got up and strolled across the clearing. His experience of women taught him that the chances were in favour of Margery's return when she recovered from the fright he had given her —"

"I wouldn't have gone back there for anything," declared Margery vehemently.

"So he walked round the Stone to examine it. The thing has its fascination. On the farther side of it he came upon Sethleigh's body. He knelt to examine it. In doing so he got a good deal of blood on to the knees of his trousers. Now mark the sequel to that. The corpse had bled from the neck. There was no blood probably on Sethleigh's trousers. They were grey flannels supported merely by —" She glanced enquiringly at Mrs Bryce Harringay.

"A coloured silk scarf, I believe," supplied that lady. "But I really must say, Mrs Bradley —"

"Thank you," said Mrs Bradley. "A coloured silk scarf. Cleaver Wright is quick-witted. He realized that Sethleigh had been murdered. He felt the blood of Sethleigh wet against his shins. At any second Margery Barnes might return."

"Ugh! Don't!" screamed Margery, covering her face.

"So Wright hastily dragged off the trousers of the corpse, pulled off his own flannels —" She glanced enquiringly at Margery. Aubrey tapped the girl on the

269

arm to attract her attention. Margery lowered her hands and nodded.

"Yes, he *was* wearing grey flannel trousers that evening," she admitted.

"Ah," said Mrs Bradley, satisfied. "I knew it. He then left his own trousers lying on the ground and darted into the woods, where he assumed the nether garments of the murdered man. Then he emerged from the bushes, went with all speed to the 'Queen's Head', and, fearful lest any undetected bloodstains might be visible upon his clothing, he promptly picked a quarrel with the biggest young fellow there, and got himself so badly knocked about that no one would suppose any blood on his person to be other than his own blood from his poor nose" — she glanced with affected commiseration at Margery — "or his poor lip." She smiled with quiet enjoyment.

"Brains," said Aubrey Harringay admiringly. "Bright man!"

"I agree," said Mrs Bradley dryly.

Felicity Broome sat noticeably still and mute. The vicar knocked out his pipe against the wooden arm of Mrs Bryce Harringay's deck-chair, lay back, and composed himself for slumber.

"Well," continued Mrs Bradley, "the vicar was much intrigued by Wright's performance with the trousers, for he was too far away to realize the implication or the significance of it. He did realize very clearly, however, that Wright had seen the dead body. That was exceedingly awkward. It meant that if possible the body had to be disposed of. He crawled towards it. It was

270

then that Margery saw him. He realized that she had seen him, did not know whether she had recognized him, but trusted she had not. He then took a big risk. He lifted Sethleigh's body in his arms — he is a very strong man, remember — and carried him the shortest way he could — except that he kept along the edge of the public woods instead of on the Bossbury road itself — to the wicket gate, up to the lych-gate of the church, through the churchyard, and over the wall into his own garden. He took exactly the same route, in fact, as that taken by his daughter Felicity" — she grinned horribly at her — "when she transported the bloodstained suitcase from the pigsty to the Manor Woods. That suitcase, I may suggest to you, was stained with blood from the murdered man's collar, tie, and white tennis shirt, and it was because Felicity knew that, and knew that her father was the guilty person, that she was so anxious to be rid of that incriminating clue."

Felicity sat up.

"How dare you say such a thing?" she demanded passionately. "It was nothing of the sort!"

Mrs Bradley waved her hand pacifically.

"You will remember that I am reconstructing on circumstantial and not upon psychological evidence," she remarked coolly. "Well, the vicar carried Sethleigh's body over to the empty pig-sty and laid it down in the inner shed. It then occurred to him that he was still in possession of the knife with which he had killed a man, and the clothes of the corpse, and also that there was a considerable quantity of blood on the cuff of his own coat. So he sallied forth again, swiftly and by devious ways, until he got nearly to Culminster. There, trading on the fact of his known absent-mindedness, he deliberately walked into the River Cullen, dropped the incriminating knife, dropped the murdered man's clothes, which he had weighted with stones —"

"How?" asked Jim Redsey.

"A handful of flints placed in the middle of the shirt, the collar and tie thrown on top of the stones, the shirt gathered up like a bag and tied round with string," said the vicar, joyously entering into the game.

Mrs Bradley looked at him in surprise. He grinned at her genially. Margery giggled. Felicity glowered. Jim Redsey picked a daisy and dropped it accurately into Aubrey Harringay's open mouth, as the boy, lying almost full length, opened his lips to speak.

"Then he returned to Wandles Parva," continued Mrs Bradley, "went into the house, and informed his daughter and the servant that he had absent-mindedly walked into the river. All unsuspecting" — she glanced at Felicity, who sat straight-lipped and pale in her chair — "the two of them dried his clothes, prepared a hot bath for him, and believed implicitly the tale he told them."

She turned to Felicity.

"Dear child," she said, "would you rather I stopped?"

"Good gracious, no," replied Felicity angrily. "I know it's only a joke on your part. Of course, it sounds rather horrid to me," she added, chin in air.

"Of course it does," said Mrs Bradley decidedly. "I won't go on. It isn't *really* funny."

272

"But *I* want to hear the rest," the vicar remarked. "You had better go away, Felicity. Don't spoil other people's pleasure!" And he chuckled lazily.

"I'm glad you're enjoying yourself," said Felicity furiously, and almost in tears. She rose hastily and ran into the house.

"Go on, Mrs Bradley," said Aubrey. "Corpse in pig-sty. Vicar in bath. Rupert missing. What next?"

"The next is where the rest of the circumstantial evidence comes in," said Mrs Bradley, with a sidelong glance at the vicar.

"How do you mean?" asked Aubrey Harringay. "Haven't we heard it all? Oh, no. The butcher's shop business."

"That doesn't interest me very much," confessed Mrs Bradley. "You see, the young man who acts as Binks's assistant belongs to the Boys' Club in Bossbury which the vicar holds on third Mondays. Note the significance of these facts. First the day. What day in the week could be so convenient for the transportation of the corpse into Bossbury? Especially as Cleaver Wright often lent the vicar his car for the journey. He could have propped up Sethleigh's body in the car and driven him into the market with the utmost ease. He could have stolen the key of the lock-up shop from Binks's boy's pocket when the lads were changing for their running practice. He is strong enough to perform the somewhat arduous task of dismembering the corpse —"

"Good heavens!" said the vicar blankly.

"Lastly," said Mrs Bradley, "at this very instant he is in possession of a tobacco-case, beautifully wrought in silver, which was once the property of the murdered man!"

She turned implacably upon the astounded cleric.

"I knew this passion of yours for secreting receptacles of all kinds about your person would get you into some ridiculous scrape one day," she said sternly. "Turn out your pockets!"

Mrs Bryce Harringay helped him. It did not take them long. Very sheepishly the vicar pulled out a small circular box with a hinged lid. It was about three inches in diameter, beautifully chased and engraved, and the engraving consisted of three letters intertwined in a maze of ornamental scroll-work, but perfectly distinguishable.

They were the initials of Rupert Sethleigh.

CHAPTER
TWENTY-ONE

Savile

I

"Well," said the inspector, "here's this list of names. She thinks one of them moved that head. We'd better check up on them in case she's right. You never know, with these funny old parties. And, to tell the truth, I'm at such a dead end with the thing myself that I'd be thankful for any trail to follow up, so that it would lead us somewhere near the truth."

He produced a sheet which at one time had formed part of Mrs Bradley's loose-leaf pad, and handed it to the superintendent. It contained the names of all the persons who had been asked to play Mrs Bradley's little table-game, in which they had written down possible hiding-places for the skull.

"Wright's name isn't here," grunted the superintendent.

"No. I noticed that."

"His pal's name is down, and so is the lady's."

"Yes."

"And young Harringay — but not his mother. The old dame's put her own name down, I see, and the vicar and his daughter. Oh, the doctor's daughter is down, and the major's two youngsters, and that gardener chap, Willows. But we can cross him off. We know all about him that Sunday night, and he's a poor fish, anyway. And we can cross off those two youngsters and Miss Broome. Oh, Redsey's name is here at the bottom. That makes ten names, not eight. Of course, Wright might have heard about the game from one of the others; and the doctor and the major could have heard from their daughters, so it doesn't rule any of them out. And look here, Grindy! What about Savile?"

"We've got nothing on Savile. Besides, he's as meek as a sheep."

"The deuce he is! And he's got muscles like a prize-fighter under those polite duds of his! Besides, he could have pinched the skull from Wright, and he could have buried it on those cliffs! He could have gone over there on the Thursday afternoon while everybody at the Vicarage was playing tennis —"

"But he was playing tennis, too."

"Yes, part of the time. Then he went into the house to look at one of the vicar's books, but I wonder whether that was an excuse for slipping away and burying the skull without anybody knowing he had left the house? You see, from the Vicarage it is the easiest thing in the world to drop over into the churchyard and take a short cut on to the Bossbury road."

"Yes, but he couldn't walk to Rams Cove and back in an afternoon, Mr Bidwell."

"Who said he could? He'd have a car waiting. He's got one, you see. We must find out about that. If he didn't go in a car — oh, or on a push-bike; that's another idea! — or on his motor-bike — I believe it belongs to Wright, as a matter of fact, but Savile borrows it, I know —"

"Or he could have buried the suitcase with that fish inside it," grinned the inspector. "Just a nice little game for a quiet summer afternoon!"

"You still think the boy Harringay did that, and then lied about it?" said Superintendent Bidwell.

"Well, don't you, sir?" asked Grindy, laughing.

"I don't know. Either he or Wright. That's the sort of silly-idiot joke Wright would think really funny. And don't forget — talking of Wright — that he can't account for that hour and a half between the time he left church and the time he went to the pub."

"I heard some rumour that he met a girl."

"What girl?"

"The doctor's daughter."

"Oh. Doesn't want to give her away to papa, I suppose. Of course, he could have hidden the skull himself, and put that coconut in its place. But the *motive* is the whole blinking point. There was nothing between him and Sethleigh any time that we know of, was there? You see, that's where I think we ought to freeze hard on to young Redsey, now that we've proved Sethleigh is dead. After all, he's the chap with the really strong motive."

"What about the doctor?"

"Eh?"

"And Mrs Bryce Harringay?"

"Eh?"

"And Savile? Why, that Lulu girl up at the Cottage as good as told Mrs Bradley that Sethleigh was her lover. 'There's one man dead for me already,' she said. What else can you make of that? A husband that's been fooled isn't the sweetest-tempered creature on earth, you know, and you say yourself the chap's got muscle enough for the job."

"What was that about the doctor?"

"Blackmail."

"Oh, that illegitimacy business. What of it? — Good Lord, if every man who has an illegitimate kid turned into a murderer, what the devil would the world come to?"

"Oh, well, a doctor, you know. Got to be pretty careful. The patients and all that. Especially when they're county families. Don't like it, you know. Family doctor's got to be a bally Joseph as far as they're concerned, or else — nah poo!"

"Was it ever proved, though?"

"Cleaver Wright."

"How much?"

"Fact. Don't you spot the likeness?"

"I — well, now you mention it — oh, I don't know, though. One's reddish and the other nearly black."

"Not an unusual result in father and son. Probably the mother was dark, too."

"But the eyes and mouth?"

"Different, yes. The mother again, I should think. But the family likeness is unmistakable, once you've got on to it. And, of course, Cleaver's been sponging on the doctor ever since he's been here!"

278

"Has he?"

"Rumour says so. May not be true, of course. But we might look into it, I think. I've often wondered why those folks came to live here. Easy money was probably the reason. The doctor wouldn't want —"

"But Mrs Bryce Harringay?"

"Well, I've been thinking a lot about young Redsey and that will, and I'm dead sure that boy's telling the truth. Put it this way. As soon as the will was altered and Sethleigh died, young Harringay came in for the house and land."

"Yes. I know that. Go on."

"Redsey swears he didn't know the will was going to be altered. Hadn't heard a word about it."

"We've thrashed all that out before. I say he did know."

"Half a minute. Just take the other side for a moment. Suppose he didn't know, but that Mrs Bryce Harringay did."

"We needn't suppose at all. We know she'd heard the will was to be altered. She said as much."

"More than once." The inspector grinned ruefully. "And always with chapter and verse, not to mention whole book of words, complete with song and dance! What I've put up with from those two old women — her and the scraggy one —"

"Bradley?"

"Ah. Never mind! Well, as I say, supposing she not only knew that the proposed alteration was in the wind, but that she actually thought the will had already been altered?"

"But she didn't think so."

"We can't prove it, either way. Neither can we prove that Redsey is telling the truth when he swears he didn't know. It cuts both ways, you see, and if you say one of 'em's a liar, you've got to keep your weather eye lifting because the other one may be lying too. See my point?"

"Oh, yes. But the crime? You don't tell me she did in Sethleigh and then carved him up?"

"I think she might have killed him. Big, hefty, very heavy woman, you know, and determined — damned determined!" said the inspector feelingly. "She could have followed the two of them into the woods, seen Redsey knock out Sethleigh, gone up and stabbed Sethleigh in the throat with her little fruit-knife —"

"Fruit-knife?"

"Ah. Poor woman's one of these vegetarians, you know. They all cart their fruit-knives about with them. At least, the Miss Mindens always do; and this one is always got up in gold chains and things, so she could easily hang a fruit-knife on herself somewhere. Silver or stainless steel they're made of, and are beautifully fashioned and finished. And nobody would think of such a thing as a weapon. You could clean it up after the murder, and go on carting it about with you, you see. Not like anything big and suspicious — like a dagger, for instance."

"That's a point. We've never discovered quite how the murder was committed. We only know the chap wasn't killed at the butcher's, because there was not enough blood. A little neat nick in the neck would have done the trick very nicely, I should say."

"Yes," went on the inspector, "and she's got no alibi at all from about a quarter to eight until ten o'clock that night."

"How's that?"

"Well, I've been nosing round that house a fair number of times now, and getting out a few ideas — you know the way — and it has sort of come out that she didn't go to church that night, and she went up to her bedroom at about a quarter to eight because she had a touch of neuralgia or something. Well, nobody saw her from then until two farm hands brought Redsey home drunk from the 'Queen's Head' that night. What do you make of that?"

"And you think she had an idea the will had already been altered?"

"Ah."

"And by doing in Sethleigh she could grab the lot for the kid?"

"Ah."

"There's something in it, but not much."

"There's as much in it as in your tin-pot idea that Redsey did it," retorted the inspector, grinning. "The fact is, Mr Bidwell, they've neither of them got the stomach to carve up the corpse. It seems to me we're up against that all the time. Those that had enough motive to do the murder couldn't rake up the guts to cover their tracks by messing up the identity of the body. And those that are blood-thirsty enough to hang bits of a dead man on hooks don't seem to have had enough motive to kick a dog — let alone commit a crime!"

<h2 style="text-align:center">II</h2>

"Then there's the question of Savile," said Mrs Bradley, after a pause. "A very vexed question, that of Savile. You see, the Stone itself would be such a temptation to him."

"How do you mean?" asked Aubrey.

"A most curious person, Savile," Mrs Bradley went on. "I've made a whole sheaf of notes about him. I shall incorporate them in my small new work for the Sixpenny Library. It is entitled *Psycho-Analysis for the Many*. You might recommend it to your mother with my compliments! No, but Savile really is a gem. I wouldn't have missed him for anything. And the vicar, too. Excellent. Surprisingly excellent, both of them."

"But Savile hadn't any reason for hating Sethleigh," said Aubrey.

"Hadn't he? You go and ask Lulu Hirst about that." Mrs Bradley pursed her lips and shook her small black head.

"Oh? Oh, really. Oh, I see." He didn't, in the least, but at fifteen and three-quarters one hesitates about confessing ignorance on any subject under the sun.

"Yes, Savile liked things done just so," Mrs Bradley went on, as though she were talking to herself. "And I wonder sometimes whether the Stone was too much for him. Somehow, though, I think he wouldn't have carried the thing through so boldly. He is consistent, I am sure; neat and tidy to a fault — it was a *very* tidy person who left that butcher's shop in such good order! — and he has a curious kink in his mentality. Have you observed it, child? But I don't think he has the requisite amount of nerve, quite, for a murder."

"I've observed he's a greasy swine," said Aubrey, without heat. "Can't stick him at any price."

"Yes. I didn't mean that. No, this that I am referring to struck me very forcibly when I went to call there one afternoon and discovered him in the act of interring a small dead bird — a canary which in life had belonged to Lulu Hirst."

"Oh?" The hot afternoon was making Aubrey sleepy.

"Yes. He was wearing a clergyman's collar."

"Clergyman's collar? Absent-minded blighter — like the vicar! Fancy two of them in one parish!" He began to laugh.

"Not absent-minded. That collar was a bit of ritual. Surely you noticed the Robin Hood suit when he nearly shot me in the Manor Woods that afternoon?"

"Robin Hood suit? Oh, yes. But he told us he was rehearsing for a play."

"Rehearsing my foot!" pronounced Mrs Bradley firmly. "He was dressed for the part he was playing in his imagination, that's all. And that's why I think he must be the butcher. You see, to him a dead body — dead flesh — would signify meat. Meat is cut into joints. Very well. He cuts it into joints!"

"But that's a bit of a skilled job, you know." Aubrey was wide awake now. "I mean, you can't just pick up a butcher's cleaver and hack about. It's scientific. I've often watched them, and I bet it takes a bit of doing, not to speak of heaps of practice." He spoke decidedly.

"Undoubtedly. But Savile had a chart hanging up in the studio. He used it to correct his drawings. It was a mass of red-ink dots and little crosses, and was annotated very freely. It was a human body with the skeleton marked in black, and had fainter lines showing the shape of the flesh on the bones. A most fascinating work. Oh, and Wright didn't like to see me looking at it, I remember. That is interesting, too."

"But Savile looks such a miserable little dago," argued Aubrey. "Butchers are generally hefty lads."

"So is Savile." Mrs Bradley drew a vivid word-picture of Savile's strength and muscular development.

"Shouldn't have thought it," said Aubrey. "Well, he had the strength, then. What else?"

"The Stone. Apart from any question of motive from the viewpoint of revenge or gain, we get the fact that the Stone is the centre of some weird and wonderful legends. It may even have been a sacrificial altar in some remote age, as its name suggests. I wonder sometimes whether the urge to offer a human sacrifice upon it would not be motive enough for a mind like that of Savile to cause him to commit murder. It is a pleasing idea. Rather fantastic, perhaps . . ."

"Then, if you are right, Savile could have been the chap who must have been sneaking about in the woods that night and boned the suitcase while I'd gone up to the house," said Aubrey.

"Yes. Undoubtedly. And it would fit in well with my theory of his guilt that he should have buried the fish with it and inscribed that peculiar legend upon the piece of paper. 'A present from Grimsby'!" She cackled with pleasure.

"I see the inspector at the gate. I wonder whether they've tried to find the origin of that piece of paper?" she continued, staring down the long garden path.

"I don't think they have. The chap kept trying to get me to confess I'd written it myself," said Aubrey. "Got quite huffy when I stuck to it that I knew no more about the bally paper than he did! But do you know who I think did that? Cleaver Wright. He's just that sort of feeble ass, you know. I say, I think the inspector wants to speak to you. Oh, no. He's gone. But I say! Wouldn't what you say about Savile apply pretty equally to Wright? I mean, he's a mad coot, isn't he? And I could more easily imagine him killing a chap than that worm Savile. And he's as strong as an ox, and he's pretty keen on Lulu Hirst, too; and he'd think it a good jape to cut up the body and hang up the limbs like bits of meat! I can see him grinning all over his face at the thought of it! And we *know* he was in the Manor Woods that Sunday night with Margery Barnes, and we know she ran away from him. And then, the chap she saw crawling out of the bushes could not have been Sethleigh, so that it may have been the murderer. Had you thought of that?"

"*Ad nauseam*," said Mrs Bradley, with no intention of snubbing him. "But then, child, don't you see? If it *was* the murderer, then the murderer couldn't have been Cleaver Wright, whom she'd just left in the clearing."

"Why not? He could have sneaked behind the bushes when she ran away from him, and started crawling out without noticing that she had run back to the clearing again."

"With what object should he hide himself then? You are not proposing to tell me that, in the few seconds whilst Margery Barnes was lost to sight, Cleaver Wright killed Sethleigh, hid the body, and crawled into the bushes and then out again, are you?"

"Well, no, but —"

"And if you are not telling me that, why then, if he *was* the murderer, that means he murdered Sethleigh at some time between five minutes to eight, when your mother saw Sethleigh and Redsey going into the woods together, and a quarter to nine, when he met Margery Barnes. Well, that part of the theory is tenable. After all, given reasonably favourable circumstances, it does not take long to kill a fellow-creature. But, supposing Wright did that, do you really think it conceivable that he immediately brought Margery Barnes to the spot where he had just committed the murder? And, even supposing that he were bold or foolhardy or cold-blooded enough to return to the spot with the girl, why should he have fled to the 'Queen's Head' in that panic-stricken way and at once set about providing himself with an alibi? You see, I'm sure he *saw* the corpse in the woods that night, and he *may* have got blood from it on to his clothes. Of course, the fight with Galloway was a capital mistake. It was a confession that he knew of, even if he did not actually participate in, the crime."

"Knew of?"

"Oh, yes. Cleaver Wright has been shielding somebody for a long time now. The curious part of it all is that I rather fancy he is shielding somebody who is not the murderer!"

"I don't follow."

"No. I expressed myself very badly, child. Take a concrete case. He is in love with Lulu Hirst. Suppose he imagined she had done it. She couldn't possibly have done it, as a matter of fact —"

"Why not?"

"Wrong type, my dear. These passionate, tigerish, rather primitive persons don't go about things so deliberately. All the details of the murder of Rupert Sethleigh have probably been planned for months. All that the murderer needed was a favourable opportunity. He prowled about, and had the wit to take advantage of one of those freaks of fortune which do occasionally occur. He saw that James Redsey imagined he had killed his cousin. I can't see why a man who had the presence of mind to take advantage of a fact like that should have made the tremendous mistake of transporting the corpse to Bossbury and attempting to get rid of all evidence of its identity. Only the fact that it was impossible for your cousin James Redsey to have dismembered the body has saved him from arrest all this long time. I dare say that if the butcher person had contented himself with stabbing the prostrate Sethleigh as he lay unconscious on the ground, and had gone away leaving the corpse undisturbed, James Redsey would have been hanged."

"Motive," said Aubrey, under his breath.

"Exactly. James had the best motive of anybody, and, in my opinion, your mother had the next best. Then come Dr Barnes and Savile, with about equal motive, I should say, and then Wright. Perhaps Wright's motive was stronger than Savile's, though. He is in love with Lulu in his crude animal fashion, whereas Savile is merely married to her. And — Aubrey!" She leaned forward and slapped his knee excitedly. "Quick! Run! Get the inspector to find out which of Lulu's admirers scorched the collar and handkerchiefs and Felicity Broome's curtains! Run, child, run! Yes, he went that way! Find out whether it was Savile or Wright, or somebody else! Particularly whether it was somebody else! It's important!"

Aubrey returned, breathless, in ten minutes.

"He's going to find out. Wants to know why you want to know."

"To-morrow he shall hear," promised Mrs Bradley.

"What was I saying? Oh, yes. About Wright shielding Lulu."

"You think he doesn't know the real murderer? You think he thinks it is somebody else?"

"Yes. Queer state of affairs, isn't it?"

"I should say so. By Jove, yes! First of all old Jim certain he'd laid Rupert out. Then everybody having such a frightful bother to prove that the — that Rupert was really dead . . . Oh, I know what I wanted to ask

288

you! Who *did* pinch the skull from Cleaver Wright's studio that afternoon?"

"Cleaver Wright, perhaps."

"Still on this false tack of thinking the murderer was — well, you know! — somebody it wasn't?"

"Yes, I think so."

"Then," said Aubrey, disappointed, "he was the one who put it in the Culminster Collection?"

"Of course, child. I've known that all along. His peculiar sense of humour again, you see."

"The — I mean — you can't prove anything from the skull being moved back to the butcher's shop."

"Well" — Mrs Bradley smiled at him thoughtfully — "it just depends who moved it back, doesn't it? Wright would be bound to share his little joke. No fun keeping it all to himself. See?"

"Yes. Well, I thought you gave the names of all the people you suspected to the police, and told them —"

"I did tell them quite a number of strange things, child. There is a surprise in store for Cleaver Wright, I think. Of course, he stole the key of the Museum from the vicar. A man like that is a menace to the whole parish! The vicar, I mean. Anybody could steal anything from him!"

"You know," said Aubrey, wrinkling his brow, "I feel in an awful muddle about all this. *Do* you know who the murderer is? And can you be certain that Cleaver Wright could get into the butcher's shop?"

"I am not quite prepared to answer those questions," said Mrs Bradley, smiling with quiet enjoyment. "Ask me again to-morrow. And now, dear me! Whoever is

289

this? Mary Kate Maloney, as I live! She seems perturbed."

Mary Kate flew up the garden path in an ecstasy of importance, terror, and blazing excitement. She had not even troubled to remove her apron.

"Glory be to God, Mrs Bradley, ma'am!" she declared, fervent but out of breath. "Do you be running over to the house with all your legs this day! Sure, and there's poor Mr Savile from the Cottage on the Hill does be hanging by his braces from the wood-shed door entirely."

"I'm glad it's entirely," said Mrs Bradley calmly, as she stood up and smoothed her skirt. "I am bored to death by mere limbs and joints. What's come over him that he should do a silly thing like that?"

"Sure, they do be saying it must be unrequited love, the poor young fellow, ma'am."

"Fiddlesticks!" said Mrs Bradley briskly. "Undigested dinner is more likely in his case!"

CHAPTER
TWENTY-TWO

The Inspector Makes
an Arrest

Inspector Grindy saluted Mrs Bryce Harringay with punctilious ceremony, and halted.

"Well, madam, you've seen the last of me," he observed with great geniality, "and I'm sorry you were ever troubled. Still, all's well that ends well, as the saying is. Could I see Mr Redsey for a minute?"

"I will cause him to be summoned," said Mrs Bryce Harringay majestically.

Jim met the inspector in the library.

"Well, what is it now?" he said ungraciously.

The inspector grinned.

"Only to tell you you're free to get off to America as soon as you like, sir," he said. "We've nothing on you at all now. We've made our arrest."

"The devil you have!" said Jim, staring. "That poor dago Savile, I suppose?"

"Well, sir, no. As a matter of fact, after I'd heard that comic fairy-tale Mrs Bradley was handing out to you all in her garden, I got quite one or two new ideas on the subject of that murder. Of course, I knew it wasn't the vicar. Hasn't got it in him. Besides, one or two of Mrs Bradley's ideas were entirely up the loop, and I knew it, and she knew it too, I reckon, and was just trying it on!"

"But how the deuce did you hear her ideas at all?" asked Jim, handing his cigarette-case to the police officer. Inspector Grindy laid his uniform cap on the table and stretched out a massive mahogany hand.

"Thank you. I will. Just to show there's no ill-feeling," he said.

They lit up. Then Jim said:

"Where did you say you were?"

"Oh, behind that clump of laurels. At Mrs Bradley's invitation," replied the inspector jovially. "And I certainly got a knock-out over that silver tobacco-case. You see, sir, she pulled my leg about that case quite a long time ago. Told me the murderer had collected some of Sethleigh's blood in it and poured it over the Stone of Sacrifice. Though, mind you, there was nothing like enough blood on that Stone for a murder! Of course I knew that was only her funny idea of a joke, so I took no notice; but, upon my soul, I was startled to see the vicar hike that case out of his pocket. Sifting it out, though, it seems as though he must have —"

"Acquired it?" suggested Jim, grinning.

"Thank you, sir. Yes, and a long time before the murder. Mrs Bryce Harringay remembers hearing Mr Sethleigh enquiring after it, and the servants all remember being questioned about it upwards of six or perhaps eight weeks ago, so I expect the vicar pouched it in that absent-minded manner of his, and that's that.

292

Then the clothes. We investigated the idea that Wright handled the body, and that bit is quite true. How the devil she tumbled to that, I don't know. I hadn't seen the significance of that scrap-up in the 'Queen's Head' all along, but that old woman got a strangle-hold on it right away. I'll hand her that. Well, Wright broke down under our interrogation and confessed he'd seen a headless corpse. Mark that, sir! The skull again, you see! Then we made him produce the trousers which he'd been wearing on and off ever since the murder. They were Sethleigh's, which was really a bit of a knock-out, because I'd put that bit of the old girl's yarn down as sheer piffle. Funny thing is, he's sticking to it that he didn't take 'em off the corpse at all! He'll go a long way if he isn't hanged. Time and again he must have had 'em on and stood and talked to me. It's a proper knock-out, that is! They're Sethleigh's flannels right enough. Tailor's mark on 'em and everything. Well, of course, the rest of the clothing wasn't dropped in the river at all, and Mrs Bradley never really thought it was. It seems as though it really must have been shoved into that suitcase with the head, and that's where those bloodstains must have come from. Well, the suitcase affair altogether was a bit tricky. I'm not dead sure I've got it right now, and we certainly haven't found the shirt and things. But it seems as though it was lent by Sethleigh to the vicar. Then the maid at the Vicarage packed some laundry in it and sent it to that daisy that hangs out with Savile and Wright in the Cottage on the Hill. From there the murderer pinched it. Had ample opportunity, it seems, because he was very sweet on Mrs Lulu, and used to visit her as often as he could crowd it in. Wonderful how many patients a country practitioner can — acquire was your word, sir, I think?" — he guffawed heartily — "and what a devil of a time it takes him to get round to see 'em all!"

"Country practitioner?" said Jim, puzzled. "What on earth are you getting at?"

"Why, Dr Barnes, sir, of course. He's the chap we've arrested. I just told you we'd made an arrest. Don't you remember little Miss Barnes saying her father was at the major's that Sunday evening? And Mrs Bradley's peculiar answer struck me all of a heap. She said they could prove whether that was so later on — or some words of that sort. Evasive, I said to myself. There's something behind that, I said. Well, it turns out on investigation that he was never at the major's at all! What do you make of that, sir? And then — another thing," he added, before Jim could reply; "the dismembering of the corpse! Child's play, sir, to a surgeon! And wouldn't disgust him and upset him like it would ordinary folks. Just science to him, cutting up a body. Just science. And Mrs Bradley confided to me herself what a tidy beggar the murderer must be! Now, sir, I ask you! What could be tidier than cutting up a body as neat as that, and hanging up the bits out of the way?"

Jim looked as he felt — sick.

"Then, again," pursued the inspector, "look at the motives! Two motives, in fact, and both different. Mixed motives, as we call it. His daughter and the blackmail business."

294

Jim, rather tired of Rupert's wide reputation as a Don Juan of the baser sort, merely nodded.

"Well, three, if you count Mrs Lulu," said the inspector, working it all out. "Both sweet on her, you see, Sethleigh and him were. Jealousy, and all that. Wonderful what a bit of passion will do to a man's character, you know. Anyway, he could have done the deed in the time; he wasn't at the major's; and we trapped him into saying he'd been in the Manor Woods before he knew what we were after. So how's that? As for the deed itself — well, Mrs Bradley talked of the vicar's penknife, but a doctor would be neater. Tidy again, sir, you see! She certainly put me on the track there again! His scalpel. And it could be put away with his other instruments and nobody any the wiser! Then the head. Takes a doctor to dissect a head nicely and leave just the bare skull like we found. The police surgeon says the head was split half-way down, and boiled to leave the bone, but you know what these surgeons are, sir — must have their nasty little jokes! Anyway, that's a small point. Well, then, sir, the Stone of Sacrifice. If you say 'doctor' where Mrs Bradley said 'vicar', you'll be about right. I should say that to the doctor that big slab suggested an operating-table! Something in that, sir, don't you think? And perhaps he could have done something about the quantity of blood. There wasn't enough for a stab in the neck, you see. That's the only flaw in our theory."

Jim nodded.

"I see," he said, still trying to readjust his thoughts sufficiently to take hold of the idea that the large, robust, ruddy, rather offensively loud-voiced and didactic Dr Barnes was a murderer.

"And then the slug business."

"How much?" said Jim, puzzled.

"Miss Barnes's own words, sir. The man that came crawling out of the bushes like a great black slug. She confessed that the form seemed somehow familiar, you remember? Well, sir, what could be more familiar than the sight of her own father? That's who she saw, and the doctor can't deny it!"

"And why should he deny it?" asked a rich voice at the open French doors. "Of course it was Dr Barnes, and of course Margery did not recognize him, although his figure seemed familiar. It is a great pity she did not, for otherwise quite a number of muddles could have been cleared up by this time."

And Mrs Bradley stepped into the library and seated herself in its most comfortable chair. Jim turned to her in perplexity.

"I'm damned if I can make this business out at all, Mrs Bradley," he confessed frankly. "Of course, we all knew that you were drawing the long-bow about the vicar yesterday, but really, to push the murder off on to the doctor seems almost as bad to me. I mean, all the people here have known the chap for years, and I'm sure he must have lived down any scandal there ever was connected with his son."

"Cleaver Wright is that son," said Mrs Bradley.

"Oh, really? I've heard rumours of it, of course. Still, there's a sight of difference between going off the end about some woman or other and doing a blooming great murder, isn't there?"

"There is," said Mrs Bradley dryly. "Curious of me, perhaps, but on the whole I prefer the murderer. The population of this country is so excessive that, looked at from the purely common-sense point of view, a person who decreases it is considerably more public-spirited than one who adds to it, and he should be dealt with accordingly."

"But the doctor?" said Jim, having digested these theses in silence. "It's a knock-out to me."

"Well, what can you expect will happen to a man who has never played bears with the children?" demanded Mrs Bradley abruptly.

"Never what?" asked the inspector, grinning.

"But, of course, to arrest him for murder is ridiculous," went on Mrs Bradley calmly. "He was in the Manor Woods — yes. He has no alibi? Are you sure of that? Go and ask Lulu Hirst. His daughter saw him — yes. And he was crawling on hands and knees, and if he had ever played bears with her when she was a child she would have recognized him, and could have said so, and that part of the business could have been cleared up. Anyway, inspector, take the advice of a sincere well-wisher and let the poor man go. Besides, what about fingerprints in the butcher's shop?"

"Oh, we don't think the actual work was done in the butcher's shop. We suspect he dismembered the body in his own surgery in the garden. More expeditious, madam, you see. Then he wrapped up the bits in Miss Felicity Broome's muslin curtains, like they wrap up meat when they deliver it to the butchers' shops, and that's how the curtains got scorched."

"Expound, O sage," said Mrs Bradley, settling down with huge enjoyment to listen.

"Well, madam, you yourself put us on to that. Don't you remember how you found out about that suitcase getting to Mrs Lulu Hirst?"

Mrs Bradley nodded her small black head.

"And don't you remember telling me her words?"

"Whose words, inspector?"

"Mrs Lulu's. She didn't name Savile or Wright as the man that scorched that ironing. All she said was 'that swine I goes with'. Well, that's the doctor, madam. Plain as a pikestaff. She washed the curtains for him and he went and scorched 'em!"

"Inspector," said Mrs Bradley, with emotion, "you will convince me in a minute that you are right and I am wrong. This is too wonderful for words!"

The inspector grinned.

"Just a little bit of deduction," he said spaciously. "Just part of our job, you know."

"Then you imply that Lulu Hirst is aware that Dr Barnes committed this murder?"

"That's right, Mrs Bradley. And that's why it's no good me going to her, as you suggest, to give the doctor an alibi, because I know she will, like a shot. Knows he did it, you see."

Mrs Bradley sighed and turned to Jim Redsey.

"This is very difficult, young man," she observed.

Jim put out his large hands helplessly.

"You see, madam, there's her own words to be thought about. She said to you, you remember, 'There's one man dead for me already, and another soon will be!' Or some expression like that. Meaning, I take it, that Sethleigh was murdered, and the doctor would be hanged for doing it."

"H'm! Doesn't sound as though she would be prepared to fix him up with much of an alibi," said Mrs Bradley tersely. "You can't have it both ways, inspector, you know!"

"Oh, yes, you can, Mrs Bradley, with ladies of the type of Mrs Lulu," contradicted the inspector gravely. "Love their loves *and* hate 'em, that's the way they go on. You'd be surprised!"

Mrs Bradley broke into an amused cackle.

"Upon my word, inspector!" she said. "I can't think what has happened to you. This is so sudden!"

"Well," remarked the inspector, winking solemnly at Jim, "I got your little book out of the Bossbury Library a couple of days back. There's some frisky reading in that there book, Mrs Bradley, and I reckon it has kind of inspired me. Keep it away from the wife, though, I had to. Wouldn't hardly do to let her know I read stuff like that! If it was fiction it would be seized by the police, and so I tell you!" He guffawed loudly.

"Frisky reading!" said Mrs Bradley, clutching her black hair. "Seized by the police! James, get me some water! This man unnerves me!"

Jim grinned.

"And as you value your professional reputation, inspector," she added, "fly, fly to the prison-house and set free that unfortunate, choleric, ridiculous man! Tidy, indeed! Is it tidy to have illegitimate children all over the place, so that blackmailers may arise from the earth and counfound you? Is it tidy to have affairs with the Lulu Hirsts of this world, so that all the village knows about them? Is it tidy to be compelled to forbid your own daughter, of whom you are very fond, to have aught to do with young men for fear that her innocent mind may be contaminated with stories of your own depravity? No, no, no! And the motive, inspector! The motive! Why, the poor man *had* no motive! Everybody in the village knew his secret. It wasn't a secret at all!"

She smote the polished table vehemently, and continued:

"No, I tell you, no! And the man who cut up that body *is* tidy! How many times must I say it? He is a maniac for tidiness! Oh, you are right enough about the curtains! They *were* used for the purpose you stated! And the corpse was *not* dismembered in the butcher's shop! Neither was it dismembered in the doctor's surgery, though! And what about the burial of that suitcase containing the fish? What about that ridiculous notice on the fish? Those were the clues you should have studied! Those were the two facts absolutely germane to your case! Man, rid your mind of this poison about the doctor's guilt! He is a fool, but he is not a madman!"

She stopped short. The inspector and Jim gaped at her in stark amazement.

"Beware of the fact that will not fit," proclaimed Mrs Bradley, more calmly. "Go home and pray, inspector. But set the doctor free first!"

She walked quickly out of the room through the French doors, leaving the two men staring after her.

"Well, I'm damned!" said the inspector solemnly.

Jim nodded. It seemed an adequate comment.

Suddenly Mrs Bradley poked her head tortoise-wise in at the French doors, and addressed herself again to the inspector.

"I couldn't bear the thought that our charming James should be suspected of murder," she said. "An unpalatable idea! Therefore I determined to look at the facts for myself. It very soon dawned upon me that we were dealing, not with a man possessing a perverted sense of humour, but with a man of such deadly seriousness of mind that the mere word 'eccentricity' could not account for his peculiar traits. The man to whom dead flesh was meat, and must be disposed of as such; the man who split open the skull and boiled it because that's what he's seen done with the heads of deceased animals; the man who, dog-like, buried the skull (after all, there *were* other ways of getting rid of it, you see!); the man who found himself compelled to write 'A Present from Grimsby' on a stuffed fish; a man whose queer mentality would never let him rest until he had seen an offering, a sacrifice — a human sacrifice — laid upon the Stone (by the way, he went back home and brought a small saw and a carving-knife as well as the suitcase back with him to the Stone, and performed that unpleasant job on the Sunday night when everybody had gone to bed. Very neat, considering the enormous handicap of having nothing but the front lamp of a car to light up the grisly work); and —"

"I say!" said Jim, open-eyed. "What a ghastly scene! But how do you know all this?"

"I don't. I deduce it. There were certainly some splinters of bone on the top of the Stone when I examined it through my reading-glass that day."

"But the police didn't spot them!"

"No, child. They were not looking for them. I was. That makes all the difference," said Mrs Bradley, looking more like some deadly reptile than ever, as she directed a serpent's grin at the inspector.

"But who on earth could be such a maniac?" asked Jim. The inspector stood by, mute but amused.

Aubrey Harringay, coming up behind Mrs Bradley, gently pushed her into the room, and entered after her.

"The person who puts on a clerical collar when he is going to inter a little dead bird," replied the terrible little old lady to Jim's question. "The person who assumes a suit of Lincoln green and its appurtenances when he is practising archery (I cannot make up my mind whether the shot in the wood was directed at me or not, by the way)."

"If not," said Aubrey, eager to display knowledge, "why did he tell a lie about where he was standing when he shot it?"

"Did he tell a lie?" asked Mrs Bradley.

"Yes, of course. Said he was in the woods on the other side of the road. Couldn't have been."

"Why not, child?"

302

"Flight of the arrow. He'd have had to shoot over the tree-tops, wouldn't he? But the arrow was less than six feet from the ground, and travelling in a straight flight. Hadn't been fired from more than twenty yards off, I should say."

"By heavens, Holmes," said Mrs Bradley, hooting merrily and poking him in the ribs, "this is wonderful!"

"No, it isn't," said Aubrey, getting out of her reach. "It's the result of patient observation. The mater belonged to an archery club a few years ago, when I was about eleven, and I used to put in a lot of time acting as sort of caddie to her. I don't know what they call it in archery, but when I read that bit in the Bible about Jonathan shooting the arrows and telling his boy the arrow was beyond him, I jolly well know what that poor kid felt like. It reminds me of my own youth." He grinned.

"Oh, well. That's that," said Mrs Bradley.

"And what about getting the parts of the body into Binks's shop? When was that done?" demanded Jim.

"That's where you got yourself into a muddle, my dear inspector! Somebody hung about Binks's shop for weeks and wondered how the thing was to be managed; and at last, seeing no other way, he bribed Binks's boy for the key. The boy did not recognize him — the man's a vegetarian, you see! — and anyway, the boy hasn't the brains to describe him for us — and there you are! He had only to load the dismembered parts into his car, each bit wrapped up in a fold of Felicity's muslin curtains, and deliver them at Binks's shop whenever the fancy took him, which was on the Monday afternoon, and that was that."

"Wouldn't the other people in the market be surprised at a delivery of meat being made in a lock-up shop on a Monday? And what about the finger-prints on the butcher's knife and cleaver?"

"Those of Binks's boy," grunted the inspector. "I tell you we made up our minds long ago the business was not done at the shop. *And* we knew the lad was bribed to give up the key."

"But how will they bring home the crime to the murderer?" asked Jim, glancing at the inspector.

"They probably won't. You don't suppose the inspector is taking any notice of my fantastic theories, do you?"

She chuckled with sardonic amusement.

"But hang it all, I mean! What price the doctor?" cried Aubrey. "Oh, and why did Savile try to commit suicide?"

"The wronged husband. He considered it was the correct way of proving that his faith in human nature was gone for ever."

"Wronged husband?"

"Yes."

"Oh, Lulu."

"Yes."

"And that blighter Rupert," interpolated Aubrey.

"A dead man, child," said Mrs Bradley solemnly.

"What about it?" demanded Aubrey sternly. "Dead or not, he *was* a blighter! Why be soft?"

"Quite, quite!" Mrs Bradley nodded sympathetically. "But not Rupert. Dr Barnes."

"Oh!"

"Yes. It was certainly Dr Barnes who scorched the ironing that day. The inspector was right there." She nodded brightly and encouragingly at him, and continued. "By the way, talking of Lulu — you realize the interesting implication now of Savile's having married her to please one school of opinion and his having demanded that they should continue to use her maiden name to satisfy the ridiculous conventions of another?"

"Oh, the New Art mob? The mater had a spasm to join them, but thought better of it, thank goodness," said Aubrey.

"Their anti-marriage point of view decided her, I imagine?" grinned the unregenerate James.

"No. Their tendency to sponge on anybody with a bit of money. The mater's an arch-sponger herself, you see, and it was a case of two of a trade, I suppose."

"But what *about* the murderer?" asked the inspector, grinning broadly.

"Inspector," said Mrs Bradley solemnly, "will anything short of a miracle convince you that the doctor is innocent and that Mr Savile dismembered the body of Rupert Sethleigh?"

"Savile?"

"Savile."

The inspector scratched his head. At that moment the telephone-bell rang.

"It's for you, inspector," said Jim, who had stepped to the instrument.

"Oh, Lord, Mrs Bradley! I must hand it to you this time, after all!" said the inspector, at the end of a minute's hectic performance at the mouthpiece. "Savile's done it on us!"

"Not dead?" said two voices.

Mrs Bradley assumed an expression of patient resignation.

"Tiresome for you, inspector," she said. "Never mind. I suppose it settles the matter once and for all. Besides, when you come to sift all the evidence, I think the doctor will probably prove an alibi."

"Not for Sunday night he won't!"

"No, inspector. I was thinking of Monday." She smiled sweetly.

"What's happened?" asked Jim.

"Savile escaped from bed in the Cottage Hospital, hustled aside two nurses, and jumped from a top-floor window. I must get along there, I suppose, and find out exactly what the poor loony darnfool did do! Mucking up my case like that!"

Much incensed, he took his leave.

CHAPTER
TWENTY-THREE

Mrs Bradley's Notebook

(SEE CHAPTER VI.)

Question: Why should Dr Barnes so deliberately run down Lulu Hirst? Does he want to create the impression that he dislikes her, in order to cloak the fact that he likes her in a way which might harm his professional reputation if it became known?

Question: Why have those three curious persons, Cleaver Wright (whose acquaintance I must be sure to make), George Savile, and Lulu Hirst, come to live in an out-of-the-way spot like Wandles Parva?

Possible Answers:
(a) Flight from London creditors.
(b) Trouble with the police.
(c) Desire for change of air and scenery.
(d) Ditto, peace and quietness.
(e) Wright and Savile want to paint the local beauty spots.

N.B.: Savile the monomaniac — still, so are we all, I suppose. His fetish seems to be exactitude and laborious attention to correctness of detail. Interesting. Expound this to F. B., I think.

Question: Why was not Ferdinand a daughter?

N.B.: The false teeth found on the Vicarage dust-heap by the boy A. H. The vicar does not possess false teeth. Neither does F. Nor the maid. Curious.

Question: Why is A. so much excited at finding them? Interesting.

(SEE CHAPTER VII.)

Quite a joke. The bishop has been presented with a skull. Reginald Crowdesley is the kind of bishop to whom things happen.

N.B.: There is more in Cleaver Wright than meets the eye.

(SEE CHAPTER X.)

N.B.: Public opinion is strongly against the youth J. R., who is suspected of having murdered his cousin R. S. J. R. — A likeable person. Cannot imagine anyone less likely to commit murder. Might be fierce when roused, though.

(SEE CHAPTER XI.)

Redsey dug a hole that night. Interesting.

N.B.: F. B. buried alive down here. A charming and beautiful child.

Question: Why do wicked old women like me have more money than they can possibly spend on themselves?

Answer: Wait and see.

N.B.: Am determined to keep my fingers out of the local pie — i.e., this absurd murder-case. But, really, the child looks so tired and worried — I suppose she is in love with that ridiculous youth J. R.

J. R.'s Confession: Knocked cousin down about 8.5p.m. on Sunday, June 22nd. Arrived "Queen's Head" — say 8.25p.m. Helped home at closing time. Arrived home — say 10.35p.m. Locked in bedroom by Mrs B. H.'s orders. Went to Manor Woods late Monday night to locate body and inter it. Disturbed by the lad A. H. Chased lad out of woods, but no evidence to show when J. R. himself arrived indoors that night ... Oho! Indeed? Interesting, but, from F.'s point of view, unprofitable. Had better keep clear of this.

N.B.: Mrs B. H. the mother. New light on her character. Passionately desirous of seeing her son set up for life. The family fortune would be attraction enough for anything, perhaps!

N.B.: Everybody seems to know all about poor Dr Barnes's little failings.

(SEE CHAPTER XIII.)

Question: What about that skull? Stolen from Cleaver Wright's studio and now in the Culminster Collection, well hidden behind a Roman shield. Who put it there? Can it possibly be Sethleigh's skull?

N.B.: Must frighten the person who put it there into moving it to a place where I can get hold of it and

309

try the dental plate, which seems to be Sethleigh's — at least, I am certain that the lad A. H. believes so.

N.B.: That dental plate could have fallen out of the suitcase. What about that suitcase? The police are not inclined to treat it as significant. They regard the message on that fish as a joke. I don't.

N.B.: The girl M. B. reminds me of somebody. Who? — Cleaver Wright! *He* may be the doctor's son, then. Brother and sister mutually attracted — kinship is a queer thing — and go off to woods together? Seems far-fetched. But M. went to the woods with *somebody* that night. The murderer? Hardly, I suppose.

N.B.: Strength of Savile.

That chart!

C. W. went to the "Queen's Head" that night and fought and was beaten. Aha! Mr Wright. Not very clever of you, that!

(SEE CHAPTER XV.)

N.B.: Trousers, pair of, flannel, grey, intact.

Savile's kink for correctness again. *Must* dress for the part. Curious.

Dr Barnes has never played bears with children.

"A great black slug." Indeed? Interesting. The vicar walked into the River Cullen on the evening of Sunday, June 22nd. Is he *really* as much afflicted as all that? Oh, those grey flannel trousers!! I dreamt they were round my neck, strangling me, last night. F. B. has seen the skull in Culminster Museum. Now what?

(SEE CHAPTER XVI.)

N.B.: That suitcase.

Lulu Hirst, washerwoman.

The scorched curtains. Muslin. H'm! I wonder!

Scorched. Indeed?

My hat! The suitcase went to the Cottage on the Hill then! J. R. — I see light!

N.B.: Rabbits' blood? Quite so.

(SEE CHAPTER XVII.)

N.B.: F. must go into Culminster again to find out whether the skull is still there.

N.B.: The murdered man's clothes consisted of:

Flannel trousers,

Silk scarf,

White tennis-shirt (with detachable collar?),

Cellular vest and trunk drawers.

Tie? . . .

Quite so.

N.B.: The blood on the Stone. Not enough.

N.B.: The Stone — a sacrificial altar.

Blood. Sacrifice. The head, then —

Aha!

N.B.: It *was* M. B. and C. W.

N.B.: Savile again. Robin Hood this time.

It is getting too easy.

(SEE CHAPTER XVIII.)

N.B.: The doctor did not react to "consanguinity" suggestion. Have concluded he is not the murderer.

N.B.: L. H. is terrified. I wonder what she knows?

Questions:

The doctor and Lulu lovers? If so:

Savile jealous?

Wright jealous?

Sethleigh and Lulu lovers? If so:

Motive for Wright —

Savile —

Dr Barnes —

to have murdered Sethleigh?

I wonder.

N.B.: The skull has gone. If Savile moved it, it is in the butcher's shop, in the drawer beneath the chopping-block where they keep the bones and the bits.

N.B.: Oh, yes! M. B. did meet C. W., and he saw the corpse, I think. That means (see plan) somebody had moved R. S. from the bushes where J. R. had hidden him, and possibly had begun dismembering the body.

Question: Who?

N.B.: That "black slug" again:

Savile?

The doctor?

Not the vicar, I suppose?

(SEE CHAPTER XIX.)

So Savile moved the skull.

Queer that J. R. should have suggested the butcher's shop.

These notes want rearranging. Let us try a timetable.

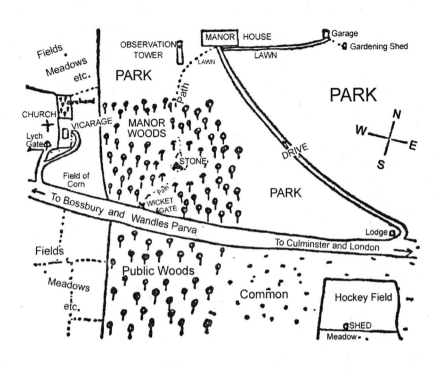

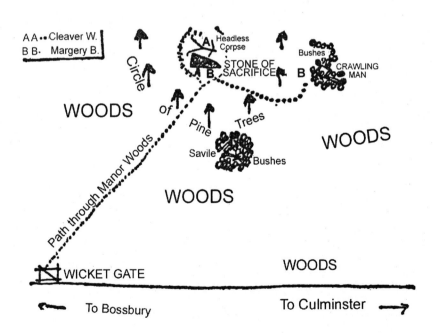

TIME-TABLE OF THE MURDER OF RUPERT
SETHLEIGH ON SUNDAY, JUNE 22ND.

7.45p.m. (N.B. — All these times are approximate.):
Savile in hiding in the Manor Woods to trap
Sethleigh with Lulu Hirst. Did not know that it was
the doctor she was going to meet. Armed with
weapon — probably axe or billhook.
Near Stone of Sacrifice.

7.55p.m.: Redsey and Sethleigh go into the Manor
Woods, quarrelling.

8.5p.m.: Redsey knocks Sethleigh down. *Fall kills him.*
Drags body into bushes. Seen by Savile.
Redsey departs for "Queen's Head" public house.

8.15p.m.: Savile drags body from bushes.
Lifts on to Stone of Sacrifice.
Decapitates with axe or billhook. Cannot decide
whether Sethleigh dead or only stunned.
Disturbed by:

8.30p.m.: (Supposition only.) Dr Barnes's and Lulu
Hirst's entry into woods. Has just time to lower
headless trunk of Sethleigh to the ground on house
side of the Stone, and disappear into bushes with
head. Dr Barnes and Lulu do not approach the
Stone, however, and Savile does not actually see
them.

8.45p.m.: Savile still in hiding with the head. Cleaver
Wright and Margery Barnes sit down on side of
Stone facing the Bossbury road (see plan), i.e.,
opposite side to the corpse.

9.0p.m.: Margery, alarmed by buffoonery of Cleaver, runs away in circle.

9.1p.m.: Dr Barnes, disturbed by the sounds of his daughter's flight, crawls out to reconnoitre, and is observed by Margery — "great black slug". Disappears hastily. Margery runs home, and arrives long before her father.

9.2p.m.: Cleaver Wright, having risen to his feet and strolled a few steps round the Stone, comes upon the headless trunk of Sethleigh. Flight to "Queen's Head" to establish alibi for himself.

9.3p.m.: Savile decides had better cover his tracks a bit, now Wright has seen the corpse. Worms way out of woods, leaving skull and billhook hidden, and returns to Cottage on the Hill, which, of course, is empty. Gets ready large knife, sharpens saw, places both in suitcase, together with muslin curtains. Takes car-lamp. Hides all these things where can easily get at them later. Sits down and awaits return of Lulu Hirst and Cleaver Wright.

9.5p.m.: Doctor and Lulu, afraid of discovery as so many people seem to be about in the woods, seek Bossbury road, and separate. Savile probably ill-treats Lulu when she arrives home, and sees that she goes up to bed early to be out of the way.

9.45p.m.: Return of Wright in bloodstained and exhausted condition from the fight in the "Queen's Head". Goes up to bed. Coast clear for Savile.

10.30p.m.: Return of Dr Barnes as though he had really spent the evening at the major's.

11.30p.m.: Savile to woods. Finishes dismembering the corpse. Wraps up the pieces and hides them, ready to take into Bossbury next day. Returns to Cottage with head and clothing of the corpse. Boils the first to remove flesh. Washes the tie (?) and shirt which are slightly bloodstained. Adds the grey flannels to his own wardrobe. (Supposition only.) Places trunk drawers, vest, tie, and shirt in laundry-basket. Lulu washes other people's clothes besides Savile's and Wright's, so her suspicions not aroused. Summer weather. Damp things will soon dry.

N.B.: Cannot see how the police will ever get on to Savile. The idiots have arrested the doctor! Poor, foolish, choleric man! I must rescue him, I suppose.

Later: What a comfort! Savile has committed suicide! I can now give him away to the police without a single qualm!

Later: I really must put the wind up James Redsey. Then, if he treats that delicious child with anything but the most exquisite kindness and consideration after they are married, he had better look out for himself!

CHAPTER
TWENTY-FOUR

The Murderer

I

"So it was not Dr Barnes, after all?" said Aubrey. "Fancy his being in the woods all the time, though, that Sunday night!"

"These woods appear to have a curious attraction for all kinds of Undesirable Persons," observed Mrs Bryce Harringay, coming into the room from the hall.

"Yes, indeed. Hampstead Heath on an August Bank Holiday is not to be compared with the Manor Woods on the night of June 22nd," returned Mrs Bradley. "By the way, I must apologize for invading your house just now."

Jim Redsey, without glancing in the direction of his aunt, went out.

"Not my house," replied Aubrey's mother grandly. "My son and I are pensioners on the bounty of my nephew James. Happily, James has seen matters in a Reasonable Light. After a certain amount of discussion, in which, I regret to say, he showed little or no disposition to meet me half-way, I have prevailed upon him to purchase a Controlling Interest in this ranch or whatever it is, and go out there to live. I shall remain in charge here with Aubrey."

"But look here, mater, dash it all," began her son, with unwonted heat. "I mean, it's a bit thick! He doesn't want to go out to Mexico now he's got this house and the money. I mean, you can't expect it. And there's Felicity to be considered."

"Felicity?" said Mrs Bryce Harringay blankly. "What do you mean — Felicity?"

"Well, I suppose they'll marry or something sooner or later. She's only waiting for old Jim to shout the odds, you know!"

Mrs Bryce Harringay looked pained.

"I do wish, Aubrey, that you would learn to express yourself in a Reasonable Manner. Are you suggesting that it is James's intention to propose marriage to this young person?"

Aubrey grinned.

"Just about," he said. "When he can get somebody to hold his coat and boots he's going to make the dive, I understand. Be practically a case of breach of promise if he doesn't, considering how the poor kid howled when she thought he might be arrested."

"You are indelicate, child," observed Mrs Bradley. "What does she want for a wedding-present?"

II

Jim Redsey returned to the library when his aunt was gone.

318

"Savile," he said slowly, "was a curious kind of devil, but in spite of everything I shouldn't have thought a murder was much in his line, somehow."

He glanced at Mrs Bradley, who appeared to have fallen asleep in the large comfortable armchair, and then began to tiptoe out of the room.

"Stop, James!" came in deep rich tones from the depths of the chair. "You are wearing grey flannel trousers!"

"Yes," agreed Jim, glancing down at them.

"If I had my way," said Mrs Bradley firmly, "grey flannel trousers should be taxed, together with dogs, automobiles, wireless receiving-sets, incomes, and the colour curiously termed beige."

"Why?" asked Jim, interested. "Certainly bring in a lot of money. Everybody wears grey flannel bags."

"Yes, that's what is so annoying to a mere seeker after truth," said Mrs Bradley sorrowfully. "You see. I am in a quandary. Either Savile or Wright could have stolen the murdered man's trousers — and his shirt and vest and drawers too, for that matter! — and either could have worn them!"

"You mean — yes, I see. Still it doesn't matter now the poor blighter's dead, does it? I mean, the police are certain to call it a day, aren't they?"

"That, being interpreted, equals —?"

"Well, I mean to say, the hunt is over, so to speak. They'll conclude Savile did the murder, now it is certain that the doctor could not have taken the body to the butcher's shop on Monday."

"I hope so, sincerely, for your sake," said Mrs Bradley, getting up from her chair and walking over to an oval mirror. She studied her unpleasing reflection for some seconds long, earnestly and in complete silence.

Jim began to feel the pulse in his right temple hammering uncomfortably. His mouth felt dry and his hands clammy.

"How do you mean?" he asked thickly.

"Well," replied Mrs Bradley, turning to face him, "although Savile had planned the murder, I suppose it was so little in his line that, truth to tell, he never committed it — a fact which, out of aunt-like affection for yourself, I have endeavoured to relegate to the background during this tiresome business. I have not actually told a verbal lie about it, but still there it is! Savile cut up the body — yes. He stole the murdered man's clothes — yes. Sometimes he wore them and sometimes, when their wardrobes got somewhat mixed — a frequent occurrence, I fancy, in that curious household! — Cleaver Wright wore them —"

"But what about Wright's own trousers you told us about? The ones he knelt on the ground in to look at Sethleigh's body? The ones that got stained about the knees with blood?"

"Eye-wash," said Mrs Bradley succinctly.

"How much?"

"He's been wearing them on and off ever since, alternately with those belonging to Sethleigh."

"Then, didn't he disturb the murderer and kneel by the body?"

"He kneel by the body? Oh no! What? Kneel by a headless corpse?"

She chuckled. In spite of the heat, Jim shivered. Cold sweat trickled down his spine.

"Afraid I don't follow," he said feebly.

"No, James?" Mrs Bradley stood up, put her bird-like black head on one side and pursed her beaky little mouth. She was enjoying herself. "Savile decapitated a dead man, that's all."

"Savile — Look here, are you calling me a murderer?" shouted Jim, hoarse with anxiety and crimson with anger. "You'd better not! I'll — I'll —"

Aubrey Harringay would have realized the significance of that chokingly thick utterance and the young man's ugly scowl, and would have made his getaway with celerity. Mrs Bradley was not blind to the symptoms, but she merely grinned in her own unpleasantly ghoulish fashion, and poked him in the ribs with inconsequent hardihood.

"Do not threaten me, James," she observed calmly. "Threats are so wearing to the threatener. As my dear good friend and neighbour, Mrs Bryce Harringay, would say, 'Conserve your energies for some Worthy Purpose.' There goes Felicity Broome. Bestow upon her my love. Be off with you!"

"But what about Rupert and so forth?" gulped Jim, cowed by the old lady's intrepid refusal to take his anger seriously. "What are you going to do?"

Mrs Bradley waved a yellow claw.

"Nothing," she said. "If I had been going to give you away, child, I should have done it long ago. However,

321

that punch of yours which knocked Sethleigh down most certainly caused his death. The shock alone would have done for that heart of his. I've never had the least doubt about that. Besides, there was *never* enough blood for a death by wounding. Even the inspector saw that, bless his heart! And morally, of course, Savile *was* guilty."